DAUGHTER OF THE BROKEN LINE

The Twelve Kingdoms of Adollith

BOOK 1

Daughter of the Broken Line

Other books in the series forthcoming

DAUGHTER OF THE BROKEN LINE

THE Last Heir. The Final Curse. The Beginning of a War.

BY: MELI PONCE

Daughter of the Broken Line   Meli Ponce   BOOK 1

Copyright © 2025 Meli Ponce
All rights reserved.

No part of this book may be reproduced…

First edition

PAPERBACK ISBN: 979827649789

HARDCOVER ISBN: 9798278648512

This book was created with the assistance of AI tools and extensively edited by the author.

Daughter of the Broken Line   Meli Ponce   BOOK 1

This book and the series to follow is dedicated to those who have changed my life for the better. To my husband, Erik, who supports every effort and endeavor—whether it makes sense or not—my love, you are my muse. To my children, whether biological or not, you are my purpose.

"When the last heir rises, the twelve shall tremble."
— Fragment from the Sundering Prophecy

Daughter of the Broken Line   Meli Ponce   BOOK 1

PROLOGUE

The Night the Heir Died (Full Integrated Version)

The bells of Orlanthia never rang at night—not unless someone was dying. On the eve of the Winter Ascension, they screamed across the high towers, their iron throats echoing through marble halls and moonlit courtyards. Princess Nilsa Nightstalker ran barefoot across the cold floor, her breath breaking in sharp, frightened bursts as she carved through the palace corridors; her dark braid slapped against her back as she ran, her usually steady stride faltering—not from exhaustion, but from dread. Known for her composed intensity and quiet strength, Nilsa felt her heart racing with a fear she had never known.

Her brother's chamber door hung half-open. A single lamp flickered inside, its flame trembling as if it, too, feared the truth. Nilsa hesitated only once, then pushed the door wide.

The room smelled of crushed jasmine and cold metal. Silk curtains billowed in a draft that should not exist; the windows were locked from within. The shadows on the far wall clung too tightly to one another, as though they were hiding something.

Kaelvar lay in his bed—still, pale, unmoving. Her only sibling. The last male heir of Orlanthia.

Kaelvar Nightstalker had always filled a room like sunlight in winter—soft, rare, and deeply treasured. At fifteen, he had carried the solemn poise of someone much older. His smile was small but earnest, his eyes bright with the warmth of a boy who loved fiercely and without hesitation. He was broader-shouldered than Nilsa despite being younger, with hair like dark copper brushed with gold when the light caught it, and he trained harder than any heir before him—not out of ambition, but out of a desire to protect the family he adored. Gentle with the servants, playful with the stablehands, kind even to the gardeners, Kaelvar was the calm in the storm of court politics—steady, patient, and beloved.

And now he was gone.

"Kael…?" Her voice cracked. "Kael, wake up. Please—wake up." His lips were blue. His eyelids stilled. His hands—once calloused from swordplay—had gone soft.

Her mother knelt beside the bed, one hand pressed over her mouth, the other reaching trembling fingers toward her son's cheek. Queen Ysolde's silver circlet had slipped sideways, cutting a cruel line across her hair. Usually regal and unshakable, she now looked small—hollowed out by a grief too great for her frame.

"The curse has taken him," whispered High Seer Elmaris from the corner, his shadowed face unreadable. Thin, pale, smelling faintly of starleaf and old parchment, the Seer watched with eyes clouded white from decades of trance-sight. "Just as it took your mother's brothers… and her mother's before that."

Nilsa shook her head violently. "No. Not Kael. He was strong. He—he wasn't supposed to—"

"It always takes them young," the Seer murmured. "Before their sixteenth year. It is the price Orlanthia has paid since the Sundering."

Nilsa pressed her forehead to her brother's still chest. She felt nothing. No warmth. No heartbeat. Only the faint shimmer of residue—like stale magic lived beneath his skin. Her tears wet the embroidered crest on his nightclothes: the sigil of Orlanthia's first kings—twelve stars encircling a blank center. The missing star. The unspeakable one. The kingdom the world pretended to have never existed.

Behind her, the Seer lit a wand of starleaf incense. The smoke curled unnaturally, rising in thin silver ribbons that twisted toward the ceiling—then spiraled downward, as if pulled by gravity from the other side of the world. The air smelled wrong—like rain on stone that had never known sunlight.

"This was no ordinary death," the Seer said softly. His white eyes glowed faintly, reflecting visions Nilsa could not see. "The curse tightens. It grows hungrier. Soon, Princess… it may reach for more than the heirs of Orlanthia."

Nilsa wiped her cheeks with trembling hands. "Then I'll break it." Her words were quiet but sharp. A promise forged in grief.

Her mother looked up. "Nilsa—"

"No, Mother." Nilsa rose, fists clenched. "I won't watch another brother die. I won't watch my sons die, someday." Her voice steadied, gaining power of its own. "I'll find what caused this. I'll break every curse in Adollith if I must."

Lightning cracked across a sky with no storm. The shadows in the corners pulsed. And the Seer inhaled sharply, as though he'd seen something behind her—inside her.

"You carry the spark," he whispered. "You, who were spared only because the curse hunts the sons alone. But the power you bear… it belonged to another kingdom once."

Nilsa's breath hitched. "What kingdom?"

He did not answer. Instead, he uncorked a vial from his satchel and poured a drop of shimmering ash into his palm. It glowed faintly, pale violet, humming with ancient song. When he opened his fingers, the ash lifted into the air, forming a sigil: twelve circles orbiting an empty core. A forgotten symbol. A forbidden one. One that had not been shown in Orlanthia for three hundred years.

Nilsa's heart faltered. "What… what is that?"

"The mark of the kingdom that vanished," he whispered. "The source of all magic before the Sundering. The reason the curses began."

She stared as the glowing symbol unraveled into the air like scattered embers.

"You must not seek it," he warned. "For its ruin was earned. Its secrets buried for good."

Nilsa lifted her chin. "Tell me its name."

The Seer closed his fist, snuffing the ash-runes into smoke. "I cannot."

"Then I'll find it myself."

He flinched—actually flinched—at the force in her voice.

And from the doorway, another shadow moved.

A boy she had not noticed. A stable lad—quiet, dutiful, unremarkable to most, though Nilsa had always sensed a strange steadiness in him. Erabor. Dark-haired, sharp-featured, with eyes the peculiar color of stormlight on stone. He carried himself with a humility that felt practiced, as though he was hiding the true shape of his presence. The other stablehands said he worked harder than all of them, that he hardly slept, that horses calmed beneath his hands as if soothed by something older than language.

He watched her with eyes too bright for a boy of the stables, too old, too knowing. He bowed his head when he realized she'd seen him, but not before she glimpsed something impossible: for a single heartbeat, his shadow didn't match his shape. It curved backward. Sharp-edged. Winged.

Nilsa blinked. The shadow returned to normal.

Erabor dipped his head deeply. "Princess," he said softly. "Say the word... and I will go with you. Wherever you must travel."

Nilsa drew a sharp breath, her grief hardening into something fierce and unyielding. "We leave before dawn." The words tore out of her—not reasoned or measured, but born of anguish and fury, a vow she could not swallow.

Ysolde rose suddenly, her breath hitching with panic, grief, and terror intertwined. "Nilsa, no—please," she whispered, catching her daughter's wrist with cold, trembling fingers. "You cannot leave yet. Not like this. Your brother is dead—your brother! You must stay. You must see to his rites, speak with the Council, settle his affairs. They will expect you to stand before them as heir. You are all I have left."

Nilsa's jaw trembled—only for a moment. Her resolve did not break, but it bent just enough for duty. "Fine," she breathed, the word tight and ragged. "I will face the Council. But it must be done quickly. I cannot linger. My departure will not be delayed."

Ysolde's eyes filled with fresh tears, not sorrow. "Nilsa... please, do not rush into danger."

But Nilsa's gaze had already turned toward the unseen horizon, toward the curse that had stolen her brother, toward the unknown kingdom whose absence had shaped all Adollith. Something inside her—something long dormant—had awakened.

Erabor bowed once more, and Nilsa didn't see the faint dark shimmer that rippled across his eyes—like starlight reflected on obsidian wings.

Outside, the bells tolled again. This time it was not a mourning sound. It was a warning.

Daughter of the Broken Line   Meli Ponce   BOOK 1

The curse of Orlanthia had claimed its heir.
And the world of Adollith had begun to stir.

CHAPTER ONE

The Morning After

Dawn crept slowly over Orlanthia, as though even the sun hesitated to touch a kingdom in mourning. Princess Nilsa Nightstalker stood at the edge of the eastern parapet, her cloak snapping against the cold wind. Her hair—dark as ravens' wings and braided tightly down her back—whipped against her shoulder as she looked out over the capital. Below her, the city slept beneath veils of pearly mist: spired rooftops muted by fog, silent market squares, shuttered windows still touched by night's chill. The palace bells had finally stopped ringing hours ago, but the echo remained in her bones. Kaelvar was gone.

Nilsa pressed her palm to the stone railing, grounding herself against the tremor in her hands. She had always been steady, with sharp green eyes that missed nothing and a presence that carried more steel than softness, but this morning her composure wavered. The cold helped. It kept her mind from slipping too far into memory—into the image of Kaelvar's face in that final moment. Peaceful. Too peaceful. As if he had simply drifted into a dream and decided not to return. Her jaw tightened. No more. She wouldn't let the curse take another heir of Orlanthia. Not her brother, not her mother's brothers before him, not the sons she hoped to have someday. Not anyone.

A soft knock sounded behind her. "Princess?" Erabor's voice, low and unsure. "The council convenes in the High Hall." Nilsa didn't turn yet. She needed one last breath of cold air—one last moment before she had to face the politics of grief: the whispers, the pity, the excuses.

"Did they send for me," she asked, "or are they already arguing without me?"

Erabor stepped beside her, leaving a respectful space. The early sunlight caught the loose strands of his dark hair, turning them copper at the ends. He wore simple clothing—a stable boy's tunic of rough spun charcoal, sleeves rolled to his forearms, revealing hands calloused from work. His features were sharper than most boys his age, cheekbones angled, jaw lean, and his eyes—gray with a strange undercurrent of blue—held a depth far older than he seemed. His frame was wiry, strong in a quiet, unassuming way, and though the wind bit at his clothes, he didn't flinch.

"They're waiting," he said softly. "Queen Ysolde asked that you join them as soon as you're ready."

Nilsa exhaled slowly. "Ready," she murmured. "The word feels wrong."

He didn't offer comfort—thank the stars. Too many courtiers had already tried, their condolences empty and afraid, as if Kaelvar's death were something contagious. But Erabor had a way of being present without pressing. It was a rare skill.

"We should go," she said.

They descended from the parapet, boots clapping faintly along marble steps. The palace halls were draped in mourning sigils—silver cloth woven with the twelve-pointed star, each point representing a kingdom of Adollith. The center circle, always hollow, was bound in black ribbon. The missing star. The erased kingdom. Nilsa's eyes followed the empty circle each time they passed it. Its hollowness had always unsettled her—like a wound in the world.

"Your brother was beloved," a soft voice said as Nilsa entered the High Hall.

Queen Ysolde stood among the assembled councilors. She was striking even in grief: tall, dignified, with hair the color of polished obsidian braided loosely down her back, strands slipping free around her pale face. Her eyes—deep blue, rimmed in red—bore the heavy lines of sleeplessness, but her posture remained unyielding: Nightstalker to the core. Nilsa bowed her head. Her mother's hand brushed her cheek, a fleeting touch, then fell away.

"We have much to discuss," Queen Ysolde whispered.

The council chamber loomed with tall windows that bathed the room in pale light. Twelve banners lined the walls—one for each kingdom of Adollith. Even the air felt heavy. Councilor Marith, the Minister of Knowledge—a thin, balding man who always smelled faintly of ink—cleared his throat. "Your Highness, the physicians found no trace of poison in Prince Kaelvar's body, no sign of illness—"

"Because it wasn't poison," Nilsa snapped. "It was the curse."

A ripple of murmurs broke across the room.

Councilor Rhyven, a broad-shouldered man with a jagged scar across his jaw and a warrior's stance, folded his arms. "The curse is centuries old, Princess. If there had been a way to break it, the queens and kings before you would have found it."

Nilsa locked eyes with him, unblinking. "The rulers before me didn't have what I have."

"And what is that, exactly?" Rhyven challenged.

Nilsa opened her mouth—but High Seer Elmaris stepped forward. The frail, silver-haired priest looked as though he were crafted from candlelight and smoke; his white eyes shimmered faintly beneath his hood. "She has purpose," Elmaris said, voice low and ethereal. "And a spark that does not belong to Orlanthia alone."

Queen Ysolde's glare snapped toward him. "Seer. You tread too close to forbidden prophecy."

Elmaris dipped his head. "Forgive me, Your Majesty. But we no longer have the luxury of silence."

The councilors shifted uneasily.

"Our kingdom can withstand many storms," Ysolde said. "But not the extinction of our line. Not the death of every male heir."

Nilsa stepped to the center of the room. Her posture straightened; her voice sharpened.

"I will leave Orlanthia," she declared. "I will travel to each kingdom and seek the origins of these curses. The answers are out there—I know they are."

Rhyven slammed his palm on the table. "You are the last surviving heir! You cannot simply wander Adollith searching for bedtime stories and forgotten legends!"

"I'm not wandering," she said coldly. "I'm hunting."

The room froze.

Erabor stood behind her, posture stiff, eyes alert. Nilsa felt the strange steadiness of him at her back—a quiet reassurance she hadn't asked for but didn't reject.

Councilor Marith wrung his hands. "The world beyond our borders is dangerous. Even the friendliest kingdoms are unpredictable. And the cursed lands—"

"Are dying slowly," Nilsa finished. "Just like us."

Her mother's voice softened. "Nilsa… where would you begin?"

Nilsa reached into her cloak and withdrew a folded scrap of parchment—the sigil the Seer had shown her the night before. The forbidden symbol. Twelve circles encircling a hollow core. A kingdom erased.

"I'll start where all knowledge ends," she said quietly. "With the kingdom no one speaks of."

Shock pulsed through the council like lightning.

"You cannot be serious," Marith whispered. "The Thirteenth Kingdom is a myth."

"No," Elmaris said softly. "It is a secret."

Nilsa felt Erabor's attention sharpen behind her—subtle, unmistakable, like the tightening of unseen wings.

Queen Ysolde studied her daughter for a long, weighty moment. "You are your father's fire," she finally said. "And your brother's courage. If you believe this journey is our only hope…"

Nilsa held her mother's gaze, heart pounding.

"Then go," Ysolde whispered. "Go, and may the stars guide you. But you will not travel alone."

Nilsa turned to Erabor. His brows lifted—surprise, then something deeper. His eyes, storm-gray with hints of silver, seemed to catch the light in an unsettling way.

"You," she said softly. "Will you come with me?"

For a heartbeat, something unreadable passed across his eyes—sharp, ancient, almost luminous. Then it vanished. He bowed deeply.

"Always," he said.

And Nilsa felt—without knowing why—that the path ahead had just shifted. Not because she chose him—
—but because he had been waiting for her to ask.

CHAPTER TWO

The Stable Boy's Oath

The royal stables of Orlanthia woke before the sun. By the time the first gray light of morning touched the palace roofs, the air in the lower courtyards already smelled of hay, horse sweat, leather oil, and the faint tang of river mist drifting up from the valley. Hooves shifted in stalls; tails swished; harness buckles clinked. Somewhere near the back, a restless mare snapped at a groom's sleeve and the boy swore under his breath, his voice blending with the low murmur of animals and men beginning another day.

Nilsa inhaled deeply as she stepped through the archway, letting the familiar scent steady her. The stone beneath her boots was worn smooth by years of hooves and feet, and her breath came out in small puffs in the cold air. She had spent half her childhood here, hiding from etiquette tutors and suffocating ceremonies, her dark braid flying behind her as she raced horses down the lower track. While her mother and the court saw horses as status—symbols of rank and ceremony—Nilsa saw them as freedom: muscle and lightning and open sky bound together.

Today, the stables felt different. Quieter. Watching.

Her boots whispered over packed straw as she walked the central aisle. Lantern light cast soft golden pools over rows of stalls, catching in floating dust motes and highlighting the worn grain of the wood. Grooms and stablehands paused in their work, bowing or dipping their heads as she passed. Some were older men with weathered faces and thick forearms, others lanky youths with straw sticking in their hair. A few looked at her with pity; others with a kind of hushed awe, as if being the last heir made her both sacred and cursed. Nilsa ignored their gazes and focused on the stalls, letting her fingertips trail along wooden doors as she passed. The wood was cool under her gloved hands, familiar. She couldn't shake the sense that once she rode out, everything would change—that she would not come back the same, if she came back at all.

"Princess."

Erabor's voice came from near the far end. He stood in the tack room doorway, sleeves rolled up over his forearms, a worn leather bridle draped over one arm. Dust and straw clung to his dark hair, and there was a smear of something—soot or saddle grease—along the sharp line of his jaw. He looked exactly as he always did: simple tunic, plain trousers tucked into scuffed boots, the posture of a boy used to lifting more weight than he admitted. And yet, after last night, Nilsa could not forget the way his shadow had twisted.

"Is she ready?" Nilsa asked.

"Almost." He nodded toward the last stall, eyes flicking briefly to her face, then away again with that careful deference he wore like another layer of clothing. "I thought you'd want to see to her yourself."

Nilsa's mouth curved despite everything. "Of course."

She crossed to the stall and unlatched it. Inside, her mare lifted her head with a soft snort. Starwind was a tall gray with dark dapples along her flanks, a thick winter coat, and clever dark eyes that glittered in the dim light. A faint scar traced along one shoulder from a reckless jump years ago, a reminder of Nilsa's impatience and Starwind's willingness to follow her anyway. The mare nudged Nilsa's shoulder with her nose, searching with practiced entitlement for a treat.

Nilsa produced a dried apple slice from her pocket. "You're as bad as the courtiers," she murmured as Starwind crunched, warm lips tickling her palm. "Always wanting something first."

Starwind snorted again, breath puffing over Nilsa's cheek in a cloud of warm, sweet steam.

Behind her, Erabor chuckled, a low, easy sound that seemed to rumble more in his chest than in the air. "At least she earns her keep."

Nilsa shot him a look over her shoulder, green eyes narrowing just slightly. "Are you suggesting I don't?"

He ducked his head quickly, a faint smile tugging at the corner of his mouth. "Never, Princess."

She turned back to the mare, but the hint of a smile lingered on her lips. Erabor's teasing was gentle, careful, like testing the edge of a blade before trusting it, but it grounded her in a way the council chamber never could.

"Which horses did you choose for the journey?" she asked, running a hand along Starwind's neck, feeling the warmth beneath the winter coat and the strength coiled beneath skin and muscle.

"I've set aside four." He moved closer, the bridle now looped over his shoulder. His steps were light for someone his height, practiced in moving quietly among skittish animals. "Starwind for you, of course. Flint for myself." He nodded toward a sturdy bay gelding with a broad chest and steady dark eyes, standing tied further down the aisle. "And two pack horses—Bracken and Moss. They're steady on bad roads and know how to keep quiet."

Nilsa nodded slowly. "Good. We'll need quiet."

"You intend to leave without escort?" His tone was polite, but there was a thread of concern beneath it, a tightening around his eyes.

"I intend to travel without a banner that screams 'assassinate me' from a league away," she said dryly. "A princess with a full honor guard draws enemies. Two riders and pack horses draw less attention."

"Two riders," Erabor repeated, as if weighing the words. "Are you certain the queen will allow that?"

"She already has." Nilsa's throat tightened, remembering the brief, aching embrace in her mother's private chambers before dawn. Ysolde's hands had been cool on her cheeks; her voice rough with unshed tears as she pressed a signet ring into Nilsa's hand and whispered, "Come back or don't—but don't die without changing something."

"My mother understands what's at stake," Nilsa finished softly.

Erabor studied her for a moment, his gray eyes thoughtful. "And the council?"

"Will complain regardless," she said. "I've left them something to argue over. It will keep them busy while we're gone."

He looked like he wanted to ask what she meant, but thought better of it, his mouth closing on the question.

Nilsa stepped out of Starwind's stall, closing the latch with a firm click. "How long until we can be ready to ride?"

"If we travel light?" Erabor considered, gaze flicking toward the tack room and back, fingers drumming once against the bridle in his hand. "Two hours. Less, if I threaten the lads."

"Do it in one," she said. "We'll take trail provisions, bedrolls, and nothing we can't afford to lose. I'll see to the rest."

"Yes, Princess."

He turned toward the tack room, then hesitated in the doorway. "You should know... rumors are already moving through the lower halls. People are saying the curse will turn next to the queen."

Nilsa's pulse stuttered. "It won't," she said, more fiercely than she felt. "I won't let it."

"I know." Erabor's eyes softened briefly, a flicker of warmth in storm-colored irises, then shuttered again behind his usual reserve. "I'll have the horses ready."

He disappeared into the tack room, the shadows swallowing him, leaving her alone in the aisle.

For a moment, Nilsa leaned back against Starwind's stall, the cool wood seeping through her cloak, pressing her fingers to her temples. It would be so easy to stay. To let the Seer and council pore over old records while she hid safely behind palace walls, playing the dutiful heir and waiting for the curse to decide whether she lived or died.

No.

She straightened, shoulders squaring, the weight of her cloak settling around her like armor. If the curse wanted to find her, it would have to chase her.

Nilsa's chambers were a riot of motion when she returned.

Maids hurried across the marble floors with armfuls of traveling gowns, cloaks, and boots. Their skirts whispered and swirled around their ankles, hands busy, eyes darting. An older woman with streaks of silver in her dark hair fussed over stacked trunks, muttering about wrinkled silks and inadequate jewelry. Someone had laid three different tiaras out on the bed, each one glittering with carefully-cut gems, as though she meant to attend a banquet rather than ride unknown roads.

"Stop," Nilsa said from the doorway.

The room stilled. One maid froze mid-fold; another clutched a cloak to her chest as though expecting it to be torn from her.

"Out," Nilsa added, more gently but no less firm. "All of you, please. Save your hands for when I come back."

The servants exchanged glances, confused and uneasy, but they obeyed. One by one, they filed out—the older woman with stiff dignity, the younger ones with backward glances—leaving her alone with the quiet rustle of curtains and the distant murmur of the palace.

When the door clicked shut, Nilsa sagged against it for a heartbeat, then pushed off and strode toward the bed. Two strides, and she swept the tiaras back into their velvet box and snapped the lid closed.

"Not this time," she muttered.

Instead of silk, she chose sturdy riding leathers—dark, worn-soft breeches that had seen more rides than receptions, a high-collared shirt that allowed for easy movement, and a fitted leather jerkin that hugged her frame without restricting her arms. She buckled on knee-high boots, flexing her ankles to ensure the fit, then reached for a cloak of deep wine-red wool, heavier than the ceremonial ones and lined with black fur at the collar. The fabric weighed comfortably on her shoulders, a practical warmth rather than a decorative flourish.

Only when she fastened the clasp at her throat did she let herself cross to the small chest near the window. It was plain, made of polished darkwood with no ornament, its surface smooth where years of hands had touched it. Her father had kept his most personal belongings in it: letters, old maps, a crude wooden horse Kaelvar had carved as a boy. After his death, Nilsa had added her own fragments of memory.

She knelt and opened the lid.

Inside, nestled among folded parchment and a few small tokens, lay a dagger.

Its hilt was wrapped in dark leather worn shiny where fingers had gripped it again and again. The pommel held a small stone that looked unremarkable at first glance, but under certain angles caught the light in shifting colors, as if a storm lived inside. Her father had worn it on his belt whenever he left the palace. After he died, it had passed to Kaelvar. Now it belonged to her.

Nilsa lifted the blade, feeling its familiar weight settle into her palm. The metal was cool and perfectly balanced, the kind of craftsmanship that whispered of old alliances and skilled hands long gone.

"I'll carry you for all of us," she said quietly—to her father, to Kaelvar, to the line of men the curse had already devoured.

The dagger slid into the sheath at her hip as though it had never left.

On the table near the window, sunlight spilled across the parchment Elmaris had given her that morning. The forbidden sigil glowed faintly in ink that never seemed to dull, no matter how long it sat in the light: twelve circles surrounding a hollow center. Nilsa folded the paper carefully, the crease lining up perfectly with the last, and tucked it into an inner pocket of her cloak, close to her heart.

A knock sounded at the door.

"Enter," she called.

Queen Ysolde stepped inside alone, closing the door behind her with a soft click. Without the crown and heavy ceremonial robes, she looked smaller, her age showing in the fine lines at the corners of her eyes and in the faint silver at her temples. But her gaze was as sharp as ever, blue eyes taking in everything from Nilsa's boots to the dagger at her hip.

"You're dressed to leave," the queen observed.

"I am." Nilsa swallowed. "If I don't go now, I might never."

Ysolde crossed the room, her fingers brushing along the back of a chair as she passed, as if reassuring herself it was solid. The simple gesture betrayed more than any words.

"There's still time to change your mind," she said.

"Is there?" Nilsa met her mother's eyes. "If I stay, what changes? We hold vigils. We light candles. We wait for the curse to decide whether it will come for you next. Or for me. Or for children I haven't had yet. I can't live like that."

"And you think wandering into stranger kingdoms will feel safer?" Ysolde's words were sharp, but her voice trembled, the edges of her composure fraying.

"No." Nilsa's chest ached. "But at least I'll be doing something other than waiting to die."

A long silence stretched between them, filled with things neither quite dared to say.

At last, Ysolde sighed, the sound soft and tired, like a curtain falling at the end of a long play. "You have your father's stubbornness."

"I hope I have some of his courage as well," Nilsa said quietly.

"You have more than you know." The queen reached into the pocket of her gown and drew out a small bundle wrapped in dark cloth. Her fingers lingered on it for a heartbeat before she extended it. "Take this."

Nilsa accepted it and unfolded the cloth. Inside lay a simple silver circlet, thinner and less ornate than the royal crown. Tiny star-shaped etchings ran along its surface, worn soft from years of use.

"I wore that," Ysolde said, "when I was your age and my mother sent me to negotiate our first treaty with Veldrian. I was scared enough to be sick, I made three diplomatic mistakes before midday, and I nearly froze riding over the border." Her eyes softened with the memory, a faint smile ghosting across her lips. "But I came home. And Orlanthia was stronger for it."

Nilsa's throat tightened. "You want me to wear it?"

"I want you to remember you are not just a girl running from a curse," her mother said. "You are a princess of Orlanthia. When other rulers look at you, I want them to see that. To remember that our line has not broken yet."

Nilsa set the circlet gently on the table, as though it might shatter. "Thank you, Mother."

Ysolde hesitated, then stepped forward and pulled her into an embrace. For a heartbeat, Nilsa was a child again, burying her face in her mother's shoulder, breathing in the familiar scent of lavender and parchment and the faint bite of winter air clinging to her hair.

"Come back to me if you can," Ysolde whispered. "And if you cannot… make sure the world you leave behind is better than the one that took you."

"I will." Nilsa's voice cracked.

The queen drew back, cupped Nilsa's face in both hands, and pressed a kiss to her forehead. "Go, then," she said. "Before I change my mind and have you locked in the tower."

Nilsa laughed through the tears threatening her eyes. "You'd have to catch me first."

Ysolde's lips twitched. "I'm the queen. I don't chase. I order."

"Then I'd have to hope you give the order too late."

"Impudent child," Ysolde muttered—but there was unmistakable pride in her eyes.

They parted with one last squeeze of hands, and then Nilsa was alone again. She picked up the circlet and, after a moment's hesitation, set it on her head. It settled lightly against her hair, cool and sure, as if made for this moment.

"Princess of Orlanthia," she whispered to her reflection in the window's glass. "Daughter of the broken line. Let's see if we can mend it."

Erabor was waiting in the courtyard when she descended the palace steps.

Starwind stood saddled and ready beside him, ears flicking as she tested the bit, silver-gray coat gleaming faintly where frost had melted under her warmth. Flint, the bay gelding, shifted his weight behind them, thick neck arched as he breathed little plumes of steam into the cold air. The two pack horses, Bracken and Moss—both plain brown with patient eyes and sturdy legs—stood nose to tail, already laden with neatly strapped bundles of canvas and leather.

Morning had brightened fully now, the sky a pale, washed gold over the city roofs. Frost glittered along the edges of the stonework like scattered glass. Guards moved along the walls above, their armor catching the light in dull glints.

Nilsa's heart hammered as she crossed the courtyard, the sound of her boots on stone ringing too loudly in her ears. The circlet on her brow felt suddenly heavier, both burden and promise.

"Travel light, you said," Erabor greeted her. He stood with one hand resting on Flint's neck, the other adjusting a strap on one of the packs. His cheeks were flushed from the cold, and a faint sheen of effort clung to him from the morning's work. "I did my best."

His gaze flicked briefly to the circlet on her brow, lingering there for just a heartbeat, but he said nothing about it—only turned back to check Flint's girth strap and a buckle on one of the packs with practiced efficiency.

"Any trouble?" she asked.

"A few questions," he said. "Some of the guards wanted to know which route we'd be taking."

"And you told them…?"

"That we didn't know yet." His mouth curved slightly, a hint of mischief softening his normally guarded expression. "Which happens to be true."

She smiled despite herself. "Good."

They mounted—Nilsa swinging easily into Starwind's saddle, cloak settling around her legs, Erabor pulling himself onto Flint with the fluid familiarity of someone who had spent more of his life in a saddle than out of one. He sat straight-backed without stiffness, hands light but sure on the reins.

At the far end of the courtyard, the massive gates of Orlanthia's inner keep loomed closed, iron-banded wood etched with the crest of their house. Two guards stood at attention, spears upright, their breath fogging in the chill air.

Nilsa nudged Starwind forward. The mare stepped eagerly, hooves clattering on the stone. Flint and the pack horses followed, leather straps creaking softly.

When she reached the gates, Nilsa reined in and looked back once.

From the highest balcony, a small figure stood watching—Ysolde, cloak wrapped tightly around her against the cold, dark hair swept back, flanked by two distant shapes that might have been councilors or simply shadows. Even from here, Nilsa could feel the weight of her mother's gaze.

Nilsa raised her hand to her brow in a silent salute. The queen's hand lifted in answer.

"Open the gates," Nilsa called.

The nearest guard hesitated a fraction of a second longer than she liked, eyes flicking to the circlet, to her cloak, to the pack horses behind her—then he barked an order. Chains rattled overhead. The heavy doors groaned and began to swing inward, revealing the road beyond—narrow at first between high stone walls, then winding down through the city like a pale ribbon toward the valley.

The world outside Orlanthia's walls waited on the other side of that threshold: twelve cursed kingdoms, forgotten histories, and the echo of a thirteenth name no one would speak. Starwind shifted beneath her, sensing the change, ears pricked forward.

"Ready?" Nilsa asked quietly.

At her side, Erabor smiled faintly, but his eyes were serious, watchful, a storm held tightly in check. "I was ready the moment you said come."

She believed him.

They rode out together, hooves striking sparks from the stone as they crossed beneath the arch. As they passed into the shadow of the gate, the air cooled for just a moment, and Nilsa felt a strange shiver along her spine—as though something old and unseen had taken notice.

She did not see the way Erabor's fingers tightened briefly on the reins, or how his shadow—just for a heartbeat—unfurled behind him, stretching into something taller, with the faint outline of wings, before snapping back into place.

The road bent away from the palace, and Orlanthia's inner gates closed behind them with a thunderous boom that echoed down the valley like the closing of a chapter.

Nilsa did not look back again.

Ahead lay the first of the twelve kingdoms—and with it, perhaps, the first piece of the truth.

CHAPTER THREE

The Road of Whispering Bones

The road south of Orlanthia twisted along the valley like a pale scar. Frost clung to the grass in fragile needles, melting in slow droplets as the morning sun crept higher, turning the world from silver to damp green. Nilsa kept Starwind's gait steady but brisk, eager to put distance between the palace walls and whatever grief might try to drag her back. Each breath of cold air burned her lungs in a way she welcomed; it made her feel sharp, awake, alive.

Erabor rode a length behind her, Flint moving with quiet discipline, the gelding's dark coat already sheened with a thin layer of sweat despite the chill. The two pack horses followed without complaint, their ears flicking lazily, breath steaming from their nostrils in soft white clouds. Leather straps creaked, saddle blankets rustled, hooves thudded in a rhythm that promised miles yet to go.

For the first hour, they passed only frostbitten pines and the occasional shepherd leading stubborn sheep along narrow terraces, hunched in wool cloaks, eyes lifting just long enough to stare at the small traveling party: a young woman in a circlet and a stable boy who rode like a soldier. But as the valley narrowed into a long ravine, the road changed. Shadows thickened as the sun's reach faltered. The air cooled, seeping into Nilsa's gloves and gnawing at her fingertips.

The wind no longer sounded like wind.

It whispered.

Nilsa slowed Starwind with a gentle pull on the reins. The mare's ears pricked forward, muscles bunching beneath Nilsa's legs. "Do you hear that?" she asked, keeping her voice low.

Erabor lifted his head, eyes sharpening as he scanned the ravine ahead. "Yes."

The sound did not belong to leaves or wind or distant water. It was too soft. Too deliberate. Almost, Nilsa thought, like breathing—long, shallow exhalations woven through the stones themselves. The ravine walls rose higher around them, gray rock crowding in as if the world were narrowing into a throat. The road's pale dirt darkened to a flat, ashy gray. Strange stones jutted from the ground—smooth, bleached-white pillars that looked too much like bones half-risen from the earth.

Starwind tossed her head uneasily, muscles tightening beneath Nilsa's knees.

Nilsa patted her neck, fingers splaying against the warm, tense flesh. "Easy, girl…"

Erabor tightened Flint's reins, his knuckles whitening around the leather. "Princess… we should turn back."

Nilsa shot him a look over her shoulder. "We're barely an hour from home."

"Exactly," he murmured. "Curses bleed outward from their source. The lands near Orlanthia were supposed to be untouched."

Nilsa's pulse quickened. The Seer's words from the night before echoed in the back of her mind like a bell tolling underwater. The lost kingdom. The spark that did not belong to Orlanthia alone. The sigil hung suspended in violet ash. She had seen the way he'd hesitated, the way even speaking of it seemed to cost him something.

So if something was wrong here…

It was spreading.

A low moan drifted across the ravine—long, hollow, mournful, vibrating through the air like sound pressed through brittle lungs. Starwind shied sideways, hooves skidding in loose gravel. Flint snorted sharply, ears pinning back.

Erabor rode closer, bringing Flint nearly flank to flank with Starwind. "We need to move. Quietly. Eyes forward."

They urged the horses into a careful trot, keeping to the center of the road. The whispering grew louder, woven now with threads of something almost like words, though Nilsa couldn't make them out. At first she thought the sound came from the stones—but then she realized, with a prickling at the base of her neck:

No. It came from under the stones.

Like something buried was speaking through them.

Her skin crawled. "Erabor," she whispered, "what is this place?"

He didn't answer immediately. His jaw tightened; his eyes flicked from bone-white pillar to bone-white pillar, as if measuring their arrangement. "A graveyard," he said finally.

Nilsa swallowed. "We have graveyards in the capital."

"Not like this."

Another moan rolled through the air, lower, closer, as if the ravine itself exhaled.

Nilsa glanced more closely at the stones—not stones, she realized. Bones. They were too curved, too smooth, too intentionally placed—arranged like ribs the size of trees arching out of the earth, half-submerged in rock and packed soil. Old. Ancient. Weathered by centuries of wind and forgotten rites.

"What died here?" she murmured.

Erabor's expression darkened, his gaze haunted. "Not what. Who."

Before she could question him, Starwind froze under her. All four horses went still at once, breath sharp and shallow, ears pointed straight ahead.

The whispering stopped.

Silence slammed into the ravine like a falling stone.

Then—

C R A C K.

The ground split ten paces ahead, dirt collapsing inward as if something had punched upward from beneath. Starwind reared, her front hooves clawing at the air. Nilsa clung to the reins, teeth gritted, thighs gripping the saddle.

Erabor shouted, swinging off Flint with a fluid motion. "Behind me!"

The earth heaved again, a wave rolling under the soil. Nilsa didn't have time to dismount—something erupted from the ground, skeletal and twisted, its skull too large, its limbs too long, its finger-bones ending in jagged claws. Its eye sockets filled with a faint violet glow that pulsed like sickly stars caught in bone.

A bone wraith.

Nilsa's breath caught. They were supposed to exist only in the ruins of the Shattered Kingdom, bound to ancient battlefields and cursed fault-lines. Not here. Not this close to Orlanthia. Not within an hour's ride of home.

The creature lunged.

Starwind screamed, a terrible, tearing sound.

Nilsa drew her father's dagger in one swift motion and kicked free of the stirrup just as the wraith's claws slashed where her leg had been. She hit the ground hard, the impact jolting up her spine; she rolled, shoulder scraping stone, and came up on her feet, breath ragged—

Too slow.

The wraith swiped again. She ducked, barely, feeling the cold wind of its claws scrape past her cheek. The stink of old dust and rot gusted around her, dry and choking.

"Nilsa!"

Erabor crashed into the creature from the side, slamming his shoulder into its ribcage with a force that sent the wraith staggering. Bones clattered like thrown dice. Its spine bent at an impossible angle, but the violet light in its eyes did not dim.

Nilsa darted forward, slashing at what passed for its spine. Metal rang against bone; the dagger bit deep, and a long crack split the creature's back—

But it didn't fall.

It laughed.

A rasping, hollow whisper that sounded like air dragged through a skull.

Nilsa's blood iced in her veins.

Erabor grabbed her arm, fingers digging in. "These aren't meant to be fought," he said harshly. "We need to run!"

No. No—she would not flee from the first danger she faced beyond the walls, not after standing before the council and claiming she would hunt the source of the curse itself.

"I'm not running!" she snapped, ripping her arm free, eyes blazing.

"Princess—"

The wraith lunged again.

Nilsa braced, raising the dagger, muscles coiling—

But Erabor moved first.

Too fast. Faster than any stable boy should be able to move.

He closed the distance in a blur, seizing the wraith by the skull with one hand and slamming it into the ravine wall with inhuman force. Bone shattered like brittle glass. Dust exploded in a pale cloud. The violet light in its eyes winked out.

Nilsa stared.

No normal man could do that. No stable boy. No human.

Erabor looked back at her, chest heaving—not from exhaustion, but from something like restraint held taut. His eyes were too bright. Too sharp. For an instant they seemed to catch the faint violet reflection and turn it to steel.

She opened her mouth to demand an explanation—

Another whispering moan rose from the ground, deeper this time, layered with others.

Three more cracks split the earth.

Then five.

Then seven.

Dozens of violet-lit skulls pushed free of the dirt, jaws yawning in silent hunger as bony hands clawed upward through the soil. The old bones that marked the ravine shuddered, rattling faintly, as though the whole graveyard were waking.

"Erabor," she whispered, throat dry, "there are too many."

"I know."

He grabbed her shoulder—not roughly, but with the iron urgency of someone who understood exactly what they faced—and pulled her toward the horses. "Get on!"

She sprinted for Starwind. The mare met her halfway, shoving her nose against Nilsa's chest, practically pushing her into the saddle. Nilsa swung up, boots scraping leather. Erabor vaulted onto Flint with a grace no stablehand should possess, reins already in his hands by the time he settled in the saddle.

The first wraith crawled fully free, ribs stretching, jaw unhinging in a silent scream that seemed louder than sound.

"Ride!" Erabor barked.

Nilsa dug her heels in. Starwind bolted, surging forward like an arrow loosed from a bow. Behind them, the ravine exploded with shrieking bone. The pack horses lunged after Flint, hooves pounding the cursed ground.

They thundered along the narrowing path as skeletal claws raked the dirt inches behind their hooves. Stone fragments flew, skittering across the road. The whispers rose into a howl—voices overlapping, some chanting, some begging, some commanding, all threaded with that same wrongness Nilsa had felt when the Seer spoke of the lost kingdom.

She risked one glance back.

A dozen bone wraiths pursued. Then two dozen. Then more, a tide of clacking ivory and violet flame. Too many.

Ahead, the ravine widened into an open plain—but a collapsed tree, thick and old, blocked the path like a fallen gate.

"Jump it!" she yelled.

Starwind didn't hesitate. The mare gathered herself, hooves striking the log in a single beat, and leapt clean over. Nilsa rose slightly in the saddle, weight shifting forward with the motion.

Flint followed, Erabor low over the saddle, expression carved from stone—grim, focused, unflinching. The pack horses stumbled but made it after them, packs creaking, hooves scrambling.

The wraiths hit the fallen trunk and shattered against it, brittle bones splintering and scattering like broken glass. Others toppled over the fragments and collapsed in heaps, skulls rolling, their violet lights flickering and going dark.

The whispering died. Instantly. Like someone had cut the sound from the world with a single, clean stroke.

Nilsa rode another thirty breaths before she dared slow Starwind. Her lungs burned; her hands shook against the reins. Sweat chilled on the back of her neck beneath her cloak.

Erabor pulled Flint beside her. "Princess. Are you hurt?"

"No," she managed, though her voice came out thin. "You?"

"I'm fine."

He didn't look fine. He looked furious. Not at her—at the wraiths. At the world. At something deeper she could not yet see. There was a tightness in his jaw, a darkness in his eyes that made him look briefly like a stranger.

Nilsa wiped sweat—and a faint smear of dust—from her brow. "What were those things doing here?"

Erabor hesitated just a fraction too long. "Bone wraiths don't wander," he said. "They're called. Summoned."

"By who?"

He didn't answer.

She turned Starwind fully toward him, anger slicing through the remnants of fear. "Erabor—"

"I don't know," he said finally. Too quickly.

A lie.

Before she could press him, the ground ahead shifted. Nilsa froze. The plain they had ridden into was scarred—massive gouges torn through the earth, as though something huge had been dragged or burned across it. Blackened soil spread in charred circles, the grass reduced to brittle ash. Stone lay cracked and splintered, some pieces fused as if melted and then shattered.

And in the center of the destruction…

A body.

Nilsa's heart slammed into her ribs. She swung down from the saddle before Erabor could stop her, boots hitting the ground with a jolt. She sprinted forward, the scorched earth crunching and flaking beneath her feet. The stranger lay face-down in the dirt, clothes torn and darkened with soot, skin streaked with ash and blood.

A faint violet glow pulsed beneath their shoulder blade, visible through the shredded fabric. Nilsa's breath hitched. Not a glow. A mark.

She knelt, fingers trembling as she pulled the cloth aside. There, burned or inked into the skin, lay the same sigil the Seer had shown her in ash and violet light: twelve circles encircling a hollow center.

The mark of the Thirteenth Kingdom.

She staggered back, pulse thundering in her ears. The image of Elmaris's face flashed before her—his white eyes, his shaking hands, the hesitance in his voice when he had said some secrets were buried for good. The Seer's words had not merely described something forgotten. They had named it. Spoken it aloud. Broken the silence that had held for centuries.

"Erabor," she whispered, "what is this? Why do they have the mark of the Thirteenth Kingdom?"

Erabor didn't move. Didn't breathe. His gaze fixed on the sigil with a look she had never seen from him before.

Fear. Real, raw fear.

"Prophecy is bound to silence," he said quietly, as if speaking more to himself than to her. "Old names are kept in the dark for a reason. When the Seer spoke it aloud in the palace, he didn't just remember it." His eyes rose to meet hers, gray irises shot through with a strange, stormy light. "He called it."

Nilsa stared at him, the world tilting around the edges. "You mean… this—" she gestured at the ruined ground, the bone wraiths still clawing at the far edge of the plain, the glowing sigil— "this is because he spoke the name?"

"I think this is the first ripple," Erabor said. "There will be others."

A shiver ran through her. The curse. The lost kingdom. Bone wraiths where none should walk. And a mark burned into the flesh of a stranger, answering a name that had not been spoken aloud in three hundred years.

"Princess," he said, voice low and urgent, "we need to leave. Now."

Nilsa stared at the glowing mark, at the ruined ground, at the distant wraiths still writhing along the ravine's edge, trapped for now but straining against some unseen leash.

"No," she whispered. "We need answers."

Erabor's voice dropped even lower, carrying a weight that felt older than the road, older than the curse. "Then we need to find them before whatever did this finds us."

CHAPTER FOUR

Ash in the Wind

The body lay still beside the scorched earth, the faint violet sigil glowing beneath torn fabric like a coal refusing to go dark. The smell of burnt soil and old smoke clung to the air, almost thick enough to taste. Nilsa knelt beside the stranger, the knees of her riding leathers pressing into blackened ground, fingers hovering but not quite touching the mark as if it might flare and burn her at the slightest contact.

"Whoever they were," she murmured, voice low, "someone wanted them dead."

Erabor stood a few paces away, scanning the horizon. The wind tugged at his dark hair and cloak, but his body remained utterly still, every line of him drawn taut. His hand rested near the hilt of his dagger, not yet gripping it, but close. "Princess, we need to move. Wraiths don't awaken on their own. Something called them."

Nilsa lifted her chin, eyes never leaving the glowing sigil. "Then that something is close."

"Exactly why we should leave." His tone was calm, but there was iron under it.

She ignored the warning in his voice and leaned closer to the corpse. There was no blood on the ground, no visible wounds, no broken bones she could see—just ash-streaked skin, scorched clothing, and the sigil burned into the flesh as though pressed there by a brand heated in the heart of a dying star. The edges of it were faintly raised, charred and yet somehow still pulsing with light.

Nilsa swallowed hard. "This mark… it's the same as the parchment."

"No," Erabor said quietly. "It's older."

Her head snapped up. "How can you possibly know that?"

For a heartbeat, something flickered across his face—regret, or memory, or something she had no name for. Then it was gone, shuttered behind his usual careful composure.

"Princess," he said carefully, each word measured, "we are standing on cursed land. We cannot linger."

Nilsa studied him, really studied him: the tension braced across his shoulders, the way his eyes never settled in one place for long, how his gaze kept flicking to the edges of the plain, to the ravine, to the bones. He wasn't afraid for himself. He was afraid for her.

She rose slowly, brushing ash from her gloves. "Help me turn him over."

Erabor hesitated just a fraction too long. "Nilsa—"

"Do it."

A muscle ticked in his jaw, but he stepped forward without further protest. Together they rolled the body onto its back. The stranger's face came into view: gaunt, cheeks hollowed by hunger or illness, lips cracked and darkened from dehydration. Strands of hair, the color indistinguishable beneath the soot, clung to his forehead.

But his eyes—

Nilsa staggered back a step.

They were open. Glass-gray, filmed and empty, staring directly at the sky as if surprised by whatever had taken him. The pupils were blown wide, the irises nearly swallowed.

"Stars…" she whispered. "How long has he been dead?"

Erabor knelt beside her, leaning close but careful not to touch the corpse. His fingers hovered barely an inch above the man's wrist, as if feeling for something deeper than a pulse—sensing, tasting the echo of magic that might linger there.

"Hours," he said quietly. "Maybe less."

Nilsa frowned. "But his body is cold."

"So is this ground." Erabor's gaze flicked to the scorched ring around them, to the frost still clinging to the burned earth. "Cold from magic."

Frost on burned soil. Nilsa didn't know enough of spell craft to understand that contradiction, but the discomfort curling in her gut said it mattered. The air itself felt wrong here—heavy, stale, as if something had exhaled once and refused to breathe again.

She reached into the man's cloak, fingers careful and searching for a patch that wasn't completely charred. She half expected to find some kind of identification—papers, a seal, a crest—but her hand brushed something else instead: a small pouch tied to a leather cord around his neck, hidden beneath layers of torn fabric.

She pulled it free.

The leather was worn and warm from years against skin, yet faintly cool to the touch now. Inside, when she loosened the drawstrings and peeked in, lay six flat stones, smooth and round, each etched with the same hollow-centered sigil that burned in the man's flesh. The carvings glimmered faintly, as if catching light that wasn't there.

Nilsa's breath caught. "He was carrying these."

Erabor's hand shot forward, gripping her wrist before she could pull another stone out.

"Don't touch them," he said sharply.

The sudden intensity in his voice startled her. Nilsa's heart stuttered. "Erabor—"

"Please." His eyes met hers, unguarded for once. There was no deference there, no stable boy humility—only stark, naked fear. "Not with your bare skin."

She stared at him a beat longer, then gave a short nod. With her gloved hand, she closed the pouch again and slid it into an inner pocket of her cloak, feeling its weight settle against her ribs. "We'll examine them later."

"Not here," he said. The words came out like an oath.

A faint tremor rippled under their feet.

Nilsa stiffened. "What was that?"

The ground quivered again, like a great beast twitching in its sleep. Then again—each wave stronger than the last, rattling loose stones, sending a fine dust sifting from the cracked earth.

Erabor's hand went to the hilt of his dagger at last, fingers tightening around it. "Something's waking the bones."

Nilsa spun toward the ravine. It lay far behind them now, but even at this distance she could see dust rising from its depths, swirling unnaturally like smoke from an invisible fire. The whispering had started again—soft at first, then slowly rising, folding over itself in layers. Hungry.

"Erabor?" she whispered.

"We run. Now."

They sprinted back to the horses. Nilsa vaulted into Starwind's saddle just as the first bone spike erupted from the earth where the dead man had lain—a jagged shard of white punching upward through the burned soil. The ground buckled, cracking outward from the corpse like a spiderweb of fractures.

Erabor leapt onto Flint in one smooth, practiced motion. "Ride for the ridge!" he shouted.

They tore across the plain, hooves pounding harder than Nilsa's racing heart. The pack horses followed, their loads jolting and swaying with every stride. Behind them, the earth buckled, cracked, split—skeletal arms clawing upward in dozens, then hundreds, fingers raking at the air. Skulls pushed through the dirt, violet eyes flaring open like distant, cursed stars.

Nilsa didn't dare look back again.

They reached the ridge only after Starwind's breath grew ragged, her sides heaving, foam flecking her bit. The pack horses had slowed to a weary trudge, every step a labor. The higher ground opened into rolling forest—tall trees arching overhead, bare branches etched in frost, trunks silvered by winter's touch. The wind changed here, thinner and sharper, carrying the faint scent of pine and cold stone.

Only when the whispering disappeared entirely, swallowed by the hush of the woods, did Erabor slow Flint to a walk. Nilsa eased Starwind down as well, letting the mare's pace settle into something less punishing.

She swallowed hard, throat raw. "What… what happened back there? That wasn't just a graveyard."

Erabor didn't answer immediately. He scanned the trees, the wind, the shadows—always watching, always measuring what she could not see. His shoulders remained tight, the set of his mouth grim.

Finally he said, "Something reanimated the wraiths. Something tied to that sigil."

Nilsa's hand brushed the pouch hidden in her cloak. The stones seemed to burn cold against her skin, like ice pressed over an old scar. "Then the sigil is the key."

"Or the lure."

She met his gaze, searching for anything he wasn't saying. "Either way, we can't solve this here. Not alone. Not without records."

Erabor nodded once. "Then we head to the nearest kingdom."

"Morrivan," she said. The map of Adollith unfolded in her mind, the eastern border a jagged line of mountains and trade roads. "Five days' travel."

He hesitated. "The roads between here and there are not safe."

Nilsa let out a humorless breath that was almost a laugh. "Erabor, the roads behind us just tried to kill us."

He didn't argue. But his eyes—those strange, bright eyes that never quite seemed entirely human—looked like a storm she couldn't read.

They rode until the sun dipped low behind frost-tipped hills, turning the sky to a bruised blend of purple and gold. Nilsa's limbs ached from the long hours in the saddle, muscles burning from the earlier fight and the desperate flight across cursed ground. Starwind's strides had shortened, her head drooping lower with each mile. The pack horses had slowed to a weary, dragging plod; even Flint's steady rhythm had begun to falter.

"We need rest," Nilsa said at last, her voice rough. "We'll collapse at this rate."

Erabor scanned the tree line, eyes catching on shadows and shapes. Then he pointed toward a darker corner of the woods where the land dipped into a shallow hollow. "There. A hunter's shelter."

She followed him off the barely-marked road into the clearing.

At first glance, the structure looked like nothing more than a half-rotted lean-to of old timber and stone, tucked beneath the spreading branches of a massive oak. Moss crawled up its posts; one corner of the roof had sagged under the weight of years. But it blocked the wind, and the surrounding boulders formed a natural barrier, shielding them from casual eyes on the road.

Nilsa dismounted, her legs protesting as her boots hit the ground. Pins and needles shot up her calves, and she winced as she straightened. "We'll make camp here."

Erabor walked a slow circle around the clearing, gaze sweeping the tree line, the underbrush, the sky visible through bare branches. "It'll do," he agreed. But his shoulders never really relaxed.

He set about gathering fallen branches and dry kindling while Nilsa unpacked a bedroll and coaxed a small fire into life in the ring of old stones near the shelter's front. The flames crackled weakly at first, then caught and rose, casting unsteady light over the clearing. They gave barely enough warmth to sting her chilled fingers, but the glow was a comfort all the same.

She sat back on her heels, exhausted, and let the firelight smooth the sharp edges of her racing thoughts. Five days to Morrivan. Five days of risk with every mile. Five days to make sense of the sigils, the corpse, the wraiths, and the way the world had seemed to tilt the moment Elmaris spoke aloud of a kingdom no one was supposed to name.

A soft rustle cut through her thoughts.

"Erabor?" she asked, glancing toward the tree line.

He had been bent to pick up a branch, but now he stood entirely still, his back to her. Too still. The branch hung forgotten from his hand.

"Something wrong?" she murmured.

He didn't answer.

Then—"Princess," he said quietly, never turning his head, "get behind me."

Nilsa rose instantly, every trace of weariness burned away by a jolt of cold adrenaline. She drew her dagger, the familiar weight steadying her. Moving closer to him, she let the fire cast their shadows long across the ground.

The woods had gone silent.

Not quiet—silent. The previous rustle of small creatures in the underbrush, the occasional creak of branches, the whisper of wind through bare limbs—gone. All of it. As if the entire forest had drawn in a breath and was holding it, waiting.

A shadow shifted at the edge of the firelight. Low. Crawling. Wrong.

Nilsa stepped closer to Erabor, watching the shifting dark. "Another wraith?" she asked, keeping her voice soft and controlled.

"No," he said. "This is something else."

The shadow crept closer, stretching long across the forest floor, licking at the edges of the firelight without quite entering it. Its form shimmered, flickering between shapes like smoke trying to choose a body—a long-limbed beast, a hunched figure, something serpentine and scaled, then nothing more than a smear of darkness.

Nilsa raised her dagger, heart pounding.

Erabor didn't move.

The creature let out a thin, metallic scream, the sound scraping along her bones like rusted iron dragged over stone—

And lunged.

Nilsa braced, dagger ready, muscles taut—

But Erabor moved before she could.

He got between her and the creature faster than thought, faster than fear. His arm swept upward, catching the shadow-thing mid-lunge, and in one brutal, fluid motion he twisted it with impossible strength and slammed it to the ground so hard the earth shuddered beneath their boots. The impact knocked the breath from Nilsa's chest.

The creature shrieked again, its sound warping at the edges like a voice torn apart by wind.

Nilsa stumbled back, blade shaking despite her grip. "Erabor— what—?"

His voice was almost too calm. "Stay behind me."

The creature writhed, its shape warping in the firelight—long limbs, draconic tail, a rippling suggestion of wings, teeth that didn't belong in the mouth of any known animal. Its body flickered again, dissolving at the edges, reforming as if made of shards of darkness held together by will alone. Where its limbs met the earth, frost spidered outward, killing what little moss and grass there was.

Erabor pinned it with one hand. One.

It shouldn't have been possible.

"Princess," he said, never taking his eyes off the creature, "this thing did not follow us from Orlanthia."

"Then where—?" Her voice faltered.

His jaw tightened. "It was tracking the sigil."

Nilsa's pulse faltered. Her hand went instinctively to her cloak, feeling the outline of the pouch pressed against her side. "The stones?" she whispered.

Erabor nodded once, barely. The muscles in his arm stood out like carved stone.

The shadow-creature shrieked louder, its body fracturing like shattered ink, edges breaking apart and reforming as if something were trying to pull it away.

Nilsa raised her dagger, stepping forward. "We have to kill it. If we don't—"

But the creature dissolved fully into smoke before she could strike, its form collapsing inward, spiraling upward in a narrow column of black light. It shot into the sky like an arrow and vanished into the darkness beyond the treetops.

Nilsa gasped. "Where did it go?!"

Erabor stood slowly, his hand falling away from the ground where the creature had been. His chest rose and fell in deep, controlled breaths, as though he were holding something fierce and dangerous inside and refusing to let it break free.

"To whoever summoned it," he said darkly.

Nilsa's blood ran cold.

"Someone sent that thing after us," she whispered.

Erabor turned toward her, the firelight casting sharp planes of light and shadow across his face. For a moment he looked like someone else entirely—older, more dangerous, more… awake.

"Not us," he said. "You."

The fire crackled, tiny sparks drifting upward like dying stars and winking out against the night. The woods at the edge of the clearing remained utterly still, the silence pressing in from all sides.

Nilsa wrapped her cloak tighter around her shoulders, as if the fur-lined wool could shield her from the weight of unseen eyes. The cold settled deeper into her bones, a chill that had nothing to do with the air.

"Erabor," she said, voice barely above a whisper, "what in the gods' names have I stepped into?"

He looked at her with something almost like sorrow, the storm in his eyes momentarily unmasked. "Not what," he murmured. "Who."

Then, softer still, as if the words themselves might carry too far, "And they are not finished."

Outside the small circle of firelight, the woods remained deathly still. Watching. Waiting. And far beyond the forest—five days' ride—lay a kingdom with records and answers and secrets older than Orlanthia's curses.

Whether those answers would save her…

Or destroy her.

CHAPTER FIVE

What the Shadows Remember

Night settled over the clearing like the slow fall of dying embers, the last threads of sunset fading into ash-gray gloom. The fire burned low, its flames crackling weakly as they gnawed at the small stack of kindling. Its warmth barely brushed the edges of the cold that seeped up from the cursed ground, a chill older than the surrounding forest, older than the kingdom whose roads they'd fled. The trees ringed the clearing like sentinels carved from shadow, their branches unmoving, stiff with frost.

Nilsa slept a few paces away, curled beneath her cloak, hair spilled across her cheek in dark waves. Her breath was soft, steady, almost peaceful. Innocent, even.

Erabor watched her for a long moment, arms folded across his knees, body still as the trees around them.

She had no idea.

No idea what hunted her name through the roots of dead kingdoms. No idea what stalked behind her shadow as easily as it stalked behind his. No idea that the danger wasn't something she was traveling *toward*—

Danger was following her.

He rose silently, the movement smooth enough not to disturb so much as a twig. The firelight caught the faint edge of his profile—cheekbone, jawline, the sharp set of his mouth—before he stepped into the fringe of darkness where the warmth faded and the true night began. Here, the air thickened. Colors dulled. The cold became a presence rather than a temperature.

The forest was too still. Not hushed with the gentle quiet of night, but frozen, as if the world had paused its own breathing.

No rustle of leaves.
No chitter of insects.
No distant hoot of owls.

Even the wind refused to move the branches.

It had been centuries since he'd felt silence like this.

Not silence.

Attention.

Something was watching.

Something old.
Something patient.
Something that remembered him.

Erabor closed his eyes, letting the darkness settle over him like a familiar cloak. He listened—not with ears. Not with anything mortal. But with the sense that pulsed beneath his skin like caged wildfire, the part of him he kept buried beneath layers of discipline and human mimicry.

A pull.
A whisper.
A thin thread of cold brushing the back of his neck.

You should not be here, little one.

His jaw tightened.
The voice wasn't heard.
It was felt—sliding into the world like frost tracing across glass.

He forced his breathing to slow. He would not answer. Not here. Not where Nilsa could hear him speak back to something that didn't belong to this world.

But the presence persisted, circling the clearing in slow, deliberate steps.

Protecting a mortal princess?
How far you have fallen.

Erabor's fingertips brushed the hilt of his dagger—not for defense. A blade would not save him from what stalked the tree line. It was a grounding touch, muscle memory from another age. A reminder to remain present. The world often blurred around him when the veil thinned. This kept him anchored to it.

He scanned the tree line. Nothing moved.

But shadows shifted between the trees, darker than night, slipping at the edges of sight—like smoke wrestling with the idea of shape.

The entity they'd fought earlier had been a weak thing, barely more than a puppet, a scrap of creation torn loose and molded into a mockery of life.

This presence was not weak.

It was ancient.
And patient.
And intimately familiar with the shape of his fear.

Nilsa stirred in her sleep, shifting slightly, the small sound bright and fragile in the dead air.

The presence coiled closer, drawn by the breath of the one it wanted.

Erabor stepped between her and the trees, posture rigid, shoulders squared, creating a barrier she would never know existed.

The shadows paused, as if startled by his defiance.

Then came the whisper, softer than frost melting on steel:

You cannot keep her from him.

Erabor's breath froze in his lungs.

Not *what*.
Not *it*.

Him.

His blood went cold.

That was no vague warning.
No shapeless threat.

Him meant a person.

A person he knew.

"One of his hunters?" he murmured under his breath, though he already knew the answer. His voice barely stirred the air, but the presence reacted anyway.

The temperature around him dropped, the air thickening in acknowledgment.

So.

It had begun.

At last.

The presence drifted closer, testing the boundary where firelight met shadow—a delicate threshold, a border that held only because it chose to. The flames guttered, shrinking in on themselves as if bowing in fear.

Erabor didn't move.

He could not.

To move meant to reveal.
To reveal meant Nilsa would know.
And Nilsa could not know.
Not yet.

The presence whispered again, its voice curling like cold fingers through the clearing:

She carries the mark. Only one bloodline ever could. And he will take her when the time is right.

Erabor's grip tightened on the dagger until the leather creaked. Something sharp and furious carved its way through his chest.

"She will never be his."

The words escaped before he could cage them.

The shadows recoiled, shrinking away as though struck. Then they twisted again, swirling like smoke caught in a sudden draft.

You cannot stop him. You are bound.

"I am bound by choice."

A lie.
Mostly.

The presence hissed, amusement sliding through the air like a slow, frigid tide.

Then you are a fool. Protect her, if you want. It will not matter.
He is coming.

Erabor's heart jolted, an old wound ripping open. Not for himself—he had stopped caring about his own fate lifetimes ago. But for Nilsa.

The presence unfurled backward into the forest, dissolving into drifting ash-dark tendrils. Its final whisper brushed the ground like embers rolling off a dying fire:

And when he finds her… he will remember you.

Silence reclaimed the clearing.

Erabor stood motionless for several breaths, the world slowly returning to shape around him. His jaw ached from how hard he had clenched it; his knuckles burned where the dagger's hilt had dug into his palm.

Only when he knew the presence was truly gone did he step back toward the fire, forcing his breathing to mimic human patterns again—slow, even, imperfect.

Nilsa shifted in her sleep, brow creasing as if sensing some distant nightmare.

He lowered himself beside her, stretching out on his bedroll with deliberate quiet, placing himself between her and the forest once more.

"Rest," he whispered.
"While you still can."

He watched the forest until dawn.

He never blinked.

CHAPTER SIX

The Forest That Watches

Dawn crept into the clearing like a wounded animal, pale and uneven. What little light slipped between the tangled branches overhead was the color of old bone. The fire had died to a ring of blackened embers and gray ash, thin fingers of smoke still twining lazily upward before dissolving into the cold air. Frost had crept over everything while they slept, crusting the bedroll edges, whitening the grass, and coating the branches above so thickly that they glittered like a thousand silent eyes staring down.

Nilsa woke with a start, heart hammering before her mind caught up. For one breath she forgot where she was—the bite of cold in her lungs, the stiffness in her limbs, the weight of the cloak over her shoulders. Then memory slammed back into place: the bone wraiths clawing from the earth, the corpse marked with the sigil, the shadow-creature Erabor had pinned to the ground like it weighed nothing at all.

She pushed herself upright, the bedroll crackling faintly with frost.

Erabor sat near the dead fire, posture too still, arms resting casually on his knees in a way that didn't fool her for a second. His gaze was fixed on the tree line, jaw clenched, shoulders drawn a little too tight. His cloak hung loose around him, untouched by sleep.

"Morning," she said quietly, voice rough with sleep and smoke.

His eyes flicked to her—just a glance, a brief sweep to assure himself she was awake and breathing—but the simple contact sent a wash of relief through her chest she hadn't known she was holding back.

"Eat something," he told her. "We're leaving soon."

Nilsa pulled a wrapped ration from her pack, the paper crinkling in the cold air, but her attention stayed on him. The gray light picked out the faint shadows under his eyes, the tight line of his mouth. He hadn't slept. She didn't need to ask to know.

"You didn't sleep," she said.

"I wasn't tired."

Another lie. A lazy one. He wasn't even trying to make it convincing anymore.

Nilsa opened her mouth to press him, but something tugged at the edge of her awareness—a subtle wrongness, like the forest had crept a few steps closer while she slept. A pressure she hadn't felt last night. The back of her neck prickled.

She rose, brushing frost from her cloak, and boots crunching softly on frozen ground.

The trees surrounding the clearing seemed… different. The line of trunks looked closer. Too many branches bent inward, their tips clawing toward the center of the clearing like fingers curling slowly. Too many roots coiled above the soil instead of beneath it, thick and knotted, looping over rocks and across the ground as if the forest itself were breathing through them.

Nilsa frowned. "The trees weren't this close last night."

Erabor stood instantly, all pretense of relaxed watchfulness vanishing. "Don't go near them."

She paused mid-step, instinctively obeying before bristling. "Why?"

"Just—don't."

He sounded almost… frightened.

That was new.

Nilsa turned slowly to face him, studying his expression. "Erabor, what's happening?"

He stepped between her and the tree line without thinking, movements smooth but edged with tension, his body forming an unconscious barrier.

"This forest is cursed," he said.

"Everything has been cursed lately," she muttered. "Land, trees, heirs, bloodlines—"

"Not like this."

Before she could reply, a soft creak rippled through the air, like old wood twisting under a weight it wasn't meant to bear.

Then another.
And another.

The nearest oak shuddered.

Nilsa's breath was caught in her throat. "Erabor—"

"Get back."

The tree twisted sharply. Bark split with the sound of breaking bones; long cracks racing up the trunk. Its roots tore upward from the earth, writhing like startled serpents, dragging clumps of frozen soil in clotted chunks. Ice cracked and flaked away as the roots uncoiled.

Nilsa stumbled back as more roots tore free—dozens, then hundreds—slithering across the ground toward the center of the clearing.

Toward her.

Erabor moved.

Faster than she could track.

One moment he was beside her, the next he was a blur in front of her, cloak snapping, steel flashing in his hand. He might as well have appeared there.

He slashed downward, severing a root as thick as his wrist. It shrieked—an awful, grinding sound like stone dragged across stone—and recoiled into the earth, spewing a spray of dirt and ice.

Nilsa drew her dagger, the familiar weight comforting. Her pulse thundered in her ears. "Why are they—?"

"Because of you," Erabor said through gritted teeth, cutting another root as it lunged for her ankles. "The sigil draws them. Everything with cursed blood can sense it."

Nilsa froze.

Not from fear—
From fury.

"So, I'm a lure now?" She snapped.

He didn't answer. His blade sang through the air repeatedly, slicing back the roots as they lunged, thrashed, writhed. Each cut sent another shriek; another spatter of black-tinged sap onto the frost.

Nilsa stepped forward, raising her dagger to strike at a root curling toward her—

The ground beneath her feet bulged.

A root shot up from the soil directly under her boots, explosive and sudden. She gasped and stumbled backward, arms pinwheeling—

Erabor caught it mid-strike.

He seized the root with his bare hand.

His bare hand.

Nilsa stared, stunned. The root was as thick as her thigh, ridged with knots, strong enough to rip boulders from the ground. A normal man should have been crushed instantly, pulled off his feet, dragged under.

But Erabor held it—held it—and forced it downward; muscles bunching under his tunic, tendons standing out along his forearm. He slammed it into the ground so hard the earth split, frost cracking like shattered glass.

For one dizzying heartbeat, the world narrowed around that motion—

And she saw something impossible.

His shadow on the frost-bright ground didn't match him.

It stretched taller.
Broader.
Winged.

Nilsa blinked—her heart stumbling in her chest.

The shadow snapped back into place. Human-shaped. Normal. Forgettable.

Just a trick of light.
Just exhaustion.
Just fear.

Right?

Erabor's voice snapped her back. "Nilsa—move!"

She lunged aside as another root whipped toward her legs. She brought her dagger down on it, blade biting through bark and sinew—but the resistance was wrong. Too soft to be wood. Too alive to be anything else. Something inside the root throbbed as it severed, spraying her with cold, sticky sap that smelled faintly of rot and metal.

"Fire!" Erabor yelled. "Get fire!"

Nilsa spun toward the dead embers. "It's out!"

"Then relight it!"

She scrambled to her pack, fingers clumsy with cold and adrenaline, fumbling for the flint and steel. Her hands shook as she struck them together, sparks leaping and dying on the blackened wood. Behind her, roots lashed and cracked against stone, Erabor's blade striking in a relentless rhythm.

The mother oak at the edge of the clearing—its trunk thicker than three men—was dragging itself closer, roots ripping free of the earth one after another, twisting its branches toward them like skeletal fingers reaching to pluck them from the ground.

Nilsa struck the flint—
A spark.
Then another, bright and brief.

The roots surged toward her, drawn by the motion, by the heartbeat pounding in her chest.

"Faster!" Erabor shouted, voice strained as three thick roots tried to pin him at once.

Nilsa's breath hitched.

She sparked again—

Flame.

A tiny tongue of fire caught on a curled scrap of bark, clinging stubbornly. She cupped her hand around it, feeding it with the smallest slivers of wood she had, coaxing it, pleading with it without words.

When it grew enough to hold, she seized the burning stick, whirled, and thrust it toward the nearest root. The moment flame touched bark, the entire limb recoiled with a ragged scream, curling away from the heat like burning paper.

Erabor saw his opening.

He drove his dagger into the base of the nearest oak with unbelievable force, the blade sinking to the hilt. He ripped downward in a long, brutal tear.

Sap—black, thick, and smoking—splashed across the frost like spilled ink.

The forest shrieked.

Not the tree. The *forest*.

Sound tore through the clearing, a chorus of creaking wood and grinding roots and a low, echoing groan that seemed to come from the earth itself. All at once, the trees pulled back as though the world had inhaled sharply. Roots withdrew into the soil, coiling down, branches twisted away, and the clearing widened by ten paces in an instant.

Then silence fell, sharp and sudden.

Nilsa sagged to her knees, clutching the burning stick like a lifeline, the flames licking dangerously close to her gloved fingers. Her lungs burned. Her heart felt like it was trying to punch its way out of her chest.

Erabor stood over her, chest rising and falling too fast for a man who "wasn't tired," dagger still in his hand, the black sap dripping slowly from the blade.

Nilsa swallowed, throat dry. "Is it… over?"

"For now."

His voice was a low rasp, more worn than she'd ever heard it.

She pushed damp hair from her face with a shaking hand. "What was that?"

"A corruption." He wiped the dagger on a patch of dead moss, the black sap smearing. "Something is poisoning the land. Twisting it."

Nilsa's hands trembled as she let the burning stick fall into the ring of cold ash. "And it wants the sigil."

He hesitated for the briefest moment. "Yes."

She stared at him, the word sinking like a stone. "Erabor… how did you hold that root?"

For a heartbeat, his eyes flicked—not away from her, but through her, as if calculating which truth would do the least damage. Then his expression smoothed.

"Adrenaline," he said. "Fear." A beat. "Luck."

Nilsa narrowed her eyes.

She didn't believe him. Not completely. The lie wasn't in the *words*; it was in the weight behind them. He was good at hiding, but she had grown up watching men lie in court and council. His silence had the same edges.

But the alternative—that he was something more—
Something other—

Was impossible.

Wasn't it?

"Pack up," he said abruptly. "We leave now."

"I haven't eaten," she protested, though the ration still sat forgotten beside her.

"Eat in the saddle."

He was already moving—stomping out the last of the embers, hoisting packs onto Flint's back, dismantling what little camp they had made with a speed that felt almost frantic. No—

Not frantic.

Afraid.

Not for himself.
For her.

Nilsa mounted Starwind, muscles still shaking, the mare shifting uneasily under her. "Is this forest alive?" she asked.

"Yes."

"Is it following us?"

"Not if we ride hard."

She tightened the reins, cloak settling around her legs. "What if it catches us?"

He looked at her then, eyes darker than dawn, colder than the frost still clinging to the shadowed side of the trees. "It won't," he said.

The way he said it made her shiver. Not a reassurance. A vow.

"Because I won't let it."

They rode fast. Too fast for tired horses, too fast for beasts that had already fled wraiths and twisting trees. The forest thinned gradually, grudgingly, the trees growing farther apart, the ground less choked by roots. The air lightened, though the cold remained.

As the land opened toward the southern road, Nilsa risked a look back over her shoulder.

The forest stood still, a dark wall of trunks and branches and frost-laced limbs. From this distance it looked inert, lifeless. But she could feel it watching, feel the weight of its silence pressing across the distance.

Watching.
Waiting.
But not pursuing.

Not now.

As they crested a low ridge, a gust of wind tore across the valley, tearing at their cloaks and scattering thin clouds of frost from the grasses. It carried with it a faint scent—smoke, sharp and metallic; metal, cold and bitter; and something sweet underneath, cloying and rotten, like flowers left too long in still water.

Nilsa wrinkled her nose. "What is that?"

Erabor didn't answer at first. His gaze was fixed on the horizon, on the faint suggestion of a distant line where land met sky. Morrivan lay somewhere beyond that invisible border, hidden by miles and whatever waited between.

Then, quietly, he said, "A warning."

Nilsa's skin prickled beneath her cloak. "Of what?"

He kept his eyes on the south, on the unseen roads and unknown dangers, but she could feel the way his attention stretched beyond them, like a sense reaching for something she could not perceive.

"Of what waits for us," he said at last. "And who sent the shadows."

He didn't add the rest aloud.

But it hung between them all the same.

And who wants you alive.

And why.

CHAPTER SEVEN

The Kingdom That Calls

Night fell faster than it should have. One moment the sun hovered low over the horizon, bleeding faint gold across the hills; the next, the sky dimmed unnaturally, washing the land in bruised violets and sickly grays. The air thickened. The shadows lengthened. The warmth fled without warning.

Nilsa and Erabor found shelter in a narrow hollow between two large, time-smoothed boulders—barely enough space for a fire, their packs, and the two bedrolls laid end to end. Wind scraped along the rocks above them, carrying the distant groan of the forest they had escaped. Nilsa didn't complain. She was too tired. Too shaken. Too aware of the forest's presence clawing like a memory at the back of her skull.

Erabor built the fire—a small, controlled flame, no more than a handful of kindling and a tightly contained spark. Anything larger might draw attention. *Attention* was the last thing either of them wanted.

Nilsa settled onto her bedroll, drawing her cloak close around her shoulders. The fire warmed her face but did nothing for the deeper chill lodged in her bones. Exhaustion weighted her eyelids like lead.

"Sleep," Erabor said softly from across the flame. His voice was gentle, but the set of his shoulders was not. "You need it."

She meant to argue. Meant to stay awake, alert, ready for whatever else the cursed land might throw their way.

Instead, exhaustion pulled her under like a tide.

She dreamed of a throne made of stars.

Not gold.
Not silver.
Stars.

Drifting, shimmering starlight braided into a spiraling seat that glowed softly with a warmth that wasn't warmth at all. The throne rose high above an endless floor of luminous stone, and around it stood twelve pillars—each one cracked in the same place, each fracture weeping shadow instead of dust. Darkness pooled at their bases, seeping outward in thin, curling tendrils.

A thirteenth pillar stood untouched.

Whole.
Unbroken.
Waiting.

Wind screamed across the empty hall, swirling around her in torrents of starlit dust. It carried voices—hundreds layered together—voices that sounded like they had been trapped beneath the earth for centuries.

She is awake.
The line has opened.
The blood returns.
The curse will break or bind.

Nilsa stepped forward, though she didn't remember choosing to move. Her bare feet were silent on the glowing floor. Her heart pounded painfully, each beat echoing through the hollow vaults above as if the hall itself were breathing with her.

She reached the throne.

Just as her hand touched the starlight—
Just as warmth and cold surged through her veins at once—

A hand seized her wrist.

Not hostile.
Not gentle.
Not human.

She looked up—

A figure stood before her, its body made of drifting smoke and starlit edges. It towered over her, tall enough that its features blurred into the shimmering air near the hall's heights. Its face was a shifting mask of shadow and luminescence—no eyes, no mouth, no features at all. Yet it watched her.

And when it spoke, its voice was hundreds layered as one:

"Daughter of the forgotten crown."

Nilsa tried to pull away.
She couldn't.

"Your brothers died because of him."

Her blood froze. "Because of who? Who did this?"

The figure's head tilted, the shape rippling like cloth underwater.

"The one who waits.
The one who remembers.
The one who wants what you carry."

The hall trembled violently. Cracks raced through the twelve broken pillars, shadows pouring faster from their wounds. Wind tore across the chamber as if something enormous stirred behind the walls—something long buried.

Nilsa's breath hitched. "What do I carry?"

The figure leaned closer, its presence cold enough to burn.

"The key."

"To what?"

Its voice fragmented the air around her:

"To him."

Before she could demand more, shadows flooded the hall, swallowing the throne, the pillars, the starlight—
And her.

Nilsa jerked awake with a strangled gasp.

Her heart hammered against her ribs, violent and frantic. Sweat clung to her skin despite the icy night air pressing in on all sides.

Erabor was at her side in an instant.
Too fast.

"Nilsa—what happened?"

His hands closed around her shoulders, steady and firm, his warmth anchoring her. His face hovered close enough that she could see the faint glimmer in his eyes—a glimmer the dying fire could not have caused.

Her breath trembled. "I… had a nightmare."

Erabor's grip tightened. "Tell me."

She hesitated.

If she told him everything—the throne, the voices, the figure made of starlight calling her *daughter of the forgotten crown*—

Would he think she was losing her mind?

Or worse…

Would he confirm it?

"It felt like a dream," she whispered, "but not a dream."

She swallowed hard. "Erabor, something *spoke* to me."

His entire body went still, every muscle coiled.

"What kind of something?"

"A… figure. Made of smoke and starlight. It stood in a hall of broken pillars." She tried to steady her voice. "It said my brothers died because of someone called *him*."

Erabor's breath left him in a slow, controlled exhale.

Not surprise.
Recognition.

"Nilsa," he said carefully, "dreams are strange when you're under stress. The mind creates—"

"Don't lie to me."

Her voice came sharper than intended.

He flinched—not visibly, but in the subtle tightening of his jaw, a flicker she wouldn't have noticed days ago.

She stared at him. "You know something."

"I know," he said slowly, "that dreams feel real when you are afraid."

It was a lie.
A beautiful, flawless, perfectly constructed lie.

But a lie all the same.

Nilsa grabbed his wrist. Her grip was not strong, but it was desperate. "This wasn't fear. This was—this was someone *reaching* for me."

His eyes darkened, pupils narrowing like a predator scenting danger. "Then don't let them in."

"How?" Her voice shook. "I don't even know who they are!"

Erabor's hand lifted—hesitated—and then cupped her cheek.

A soft, steady touch.
Warmer than fire.
Too gentle for the creature she'd seen tear roots from the earth.

"Nilsa," he murmured, "listen to me."

Her breath hitched, caught between fear and something else she didn't have a name for.

"You are strong enough to resist anything that hunts you."

Her voice wavered. "And if I'm not?"

His jaw tightened, thumb brushing her cheekbone with a gentleness that stole air from her lungs.

"Then I am," he said.

Silence settled between them—heavy, fragile, frighteningly warm.

Nilsa swallowed hard. "You're hiding something."

He didn't deny it.

Not this time.

He only said softly:

"It is safer for you not to know it."

Anger flared. And fear. And the aching pull of trust she wasn't ready to give, yet could not stop feeling.

"Erabor—"

He stood abruptly, stepping back into the shadowed edge of the hollow, cloak sweeping around him as though putting a wall between them.

"We ride at dawn," he said, voice cold enough to shatter. "Morrivan is four days away now. And every mile will be worse than the last."

Nilsa's throat tightened.

He was retreating.
Closing the door she didn't know how to open.

But as he turned away, the firelight shifted—
And for a heartbeat, she saw it again.

His shadow.

Not human.
Not even close.

Long.
Tall.
Winged.

And then it was gone.

Nilsa wrapped her cloak tighter, settling onto her bedroll though she knew sleep would not return. Not with the throne burning behind her eyes. Not with the sigil heavy in her pocket. Not with Erabor's touch still warm on her cheek.

And not with the question the dream had carved deep into her bones:

Who waits for her?

And why did Erabor fear him more than the curse itself?

CHAPTER EIGHT

The Empty Outpost

They reached the border outpost just after midday, the sun a pale disc behind thickening clouds, as if even the sky was losing interest in shining on this stretch of land. The wind had sharpened with the bite of early winter, cold and restless, slipping icy fingers under Nilsa's cloak and into the seams of her gloves. It raced ahead of them across the road, as if it hurried to whisper warnings farther down the valley.

Nilsa slowed Starwind as the small stone fort came into view. It clung to the side of a low ridge overlooking the valley, squat and unadorned, built for function more than pride. By all rights, it should have been bustling—border scouts exchanging shifts in the training yard, gruff voices calling rotations from the walls, the distant rumble of boots on stone. Smoke should have risen from the watchtower's hearth. Flags should have snapped in the wind, marking Orlanthian colors or, at the very least, some banner of allegiance.

From the moment she saw the outer gate hanging crooked on a broken hinge, her stomach dropped.

"Erabor," she murmured, the name rough in her throat.

"I see it."

Everything was wrong.

The training yard was empty—no sparring soldiers, no discarded practice spears, no scuffed dirt from boot tracks, just a crust of brittle frost. The signal tower stood dark and cold, its brazier unlit, no smoke, no embers. The flagpoles that should have borne Orlanthia's colors—or any colors at all—were bare. Ropes fluttered loosely in the wind, snapping occasionally against wood with a sound that made her flinch.

The silence was unnatural.

Smothering.

Nilsa guided Starwind through the courtyard arch, every sense straining, eyes sweeping the corners, the battlements, the shadowed alcoves. Her mare's hooves rang too loudly on the stone, each step echoing against empty walls. The air smelled faintly of ash…and something metallic beneath it.

Blood.

Her pulse jumped.

"Stay close," Erabor said quietly.

He dismounted first, boots landing with a controlled thud. His eyes cataloged everything—the empty sentry posts, the unmanned murder holes, the abandoned ladders at the tower's base. His hand hovered near his dagger, not drawn yet, but only a thought away.

He moved to the stablehouse door with a predator's caution, weight balanced, steps sure. Nilsa slid out of the saddle, dagger already in her hand, heart pounding as she followed him.

The door creaked open, the sound loud enough to feel sacrilegious.

Inside, the stables were empty—no horses shifting in their stalls, no soft snorts, no rustle of hay. The air held only the stale ghosts of those smells: old straw, dried sweat, leather oil. Bedrolls lay abandoned in a corner, tangled and unrolled. A pot of stew sat on the coals of a dead firepit, the surface congealed, ladle half-tipped where someone had dropped it mid-serving. Cold fat gleamed dully along the rim where it had spilled.

Nilsa's breath hitched. "Where is everyone?"

Erabor crouched near a dark streak in the dirt—a drag mark, long and uneven, as if something heavy had been pulled toward the door and out. His fingers hovered over it without touching.

"Taken," he said.

"By wraiths?" The word tasted like old fear.

"No."

He didn't say what.

He didn't have to—the weight in his voice said enough.

Nilsa stepped back outside, letting the cold wind hit her hard. She forced her gaze to sweep the outpost again, looking for any sign of life. The walls, the yard, the doors, the tower. A loose shutter rattled weakly against a barracks window, banging in a slow, uneven rhythm that echoed far too loudly in the emptiness.

They crossed the courtyard to the main hall. Erabor pushed the heavy door open, muscles flexing under his sleeves, and a gust of stale, cold air rushed out, brushing past them like something fleeing.

Inside, chaos.

Tables overturned, benches on their sides. Maps lay scattered across the floor, some torn, others trampled, ink smudged by hastily dragged boots. Quills lay snapped in half beside dried pools of ink. A lantern had been thrown against the wall, glass shattered, oil smeared in a long, ugly streak.

Nilsa's throat tightened. "Oh, stars…"

Erabor moved with the precision of someone who expected danger behind every door. Each step was calculated, each shift of weight deliberate. His gaze flicked from beam to beam, corner to corner, cataloging threats even in the stillness.

Nilsa followed him deeper into the hall, dagger ready, eyes straining to adjust to the dim light.

They found the body in the war room.

Nilsa gasped and stumbled back, her shoulder hitting the doorframe.

A border scout lay slumped against the far wall, legs sprawled awkwardly, head tilted at an unnatural angle. His eyes were wide open, glassy and empty, frozen in a look of terror that had never had time to fade. Across his throat, burn-marked into the skin in faint violet, was a familiar hollow-centered circle.

The sigil.

The same sigil on the corpse in the plain.
The same sigil hidden in the pouch against her ribs.

Nilsa forced herself forward and knelt beside him. He was young. Barely more than a boy. Maybe a year or two older than Erabor. His hair stuck to his forehead in dried clumps. His lips were parted, as if the last thing he'd done was try—and fail—to scream.

Fear was frozen in his eyes.

Erabor knelt too, but he didn't touch the body. He never touched the dead. His presence beside her felt like a shield, cold and steady.

Nilsa's gloved fingers brushed the violet stain, hovering over it, close enough to feel the residual heat that shouldn't still be there. "Why would the sigil be on him too?"

Erabor didn't answer.

"Erabor." Her voice sharpened.

"It wasn't burned into him," he said quietly. "It was cast onto him."

"Magic?"

"Yes."

Nilsa stared at the mark, at the sickly light that seemed to cling to it. "Is this a warning?"

"Or a claim."

The air in the room felt suddenly thinner. Colder. As if something was listening to them breathe.

She swallowed. "What could take an entire outpost in a single night?"

Erabor looked at her with an expression she couldn't read—anger coiled under restraint, something sharp and controlled and dangerous. "Something hunting."

Nilsa pushed to her feet, legs unsteady. "We need answers."

"And we will not find them here."

He reached out, two fingers hovering just above the scout's eyelids, and with a small motion, he drew them closed. He still didn't touch skin. Nilsa had the sudden, unsettling sense that this was not a habit he had learned from Orlanthian customs.

A gesture that felt ancient.
Ritualistic.

Nilsa turned toward the map table—and froze.

Something had been scratched into the wood.

Not with ink.
Not with a knife.

With desperate fingernails.

She leaned closer, heart pounding, and traced the jagged letters with her eyes.

DON'T STAY AT NIGHT

Her breath trembled.

Underneath it, in smaller, more uneven letters—as if written by a hand already shaking with pain:

HE'S COMING

Nilsa stepped back sharply, every instinct screaming.

"Erabor…"

He was at her side in a heartbeat.

His eyes darkened as he read the words, something like fury and dread warring behind them.

"Pack your things," he said.

"We are leaving. Now."

"Wait—what about—"

"No, Nilsa."

His voice cracked like a whip. Sharp. Commanding. It hit her in the chest and pinned the rest of the question in her throat.

He caught himself a heartbeat too late, swallowing the edge of fear, but the echo remained.

She stared at him, heart thudding. "You know who 'he' is. The dream. The body. Now this—who is he?"

Erabor closed his eyes for one brief moment, as if steadying himself against a wave she couldn't see. When he opened them again, they were shuttered, every thought locked away.

"You are safer not knowing," he said.

"That's not good enough."

"It has to be."

"Erabor—"

He stepped closer, lowering his voice so the shadows couldn't hear. The barely-lit war room suddenly felt too small, the walls too close.

"If you knew his name," he said, "even speaking it could draw him."

A chill raced down her spine. Names had power. She'd grown up hearing that in stories and legends, but now it sounded less like myth and more like a rule of survival.

Nilsa lowered her voice to match his. "Then why is he coming for me?"

Erabor hesitated.

And she knew—*knew*—he would lie again.

So she asked the one question he couldn't lie around.

"Is it because of the curse?"

His jaw tightened. Hard. A muscle jumped in his cheek.

"No," he said at last, voice barely a whisper.

"It is because of you."

The words landed like a stone dropped into deep water. No splash. Just a sinking weight.

Before she could speak again, a sudden gust slammed the outpost doors somewhere behind them. The impact rattled the walls, sent maps fluttering, and shook dust from the rafters in thin, drifting streams. The fire in the distant hearth—a mere ember they hadn't even noticed—sputtered and died as if choked by invisible hands.

The temperature plummeted.

Nilsa's breath caught in her chest.

"Erabor—"

"I know."

He grabbed her wrist—not harshly, but with an urgency she had never felt from him before—and pulled her toward the courtyard.

"Mount up," he ordered. "Keep your eyes forward. Don't look at the windows. Don't look at the shadows. And no matter what you hear—don't look back."

Her heart hammered so hard it almost drowned out his words. "Are we being followed?"

"No."

The wind screamed against the shutters as if in denial.

"We are being watched."

They ran.

Out of the war room.
Through the main hall.
Across the empty courtyard.

The outpost felt smaller now, as though the walls themselves were leaning inward.

They reached the horses. Nilsa swung onto Starwind's back with more haste than grace, fingers clumsy on the reins. Erabor was already in Flint's saddle, every line of him tense and ready.

He threw the reins forward, shouting, "Ride!"

Nilsa kicked Starwind hard, and the mare leapt forward, surging toward the broken gate. The pack horses strained to keep pace, hooves striking sparks from the stone.

As they tore through the ruined arch, something rattled across the outpost roof—light and quick, like claws or bones or wings skittering over tile and stone. The sound chased them into the open air.

Nilsa didn't look back.

But she felt it.

Whatever waited in the shadows…
whatever had emptied the outpost…
whatever had carved those desperate warnings into the table…

It had seen her.

It had marked her.

And now it knew she was coming.

CHAPTER NINE

The Road of Half-Remembered Prophecies

The road wound south through low, rolling hills, each one brushed with frost and winter-brown grass that whispered faintly under the wind. The dirt path had hardened to a pale, rutted ribbon, the edges crusted with ice where old puddles had frozen solid. Above them, the sky stretched pale and washed-out, a color between gray and exhausted blue, the fading light stretching long, skeletal shadows across the ground as the sun dragged itself slowly toward the horizon.

Nilsa and Erabor rode in silence for nearly an hour after leaving the empty outpost. The only sounds were the steady clop of hooves, the creak of leather, the soft jingle of tack, and the faint rasp of frost-stiff grass crushed beneath their horses' weight. Neither of them spoke of the body. Or the sigil burned into the scout's throat. Or the words carved into the table with torn fingernails.

HE'S COMING.

The memory of those letters sat like stone in Nilsa's chest, heavy and cold. Her fingers tightened around Starwind's reins until her knuckles ached inside her gloves. The air tasted wrong—thin and metallic, like it had scraped across old blood and ash before filling her lungs.

"Erabor?" she said at last, her voice quieter than she meant it to be.

He turned his head just enough that she knew he was listening, profile carved in hard lines against the dimming sky.

"Why would an entire outpost be abandoned?" she asked. "Without bodies. Without signs of retreat."

"Because the soldiers weren't killed," he said quietly. "They were taken."

A shiver ran down her spine. "By who?"

He hesitated a long breath. Then another. The silence between them stretched taut as a drawn bowstring.

"By something older than curses," he said finally. "And smarter."

Nilsa swallowed against the dryness in her throat. Older than curses. Older than the Sundering. Older than the stories whispered in Orlanthia's dark corners. The wind picked up, tugging at her cloak, its icy teeth nipping at her exposed skin. She didn't press him further—not because she didn't want answers, but because she could feel how hard he was fighting himself just to say that much, holding something back with every ounce of will he had.

They crested a ridge just as the sun bled into the horizon, turning the edge of the world into a smear of molten gold and bruised purple. A soft glow lit the valley below, bathing the distant trees in amber light that made them look almost gentle, almost harmless, from this distance. The sky thinned, the clouds streaked like smoke.

"Let's rest a moment," Nilsa said, sliding out of the saddle before Erabor could object. Her legs ached from hours of riding; her shoulders felt like carved stone.

Erabor opened his mouth anyway, because of course he did—

Her raised brow stopped him.

Starwind lowered her head to drink from a narrow stream that wound its way through the dip between hills, the water dark and clear, edged with fragile lacework ice. Nilsa knelt with a soft grunt and cupped water into her hands. It was shockingly cold, biting at her skin as she splashed it over her face, along the back of her neck. Her reflection wavered on the ripples—tired eyes ringed with shadows, cheeks reddened by the wind, a smudge of dirt near her jaw, hair mussed from the long ride and half-fallen from its ties.

She didn't look like a princess of Orlanthia.

She looked like someone running from something she didn't understand.

Erabor approached with two wrapped ration squares, the simple, practical gesture somehow grounding. "Eat."

Nilsa took one with a sigh, the corners of her mouth twitching. "You know, you're starting to sound like my mother."

He blinked at her, caught off guard.

Then—

A smile tugged at the corner of his mouth. It was faint. Barely there. But real—softening his features, warming his eyes for the briefest flicker of a moment.

Nilsa stared. "Did I… actually make you smile?"

His expression shut down instantly. "No."

"You did."

"I did not."

She leaned in, smirking despite the cold, despite the outpost, despite the heaviness in her chest. "I saw it."

Erabor looked away too quickly, like the horizon had suddenly become fascinating. "You're imagining things."

"Oh? Should I dream it again?" she teased.

The joke slipped out before she could stop it—light, easy, reflexive.

She instantly regretted it when she saw him stiffen, shoulders tightening, eyes going flat in that way they did when something cut too close.

Nilsa looked away, shame burning hot against the frozen air. "Sorry. I just—things have been so tense. I needed to… breathe."

Erabor exhaled slowly, as if reminding himself to. "You have nothing to apologize for."

When he looked at her again, the wall in his gaze had cracked—just a little. Enough for her to glimpse something raw behind it.

"Nilsa," he said softly, "I'm not good at—this."

"Talking?" she offered, one corner of her mouth lifting.

"Being…" He paused, searching for the right word, as if the language of vulnerability were one he only half remembered. "Open."

"You don't have to be," she said gently. "Just honest."

Erabor's throat worked, his gaze dropping briefly to the ground before returning to her. "I'm trying."

Her heart tightened, an ache that had nothing to do with curses or prophecies. "I know."

For a moment, the world felt still. Quiet. Almost peaceful. The hills rested under the bruised sky. The stream whispered its small secrets. Starwind's steady breathing and Flint's soft snort filled the silence between them with something almost like normalcy.

Then something glinted beneath the water.

Nilsa blinked, frowning, and leaned closer to the stream. "What is that?"

She crouched, cloak trailing through the frost-damp grass, and reached down. Her fingers slid between two slick rocks and closed around something smooth and hard. When she pulled it free, water streamed from polished metal, cold and heavy in her hand.

A pendant.

Round. Smooth.

Etched with a symbol she knew too well.

Twelve circles—
and a hollow center.

Her breath stuttered. "This mark—"

Erabor was beside her in an instant, moving so quickly the air seemed to shiver in his wake. His gaze dropped to the pendant, sharpening like drawn steel.

"Where did you find that?"

"In the river," she whispered. "How did it get here?"

He took the pendant carefully between two fingers—barely touching it, as if contact carried a price. His jaw tightened. "It shouldn't be here. Not this far north."

"North?" she echoed. "You've seen this before."

He froze, the small motion of his breath the only sign he was still alive.

Nilsa stepped closer, refusing to let the moment slip away. "Erabor. Tell me."

He didn't answer. But his eyes betrayed him—darkening with recognition and dread, the way they had in the war room, in the clearing, in the forest that watched.

She held out her hand. "Let me see it."

"No."

She frowned. "It belongs to whoever dropped it. It's a clue. It might tell us—"

"It is not safe for you to touch," he said sharply.

Then, softer—painfully honest—

"It is not safe for *it* to touch you."

Her pulse quickened. "Is it cursed?"

"Cursed?" He let out a breathless, humorless sound that might once have been a laugh if it weren't so thin. "If only."

Nilsa stepped closer again, so close she could feel the heat radiating off him despite the freezing wind, smell the faint scent of leather and smoke clinging to his cloak. "Then what is it?"

His fingers tightened around the pendant until the metal clicked softly against itself. "A sign."

"Of what?"

He met her gaze, and for a heartbeat she saw fear there—not of the pendant, not even of what hunted them, but of the answer itself.

"Of prophecy."

A chill rippled down her spine, colder than the stream water, colder than the border winds. "What prophecy?"

"The oldest one," he whispered. "The one that sparked every curse in Adollith."

Nilsa's throat tightened. Her mind flicked to the broken pillars in her dream, the throne of stars, the voices calling her *daughter of the forgotten crown*. "And how does it involve me?"

Erabor's gaze softened in a way that hurt to look at. He looked at her like he wished he could lie—
but couldn't.

"Because it began with your bloodline."

She sucked in a breath, the air cutting like glass in her lungs. "What?"

He closed his fist around the pendant, as though he could crush fate itself in his hand if he only tried hard enough. "Nilsa," he said, voice rough at the edges, "I need you to trust me when I tell you that we cannot stay here. We cannot rest. We cannot wait for answers."

"Why?" Her voice trembled on the word. "Why can't you just tell me—?"

"Because if he finds you before we reach Morrivan," Erabor said, "not even I will be able to keep you alive."

Her heartbeat stalled. The world seemed to narrow to the space between them—the pendant hidden in his hand, the wind, his eyes. *Not even I.*

Erabor realized a second too late what he had admitted.

Nilsa stepped closer, breath trembling in the cold. "Erabor… what do you mean *not even you?*"

He flinched.

Actually flinched.

A sound rose from the trees then—a long, distant howl that rolled across the hills like a wound remembering how to ache. It wasn't animal. It wasn't human. It was something stretched and wrong, as if a voice made for another world had been forced into a shape this one could hear.

Erabor's face hardened, all softness burning away. "We need to ride."

Nilsa didn't argue. Not when the wind shifted and the howl came again—closer this time, shivering through the grass at their feet.

Erabor slipped the pendant into his cloak, tucking it close against his chest where it vanished beneath worn fabric.

Nilsa caught his wrist before he could pull away. "Promise me something."

He turned, the faintest crease between his brows.

"Promise me," she whispered, voice tight, "that when the time comes… you'll tell me the truth."

Erabor looked at her for a long, fractured moment. The kind of moment that stretched between heartbeats and felt as though it could break the world if handled carelessly. Something raw flickered in his gaze. Regret. Fear. Devotion.

Then he said the only thing he could: "When the time comes," he murmured, "I will tell you everything."

It wasn't a lie.

But gods—it wasn't a comfort.

They mounted quickly, the wind rising around them like the breath of something enormous and unseen. Nilsa settled into Starwind's saddle, urging the mare forward as Erabor fell into a protective flank at her side, every line of him ready to put himself between her and the world.

Behind them, the howl came again—echoing across the hills like a broken prophecy remembering itself.

And somewhere in the depths of his cloak, pressed close against his chest, the pendant pulsed faintly.

As if answering the call.

CHAPTER TEN

What He Cannot Say

They made camp beneath a jutting cliff face where the dark stone rose like a broken tooth against the dimming sky. Thornbrush crowded the edges of the hollow, their bare branches clawing upward as if trying to scrape heat from the night. The air was sharp with cold—the kind that bit through cloaks and stung every patch of exposed skin, the kind that layered frost on breath and numbed fingers until they ached.

A small fire crackled weakly in the center of their camp, barely more than a handful of flames licking at the gathered kindling. Its warmth touched only a circle of earth no wider than a crouched body. Nilsa sat near it, legs folded beneath her, her cloak wrapped tightly around her shoulders as she stared into the wavering glow. Sparks drifted upward like dying fireflies. Her expression was still and faraway. She hadn't spoken since they found the pendant.

Erabor moved in the shadows beyond the fire's reach, the same silent, purposeful way he always moved when something hunted them. He walked the perimeter with mechanical vigilance: checking the direction of the wind, the slope of the ground, the shape of the rocks, the tree line beyond. Every few steps he knelt, pressed his palm to the cold earth, and listened—not with ears, she suspected, but with whatever deeper sense he was always refusing to name.

Only when he'd traced a circle around their campsite—an invisible boundary only he understood—did he return.

Nilsa didn't look up.

"You're quiet," he murmured, his voice a low rumble softened by the fire's crackle.

Nilsa traced a stick absently through the dirt, her motions slow and distracted. "You almost told me something today."

Erabor lowered himself to a kneeling position across from her. The firelight caught the hard planes of his face—cheekbones sharp, jaw shadowed, eyes reflecting the flames like molten bronze.

"I told you what I could."

"That's not true."

A muscle feathered in his jaw. "Nilsa—"

"You said you'd protect me," she whispered, finally looking up to meet his gaze. "But how can you protect me from something you won't even name?"

His breath caught—not audibly, not dramatically, but in the subtle tightening of his shoulders, the faint hesitation before he looked toward the trees. Frost clung to the branches there like white scars, the tips glittering like fragments of shattered stars.

"It is not the naming that is dangerous," he said softly. "It is the knowledge."

"Knowledge won't kill me."

"It could."

The fire crackled louder then, as if the flames themselves leaned in to hear.

"It could kill you faster than any wraith or shadow," he finished, barely above a whisper.

Nilsa swallowed hard. "Then I should know how to defend myself from it."

Erabor's jaw clenched so tightly she thought she could hear the faint grind of his teeth. "You can't."

"Why not?"

His hesitation stretched long enough she thought he might retreat back into silence. But then—

"Because it wants you," he said.

The words were a dull blade dragged down the length of her spine.

"And you can't defend yourself from something that has already chosen its prize."

Her stomach dropped. The fire seemed smaller suddenly, the night darker. "Why me?"

"Because you are marked," he whispered.

Nilsa's hand flew to the fabric over her chest. "The sigil?"

"No."

He shook his head, shadows shifting across his face.

"Something older. Something you were born with. Something buried so deep you don't even feel it."

Her breath trembled. "How could you possibly know that?"

He froze.

Just for a heartbeat.

But that heartbeat was enough—because in it, she saw a flicker of panic in his eyes, bright and sharp as exposed metal.

She leaned forward. "Because you've seen this before, haven't you?"

Silence crackled between them. The wind shifted, carrying the faint scent of pine and cold stone.

"You know exactly what I am," she said quietly.

Erabor's fingers curled into the dirt, the faint tremor of contained emotion skimming the surface of his composure. "I know what hunts you."

"And what does that make me?"

He lifted his gaze. Pain. Torture. A softness so achingly gentle she felt it physically.

"Important," he whispered.

The word shouldn't have shaken her.
But gods—it did.

Nilsa folded her arms tightly, whether to hold in warmth or emotion she couldn't say. The fire's glow brushed her cheek, warming one side of her face while the other remained cold.

"Erabor… when you touched my cheek earlier—"

He stiffened instantly, almost violently. "I shouldn't have."

"Why not?"

His breath hitched. The sound was so slight most people wouldn't have noticed—but Nilsa did.

"Because you shouldn't trust me that much."

She blinked. "I *do* trust you."

"You shouldn't," he repeated, voice cracking on the edge of the words. "It makes my job harder."

"What job?"

He flinched.
Not a big movement—just a flicker of tension around his eyes. But it was enough to tell her she'd brushed against truth.

Nilsa reached across the fire and touched his hand. Her fingers were cold. His were colder.

He inhaled sharply. Like her touch burned. Or branded.

"Erabor," she whispered, "if I can't trust you, then I trust no one. And if you can't trust yourself…"
She swallowed.
"Let me decide what risks I take."

His gaze dropped to their hands—their fingers barely touching, the faint tremble in his breath betraying more than he ever would in words.

For a moment, he didn't breathe.

Then—

He pulled his hand away.
Gently.
Slowly.
Like it hurt him to do it.

"You don't understand," he murmured.
"If you reach for me… I might reach back."

Her pulse stumbled.
Heat flushed her chest despite the cold.

And for the first time since leaving Orlanthia, Nilsa felt a new kind of fear—
one that had nothing to do with curses or wraiths or ancient things in forests.

"Erabor," she whispered, "what are you afraid you'll do?"

He lifted his gaze.

His eyes—bright in the firelight—looked like embers submerged under water.
Not reflecting the fire.
Not human.

"More than I should," he said.

Nilsa's breath caught in her throat.

"But I won't," he added, voice forced into steadiness. "Because when he comes—when he finds you—I need every part of me focused on keeping you alive."

Her heart thundered painfully.

"Then what are you giving up to do that?"

Erabor looked at her as if she had struck him.
As if the question had pierced a place he had spent centuries defending.

And for one moment—just one—he let something real slip through the cracks.

"Everything," he whispered.

Raw.
Bare.
A wound laid open.

Nilsa opened her mouth to speak, throat thick with emotion—but before her voice could form, a distant sound rolled across the darkness.

A howl.
Low.
Resonant.
Wrong.

Followed by another.
Closer.

Erabor stood instantly, every muscle coiled, his shadow stretching long across the stone behind him. He moved in front of her without thinking, instinct snapping into place like armor. Nilsa rose too, dagger in hand, heart slamming against her ribs.

"What is that?" she whispered.

"Not a creature," Erabor said.
"A message."

"From who?"

His eyes darkened, swallowing what little warmth remained in them. The dying fire flickered, and for a heartbeat, the shadows behind him seemed to bend toward the sound.

"From the one who wants you."

Nilsa's breath froze.

"Erabor—"

He stepped closer, his voice low and fierce.

"You stay behind me tonight. No matter what happens. No matter what you hear. Understand?"

Nilsa nodded slowly, throat tight, the fire's warmth suddenly a memory.

He wasn't just afraid.
He was terrified.
Not of the thing in the dark—
but of what he might have to reveal if he fought it.

CHAPTER ELEVEN

Moonblood and Shadowfire

The wind died so suddenly that Nilsa felt the silence before she understood it. One heartbeat the air hissed through the thornbrush, rattling dry branches against the cliff face; the next it collapsed into suffocating stillness, as though someone had cupped a giant hand over the world and pressed down. Even the cold changed—sharp winter chill replaced by a deeper, older cold that crawled beneath her skin and settled in her bones.

"Erabor…" she whispered, but the name barely reached her own ears.

He didn't answer. He was already in front of her, body angled just enough to shield her, one hand extended behind him—not touching, but blocking, a silent barrier carved from tension and instinct. His silhouette was rigid, coiled, every line of him reading danger. The fire in their small pit sputtered once, crackled weakly—

—and died completely.

Darkness swallowed the hollow in a single gulp. It wasn't the gentle dark of night or clouds crossing the moon. It was thick, absolute, a curtain drawn with violent intent. Nilsa blinked, expecting her eyes to adjust, but they didn't. They couldn't. The darkness was wrong—too complete, too heavy, too deliberate.

Her breath fogged in a short, sharp gasp. "Erabor… the moon—"

"Gone," he murmured. His voice was steady, but beneath the smooth surface she heard something else. Not fear. Recognition. Something he had hoped not to hear again.

A sound drifted through the dark.

Not a howl. Not a growl.

Something softer. Worse.

A wet dragging, like flesh sliding across stone, like something pulling a broken limb through dead leaves. The noise crawled along the ground, scraping at her nerves, whispering promises she couldn't understand.

Nilsa's heart slammed against her ribs. "Where is it?"

Erabor's answer was barely breath. "Everywhere."

Then—far between the trees—a pulse of faint light flickered. Violet. Cold. Familiar. A color she had begun to dread.

"The sigil," she whispered. Her fingers curled against her ribs where the stones were hidden. "It found us."

"No," Erabor said, voice dropping to something low and threaded with an ancient cadence. "We stumbled into its reach."

A shape peeled itself from the darkness. It unfolded like unraveling smoke—tall, too tall, limbs several joints too long, its body a shifting silhouette stitched together from shadow. Beneath that darkness, faint violet veins pulsed like corrupted starfire. Its head twisted sharply, vertebrae cracking like snapped twigs until the hollow, faceless gaze fixed on them.

Then it opened its mouth.

There were no teeth.
Just light.

A blinding, violet tremor of hollow-centered radiance mimicking the cursed sigil.

Nilsa staggered backward. "Erabor, what—?"

The creature lunged.

Not walked—launched, a blur of shrieking light and clawed shadow.

Nilsa raised her dagger—too slow—

Erabor moved.

Not human-fast.

Faster.

He was beside her one moment, and directly in front of the creature the next. He caught it—*caught it*—with one bare hand clamped around the convulsing mass of shadow. The creature thrashed wildly, claws slicing the air, violet veins pulsing so brightly Nilsa's eyes watered. Its scream split the night, a metallic wail scraping along her skull.

Erabor didn't flinch.

"Stay behind me," he said, but his voice had changed.

It was deeper. Resonant.
Older.

The creature tried to writhe around him, shadowy limbs whipping toward Nilsa, but the darkness recoiled when it touched Erabor. It didn't just withdraw. It burned.

Nilsa's breath stuttered. "Erabor… what are you—"

He snarled.

No words.
A sound of strain, fury, pain—and something far more primal.

He slammed the creature into the ground. The impact cracked the earth. Stone split, dust rising in choking plumes. The creature shrieked again, violet light bursting from its body in jagged flares. Its chest began to split open, tearing like cloth soaked in acid, revealing a black maw inside.

A tendril of shadow whipped out, lightning-fast, aimed directly at Nilsa's throat.

Erabor was there before she could scream.

His hand clamped around the shadow mid-air.

And the world trembled.

Not the ground. Not the trees.
Reality.

The air around them rippled like fabric stretched too far. A cold breeze hummed through the hollow, carrying whispers, voices she had heard only in dreams—

Daughter of the forgotten crown...

"Don't look at it!" Erabor roared.

Nilsa squeezed her eyes shut, but not before she saw a flash of violet light—

—and behind it, a silhouette.

Tall.
Crowned.
Winged.

Watching.

Her heart froze.

"That—that wasn't the creature," she choked. "That was him—he's here—"

"Not here," Erabor growled, voice tearing with effort. "*Reaching.*"

The shadow-tendril crawled up his arm, wrapping around his skin like something hungry. Violet light seared down his wrist, sizzling. Nilsa lunged forward—

"NO!" His voice broke into something not human. "Stay back!"

The creature convulsed violently, pulling, dragging, trying to draw him into that tearing violet maw. Erabor's shadow stretched across the ground—

—and this time she saw it clearly.

Tall.
Broad.
Wings unfolding behind him.

Slow.
Massive.
Impossible.

Her mouth opened soundlessly. "Erabor…"

Pain slashed across his face. "Nilsa…"

His voice cracked.

"Close your eyes."

She shook her head. "No—you'll die—"

"CLOSE THEM!" The command hit like a physical shove.

She obeyed.

Heat surged across her skin—heat without fire. Wind whipped around her, furious, swirling, lifting her hair and cloak in a storm-tossed frenzy. Something burned in the air—metallic, sharp, like heated iron.

Then she heard it.

A sound like wings.

Not the beating of feathers.
Not flapping.
But unfurling.

Like stormlight unfolding from a creature too large for the hollow that held it.

The creature screamed—high, awful, primal—and Nilsa felt the world rip open with it.

Silence followed.

A crushing, deep silence that seemed to suck the air from the hollow.

Then—
A thunderclap.

Nilsa's eyes flew open.

The creature was gone.

Not dissipated.
Not slain.
Gone.

As if pulled backward through a tear in the night.

Erabor stood at the center of the hollow, shoulders heaving, chest rising and falling in raw, ragged bursts. Smoke curled from his skin like the remnants of fire. His tall frame—lean muscle, broad shoulders—looked carved by the moonlight that had finally returned. Sweat clung to his temples, darkening wild strands of hair that curled in damp twists across his forehead. The faint scar at his throat caught the moonlight like a thin line of silver.

His hands shook violently. His right palm glowed faintly—like the echo of something too powerful to name.

Air shimmered around him in rippling waves. Cold pressed in, but heat radiated from him—contradictory, unnatural. His shadow lay still at his feet.

Normal again.

Nilsa stumbled toward him. "Erabor—are you hurt? What did you—what happened—"

He didn't look at her.

Not at first.

When he finally did—
His eyes glowed.

Not bright.
Not fully.
Just enough.

Nilsa froze.

He blinked—
the glow vanished.

He straightened painfully. "We move."

Nilsa stared, trembling. "Erabor. Your shadow. Your eyes. That thing—you—"

"I said we move." His voice cracked with raw exhaustion. "Not here."

She stepped closer. "Erabor, you saved me. That was—whatever that was—"

He looked at her then, truly looked at her, and something inside him splintered.

"Nilsa... please trust me."

Her throat tightened. "I do."

He closed his eyes, anguish bleeding through his voice. "Then don't ask me what I am. Not yet."

Nilsa's heart twisted painfully. "Erabor..."

She reached for him.

He stepped back—not from her, but from fear of what her touch might reveal.
"Because if you know the truth now," he whispered, voice breaking,

"he will sense it through you."

A cold wave slid down her spine. "Who is he? The one in my dreams? The one behind the creature?"

Erabor's jaw tightened. His eyes closed, as if bracing for a blow.

"He is the reason your brothers died."

Nilsa staggered, air punched from her lungs.

"And he is coming," Erabor said, voice torn open, "because you are the one he lost."

The night swallowed her breath whole.

CHAPTER TWELVE

The Cost of Power

Night clung to the hollow like a low-hanging shroud, heavy and unsettling, as though the darkness itself had weight. The moon had returned, thin and uncertain through a veil of drifting clouds, its pale glow barely able to slip between the thornbrush that bent inward around their camp. The firepit at Nilsa's knees stank faintly of burnt coal, stubbornly cold no matter how many sparks she coaxed from her flint. Each strike gave a fleeting flash of orange and nothing more. Even the embers resisted her, as though the night had swallowed the fire's spirit whole.

Just beyond the dying circle of light, Erabor stood exactly where the creature had nearly dragged him into the void. He hadn't moved since the moment its shriek vanished into the torn air. His silhouette remained rigid and steady, shoulders locked in a trembling he refused to acknowledge. The faint distortion that clung to him—like heat shimmering above smithing stones—hadn't settled. The air around him wavered as though reality was still trying to restitch itself around his presence.

Nilsa stepped toward him carefully, the frost-crusted ground crunching beneath her boots. "Erabor," she murmured, voice shaking with concern she didn't bother to hide. "Look at me."

He didn't. His breath sawed in and out of his lungs in shallow, controlled pulls—too controlled. That wasn't exhaustion. It was pain. Pain held tight with teeth and stubbornness, the kind of pain that made a person quiet in all the wrong ways. Her stomach knotted. She reached for him.

"Erabor—"

He flinched so hard she nearly froze, recoiling from her touch like it burned.

"No." The word scraped raw out of him, brittle as splintered bone. "Don't."

That single refusal cut deeper than any monster's claws. He staggered then—not a fall, but a falter—and Nilsa surged forward to catch his forearm as his knees buckled beneath him. His skin burned under her fingers, hot enough she almost pulled away.

"Stars," she breathed. "You are hurt."

He tried to wrench his arm free, but even that small movement twisted agony across his face. Nilsa tightened her grip and lowered him carefully until he sat on a half-rotten fallen tree. When she pushed back his sleeve, she felt her breath punch out of her chest. A bruise—if it could be called that—spread beneath his skin in thick, branching veins of dark violet light, growing upward from his wrist to disappear beneath his shoulder. The glow pulsed like a heartbeat gone wrong.

"Why didn't you say anything?" she whispered.

"Because I can handle it," he rasped.

She cupped his cheek and angled his face up toward her own. "Can you? You're shaking."

His shudder had nothing to do with cold. "Nilsa… please." The way the words left him—bare, pleading—sent something sharp through her chest. "You shouldn't be touching me."

"Why not?" she whispered.

He looked at her then, eyes storm-dark and fractured, and she saw emotion gathering behind them like a rising tide he couldn't stop. She kept her hand on his cheek, refusing to let him retreat. "You saved my life. I'm not letting you sit here and suffer alone like some wounded animal."

The words seemed to strike something deep in him. His expression tightened, but he didn't pull away. "I'm not suffering," he said again, quieter. "I'm fighting."

"Fighting what?"

A breath hitched out of him, and his gaze slid away toward the cliff face as if the rock might give him courage. "You don't want the answer."

"Erabor," she whispered, "I'm not afraid of you."

His eyes snapped back to hers, sudden and anguished. "You should be."

Her throat tightened. "I'm not."

His chest rose sharply, as though the words physically wounded him. She shifted, allowing her hand to slide from his cheek down to the side of his neck. She felt his pulse hammer beneath her fingertips—fast, unsteady, too hot.

He sucked in a tremulous breath. "Nilsa… don't."

"Why?" she asked softly.

"Because I…" His jaw clenched and the rest caught in his throat. When he managed to force breath around the words, it came out shattered. "Because I cannot afford this."

"Afford what?"

"You."

The single word stole her breath.

He lurched forward as if to stand, but pain ripped through him so violently that his legs nearly gave out again. Nilsa caught him, guiding him down onto the ground until he leaned against the cold stone wall of the hollow. She knelt in front of him, her face inches from his, her voice low and trembling. "Erabor… tell me where it hurts."

He let out a broken, humorless laugh. "Everywhere."

"Then let me help."

"You can't."

"You don't know that."

He closed his eyes, fighting some silent war within himself. At last, with a defeated exhale, he said, "Fine."

She helped him shed his coat, her fingers brushing across his shoulders when his hands faltered. He inhaled sharply, not from pain—but from her touch. When the coat fell away, Nilsa saw the full extent of the corruption. The violet glow crept like poisoned lightning up his arm, pulsing beneath his skin. It was wrong, unnatural, alive.

"Oh gods…" Her hand flew to her mouth.

"It will fade," he said quietly.

"Fade?" The word broke out of her. "Erabor, this looks like magic rot."

"It's worse," he murmured, "but not for the reason you think."

Nilsa pulled a cloth from her pack and dipped it in the remaining water. When she reached for his arm, he caught her wrist in a grip that was gentle only because he was forcing it to be.

"No."

"I won't hurt you."

"That's not—" He swallowed hard. "If you touch it… it might hurt you."

She froze—just for a heartbeat—then lifted her other hand and set it firmly against his chest over his heart. His body stilled instantly, breath caught between one moment and the next.

"Look at me," she whispered.

He did.

"I trust you," she said. "And I trust myself. Let me help you."

The tremor that went through him was not pain. It was surrender. And it nearly broke her.

He nodded.

Nilsa pressed the damp cloth to his shoulder. His breath hissed through his teeth, muscles tensing, but he didn't pull away. The violet veins flared beneath her touch, pulsing brighter, then slowly dimming again. She felt the tightness in his body loosen by degrees.

"You shouldn't…" he said suddenly, voice low and frayed.

"Shouldn't what?"

"Care." He stared at the ground. "It makes everything harder."

"I can handle hard things."

"This isn't that simple."

"It is to me."

His eyes softened, sharp edges melting into something unbearably vulnerable. "You don't understand what you're asking for."

"And you don't understand that I decide who I'm afraid of," she murmured.

Silence enveloped them then—the kind that held two people in a fragile balance between closeness and collapse. Finally, he whispered:

"I wish I could be what you think I am."

Her breath caught. "What do you think I see?"

He hesitated—the longest hesitation she had ever seen from him. When he spoke, it was barely a breath.

"A man."

Nilsa swallowed hard. "You are a man. Whatever you're hiding—whatever you are underneath—I don't care. You bleed. You break. You shake when you're hurt. That's human enough for me."

His eyes closed slowly, pain and longing crossing his features like shadows. He leaned forward, not enough to touch her, but close enough that she felt the warmth of his breath brush her skin. His forehead touched hers by the smallest, trembling margin—an accidental brush, a fleeting surrender—and she felt his entire body shiver around the contact.

"I don't deserve you," he whispered.

"Good," she whispered back. "Then we're even."

A sound escaped him—soft, cracked, something between a laugh and a sob—before he pulled away abruptly, as if the closeness itself was dangerous. "Sleep," he murmured. "Please."

"You need it too."

"No," he said quietly. "If I sleep tonight, I may not wake."

Her heart lurched painfully. "Erabor—"

"Rest," he whispered again, softer. "For me."

And despite the fear clawing at her chest, despite everything unanswered and everything unraveling, she did.

Erabor stayed awake, back against the stone, arm glowing faintly as the corruption pulsed beneath his skin. He watched her sleep with eyes that never fully blinked, breathing shallowly through the pain and the terror threading through his bones. And long after Nilsa's eyes closed, when her breathing steadied into the fragile rhythm of exhausted sleep, silent tears slid down his face—slow and unwilling. Not because of the wound.

Because for the first time in centuries, someone had touched him like he was worth saving.

CHAPTER THIRTEEN

A Voice in the Dark

Night settled over Nilsa like a heavy velvet shroud, soft enough to lull but weighted with exhaustion so deep it smothered thought. She slept curled in her cloak, the dying chill of the hollow sinking into her bones even as the last traces of Erabor's quiet, uneven breathing soothed her. The fire remained dead, its ashes cold and gray, refusing to catch no matter how many sparks she'd coaxed from the flint before sleep claimed her. Darkness pooled across the ground in a low, unmoving sheet, and though Nilsa's body finally surrendered to rest, some part of her felt the hollow watching her.

Her dream began wordlessly. Not with sound, not with light, not even with color—just silence, thick and soft and dense enough she felt suspended within it. The darkness rippled faintly around her, pulsing with a slow, steady rhythm that felt like breathing, or perhaps the echo of some ancient heart beating somewhere far beyond her sight. Then a thin strand of pale light wove itself into the void. It stretched slowly, widening, brightening, threading itself into the familiar silhouette of the starlit throne she had seen before. The floating shards of light outlining the throne flickered like dying stars.

Behind it rose the thirteen pillars—twelve jagged and cracked as if broken by time or violence, the thirteenth whole and unmarred. Tonight, they pulsed faintly with a rhythm that matched the quickening pace of her own breath. Nilsa stepped forward, though she was no longer sure whether her feet touched the ground or if the world simply shifted to meet her. The air around her felt both weightless and suffocating, as though she walked through deep, calm waters under a moonless sky. And the farther she moved toward the throne, the farther away it seemed, receding inch by maddening inch.

She reached toward it—and the hall inhaled.

The sound wasn't a sound at all, but a seismic shift, a ripple through air and stone and ancient memory. The broken pillars shuddered. Cracks widened with a gritty crunch that echoed like bones splitting after centuries of tension. Dust fell in hushed cascades. Light trembled inside the fractures. The hall itself felt alive, awake, aware.

That was when she felt him.

Not seen. Not fully shaped. But present—so close she felt warmth and chill sweep over her shoulders in the same breath, as if a hand both fevered and frozen pressed to the back of her neck. A voice slid into her mind—not through her ears, but through the marrow of every bone.

Little star.

Nilsa froze as the smoky figure stepped into her view. It drifted into a shape that almost resembled a man but never truly committed to it. A tall silhouette formed of darkness and starlit edges, as though a constellation struggled to remember its original form. Where eyes should have been, two hollow pits glowed with deep violet light.

"You are late," he murmured, voice layered with too many tones, as if several echoes spoke in unison.

She couldn't breathe—wasn't sure she even could in this place. "Late... for what?"

The shape tilted its head with the easy amusement of someone who already knew her answers. "For me."

Her heart pounded painfully. "I don't know you."

"You will." The voice was a soft purr, coaxing and cold. "You knew me once. In another life. In another kingdom."

Nilsa stepped back—or tried to. The ground shifted beneath her, becoming viscous and unsteady, anchoring her in place. "My brothers," she whispered. "Did you kill them?"

The starlit edges around the figure sharpened, flaring with brief intensity. "Their deaths were a consequence, not a desire."

"Consequence of what?"

His shadow reached toward her, drifting through the air in lazy motions like smoke caught in a breeze. "Of finding you."

Dread coiled low in her stomach. "Why me?"

The violet light within his hollow gaze pulsed brightly, illuminating cracks in the hall. "Because you are mine."

Her pulse stuttered violently. "I belong to no one."

"Not now." His voice softened again, almost tender, almost reverent. "But fate is patient. And so am I."

The pillars trembled—reacting to his presence or warning her, she couldn't tell. Dust flurried from the fractures. Light stuttered. The hall began to shrink, collapsing inward, walls bending in a slow, inevitable fold as though the dream sought to trap them together.

The starlit throne pulsed—one bright, violent flash.

The figure's head snapped toward it. His form wavered, flickering at the edges.

Then his voice slammed straight through her skull.

Wake.

The command cracked like thunder.

Wake, little star, or I will come for you myself.

The dream shattered.

Nilsa jerked upright with a gasp, hand clutching her chest as though she could steady the frantic pounding of her heart. Cold air rushed into her lungs, dizzying and sharp, and it took several breaths before she understood she was back in the hollow, dawn dimming the darkness into a muted gray. Her fingers trembled against her brow.

A sound rasped to her right.

Erabor.

He was slumped against the stone wall, head bowed, one hand pressed tightly to the glowing bruise along his arm. The violet light beneath his skin had dimmed but not disappeared; it pulsed weakly like embers buried under ash. The tension in his jaw made the tendons in his neck stand out sharply. Every breath looked like it cost him something.

Nilsa crawled toward him, ignoring the numb heaviness in her limbs. "Erabor?"

His head lifted sharply. His eyes—storm-gray and raw—locked onto hers with a force that stole her next breath. "What happened?" The words were hoarse, scraped thin by pain and fear.

Nilsa swallowed hard. "A dream. Or a vision. He was there."

Erabor's body went rigid. "Did he speak to you?"

She nodded.

"What did he say?" There was urgency now, sharp and desperate, swallowing whatever pain carved through his voice.

Nilsa hesitated. The echo of *mine* still thrummed in her bones. "He said... he said he knew me once."

Something broke in Erabor's expression. Guilt, grief, and terror fought for dominance beneath his strained composure. "And?"

Nilsa's voice strained. "He's coming for me."

Erabor shut his eyes, breath leaving him in a slow, devastated exhale. "Of course he is."

Anger sparked in her chest. "You knew."

His eyes snapped open. "I didn't want that connection awakened this soon."

"Connection?" she demanded. "What connection?"

Erabor looked away toward the horizon, dawn spreading a thin line of gold across the distant ridge. His voice was quiet, almost reluctant. "Nilsa... something binds him to you. Something none of us understand. Something very old."

"And something you're still not telling me."

His jaw tightened. "If I tell you too much too soon, I will lead him straight to you. Through your dreams. Through your thoughts." His voice faltered. "Through me."

A faint ache spread through her chest. "He called me 'little star.' What does that mean?"

Erabor's eyes softened—a dangerous softness, full of sorrow and longing and fear. He reached toward her, then stopped with visible effort, his hand trembling where it hovered in the space between them. "It means you are part of something he has sought for centuries. Something powerful. Something dangerous."

Nilsa's breath hitched. "Should I be afraid of him?"

"Yes." The answer came instantly.

She swallowed hard. "And of you?"

The question froze him.

Silence stretched thin between them until his throat worked around an answer that sounded like it had been torn from the deepest, hidden part of him.

"Only if I fail."

Nilsa reached for his wrist before he could retreat into himself. Her fingers touched his skin lightly—just enough to ground him, just enough to steady his unraveling edges. He closed his eyes, the touch affecting him more than she expected, like it kept him anchored to a body that was fighting too hard to remain steady.

When he opened his eyes, the walls he kept so carefully built had cracked, revealing something raw and fiercely protective beneath the surface.

"I will not let him take you," Erabor said softly, voice thick with emotion he couldn't hide. "Not again."

The word *again* sent a cold ripple along Nilsa's spine.

She leaned closer. "Then tell me something. Anything. Even one piece of truth. Please."

Erabor swallowed hard. Carefully, almost reverently, he brushed a strand of hair behind her ear. His fingers lingered a heartbeat too long. "Then hear this, Nilsa Nightstalker: whatever he claims, whatever he whispers, whatever he shows you in dreams…" His hand cupped her cheek, thumb brushing her skin with fragile tenderness. "…you are not his."

Her breath trembled. "Then whose am I?"

His hand fell away as if burned. "Yours," he whispered. "Until you choose otherwise."

Behind him, unnoticed in the growing morning light, his shadow flickered once—its outline stretching wider, taller, the faint suggestion of wings unfurling before snapping back into something human.

CHAPTER FOURTEEN

Through Frost and Firelight

Morning seeped slowly into the hollow, a thin wash of pale gold filtering across the frost-bitten ground as if the sun itself approached with caution after what the night had witnessed. The light touched the cold stones reluctantly, hesitant to warm the place where shadows still clung in memory. Nilsa saddled Starwind in the muted hush, fingers working with a steadiness she did not entirely feel, while Erabor gathered their packs with movements that were too controlled, too deliberate—showing strain only when she looked away. Yet she saw it every time a breath hitched, every time his posture stiffened, every time his left arm trembled beneath his cloak. He was in pain, he was hiding it, and it was worsening.

They rode in measured silence along a slow descent of hill and frost-washed meadow, the cold air sharp against their cheeks, the land stretching wide and bleak beneath the timid sun. Thin sheets of snow clung to the shadows of rocks and brush, glinting like shards of crystal. It should have been peaceful—almost beautiful—but a heaviness lingered between them, quiet and watchful, the echo of last night's terror clinging like frost to their cloaks.

Nilsa watched Erabor from the corner of her eye. He rode straighter than usual, rigid as iron, as though the only thing keeping him balanced was sheer will. Flint's reins were curled in his right hand with a grip that whitened his knuckles, and beneath the dark wool of his sleeve, she could see the faintest, wrongest pulse of violet light. He hid the glow well, but not from her. Not anymore.

"How far until we reach Morrivan border?" she asked softly, guiding her mare closer.

"Two days if we keep pace," he answered. His voice had gained a roughness, stretched thin by pain he refused to acknowledge. "Three if we slow."

"We need the three," Nilsa murmured.

His jaw tensed, a flash of stubbornness tightening his expression. "We don't."

"We do," she insisted, easing Starwind to a slower walk until he was forced to match it. "Otherwise you're going to fall off your horse, and I don't feel like scraping you off the road."

He shot her a sharp look, storm-gray eyes narrowing with irritation and an edge of embarrassment. "I'm fine."

"Erabor," she whispered, "you are not fine. You haven't been since last night."

He looked away, jaw working, and for a long moment neither spoke. The wind carried the scent of freeze-cracked pine and distant snowfields, and the horses' hooves crunched rhythmically over icy soil.

Nilsa eased Starwind closer still until her knee brushed his stirrup. Gently, she reached out and laid her hand on his forearm. His breath hitched, his whole body tensing at the contact—but he didn't pull away.

"You don't have to pretend with me," she murmured.

A heartbeat passed. Then another.

"I do," he said quietly. "Because if I let myself feel any of this… I won't be able to protect you."

"You already are protecting me," she said. "You always are. But you're not protecting yourself."

His eyes closed for a brief moment, lashes dark against his pale cheeks. Even in daylight, she could see the lines of pain etching his expression, carving deeper into the tight set of his jaw each time Flint jolted beneath him. When he finally looked at her again, the barrier she knew so well—his emotional shield, his impossible restraint—had thinned to something fragile, almost luminous.

"You shouldn't care this much," he whispered, voice fraying.

Nilsa's chest tightened. "But I do. And I won't apologize for it."

His breath left him in a trembling exhale, misting in the cold morning and fading into the vast quiet around them. For a moment, he looked at her as though she were a path he feared to walk, yet could not turn from.

An hour later the land shifted beneath them, rising into rocky slopes veined with snaking tree roots that broke the earth in jagged lines. The horses slowed, picking their way through brush and boulders. Each jostle, each stumble of Flint sent a flicker of pain across Erabor's face; he tried to mask it, but Nilsa saw every flinch.

She halted Starwind abruptly. "We're taking a break."

Erabor rode several paces ahead before reluctantly stopping and turning back. "Nilsa—"

"Dismount," she said, voice gentle but immovable. "Now."

His jaw tightened stubbornly. She didn't blink.

At last, he exhaled and swung down from Flint's saddle. His boots hit the ground—and his legs nearly gave out beneath him. Nilsa rushed forward, slipping her arm around him, steadying him before he fell.

"You are not fine," she repeated, fury and fear twisting together in her chest. "And you don't get to lie to me about this."

He didn't argue. That frightened her more than anything.

They led the horses into a sheltered alcove between high boulders where the wind broke into harmless whispers. Erabor sank to the ground slowly, his breath shuddering when his back touched the rock. His face had gone pale beneath the strands of dark hair clinging to his cheek, and Nilsa felt her own pulse stutter at the sight.

"Let me see your arm," she said.

He didn't move.

"Erabor."

Slowly, as though lifting the sleeve hurt more than the wound itself, he rolled back the fabric.

Nilsa inhaled sharply.

The violet pattern had spread—fanning outward like dark roots, delicate and sinister, threading along the veins beneath his skin. The glow was faint but deeper now, the edges shifting toward black as though the color itself were bruising into something darker.

"Oh gods..." she breathed, reaching out but stopping just before touching the afflicted skin. "Does it hurt?"

"Yes," he admitted. His voice cracked. "But that isn't the problem."

"Then what is?"

He hesitated, eyes shifting to hers with a look she had never seen on his face—fear not for himself, but for her.

"The more it spreads," he murmured, "the harder it is to stay... contained."

Nilsa's heart stumbled. "Contained?"

He looked away, muscles tightening down the length of his jaw. "This curse—this magic—it pulls at parts of me you're not supposed to see. Parts that want out."

The cold around them seemed to deepen. "So what do we do?"

"You leave me here," he said quietly, "and keep riding."

Nilsa stared at him, stunned by the sheer audacity of the suggestion. "Absolutely not."

"Nilsa—"

"No," she snapped, catching his hand before he could pull it away. His fingers twitched in hers, warm despite the cold. "I'm not abandoning you. Not now. Not ever."

Something fragile broke across his expression—shock, grief, longing wrapped in pain.

"You don't understand what I am," he whispered.

"You don't understand who I am," she countered. "We're staying together."

Silence unfolded slowly around them, thickening in the cold alcove. The wind sifted through the pines above, carrying the scent of resin and distant snow. The horses pawed restlessly at the frosted ground, sensing the heaviness neither rider spoke aloud.

Erabor's hand finally tightened around hers. Careful. Slow. As though anchoring himself to life with her fingers alone.

"Nilsa," he said softly, voice breaking, "if I lose control—"

"You won't," she said, leaning closer. "Because you're not alone. I'm right here."

His eyes closed, torment and need flickering across his face. "That's what I'm afraid of."

"Then let me be afraid with you."

He opened his eyes again, and for the first time since she'd met him, the storm in them calmed—just enough for her to see the man beneath the shadows.

They stayed like that, hands clasped, the world narrowed to the small, frost-bound alcove and the warmth between their palms. Only when the wind shifted—carrying the scent of pine needles, damp earth, and something sharp and metallic from the south—did Erabor's gaze lift.

Morrivan was drawing near.

And with it, everything waiting in its depths.

CHAPTER FIFTEEN

The Healer in the Pines

The forest thickened around them as they rode, the narrow trail weaving through ancient pines whose trunks rose like pillars into a canopy heavy with needles and shadow. The air turned colder beneath their boughs, sharpened by the scent of resin and damp bark, and the ground beneath the horses' hooves softened into a muted green carpet strewn with frost-dusted pine needles. Nilsa kept Starwind close beside Erabor, watching the stiff, deliberate way he held himself in the saddle. He no longer masked his pain well; he sat too straight, as if rigid posture alone could hold him upright, and each breath was too carefully measured to be anything but forced. He didn't speak—not out of indifference, but because every movement of his jaw seemed to cost him.

By late afternoon the shadows stretched across the trail like long, thin fingers reaching for their reins. The air carried the brittle edge of oncoming dusk. Then a thin curl of smoke rose beyond the ridge—a wavering column drifting into the pale sky. Relief washed through Nilsa so swiftly she nearly sagged from the saddle. "I see a chimney," she whispered, her voice soft and hopeful.

Erabor blinked slowly, as if dragging his vision back into focus. "Then we're close…" His breath hitched, almost a groan. "Thank the stars…"

The trail opened suddenly into a clearing cradled by leaning pines. A lone cottage sat at its heart, its roof bowed slightly beneath old snow, its stone chimney releasing a gentle plume of fragrant smoke. Warm, herbal scents—juniper, cedar, crushed leaves—drifted across the crisp air. Faint lanternlight glowed through the shuttered windows, flickering like captured fireflies against the dusk.

A refuge.
Or a trap.
Nilsa felt both possibilities settle into her bones.

She steered Starwind forward, but Erabor reached out with his good hand, stopping her with a faint tremor in his arm. "Let me go first."

"You can barely sit your horse," she murmured.

He mustered the smallest, strained smile. "I can still fall on someone if needed."

A quiet laugh escaped her—thin, anxious, but real. She slid off Starwind and moved quickly to help him down from Flint before he toppled on his own. His boots touched the frost-nipped ground, and his knees nearly buckled. She caught him instantly, her arm slipping around his waist to keep him upright. His weight leaned into her—not willingly, but because he had no strength left to hide behind—and she could feel the feverish heat radiating through his cloak.

She led him to the door and knocked.

For a moment, only the forest answered, the wind stirring high branches with a whispering rustle. Then footsteps sounded inside—slow, steady, unhurried—and the door creaked open, releasing a wave of warm air perfumed with herbs sharp enough to sting the nose. A woman stood framed in the doorway, wiry and small but radiating the brisk authority of someone accustomed to being obeyed. Her hair was braided in gray coils atop her head, and her pale blue eyes were keen enough to feel like a blade tracing skin.

Those eyes landed on Erabor.

"You brought something sick into my woods," she announced flatly.

Nilsa stiffened. "He's injured. We need help."

"Injured?" the woman echoed, stepping forward with surprising speed. She grasped Erabor's chin in one firm hand, turning his face toward the lanternlight. "No. Not injured. Marked."

Erabor tried to flinch away, but even that was weak. "It's… nothing."

"Lies." She clicked her tongue sharply. "Get him inside before the roots spread farther."

Inside, the cottage wrapped them in warmth. A fire crackled gently in the hearth, filling the space with the scent of cedar and simmering herbs. Shelves lined every wall, heavy with jars of dried flowers, twist-root bundles, vials of cloudy liquid, and strange powders that shimmered faintly in the dim light. The air was thick with healing smoke—so thick Nilsa felt it settle along her tongue like an earthy tang.

The healer gestured sharply to a padded bench. "Sit."

Erabor obeyed only because Nilsa guided him. As he lowered himself, his body shuddered in pain he couldn't quite swallow. Nilsa knelt beside him, but the healer nudged her aside with her elbow. "Let me see it."

Erabor's gaze flicked toward Nilsa—seeking permission, or perhaps courage. She nodded gently. "Let her."

He unwrapped the cloth binding his arm. The healer's expression hardened immediately. The violet marks had spread into dark branching lines, threading across his shoulder like roots seeking purchase. The pulses beneath his skin had deepened to a dangerous glow.

Nilsa felt sick. "Can you help him?"

The healer didn't answer immediately. She pressed her hand lightly above the worst of the darkness. Erabor hissed, muscles seizing as pain arced through him. The healer withdrew as if burned, her fingers trembling ever so slightly. "This is no poison. No curse I know." Her gaze snapped to Nilsa. "Where did he touch what bit him?"

Nilsa's stomach tightened. "It wasn't... exactly a creature."

"A shadow-beast," Erabor murmured hoarsely, eyes half-lidded. "From the Fellwood."

For the first time, the healer went still. A flicker of recognition—and real fear—passed over her face. "And you lived?"

Erabor didn't answer. He didn't need to.

The healer moved with sudden urgency, gathering jars, powders, dried leaves, and a small clay pot of shimmering ash. "Shadow-poison eats at a man's essence," she said, voice brisk and sharp. "It pulls at what lies buried beneath his nature. If he had less strength, he'd be dead already." She paused. "If he had more…"

Nilsa caught the tail end of that hesitation and felt it pierce her. "If he had more what?"

The healer ignored the question. "Hold him."

Nilsa blinked. "Hold him? Why—?"

But Erabor had already braced himself, his good hand gripping the edge of the bench until his knuckles went bone-white. "Nilsa," he rasped, "stand behind me. Hold my shoulders."

She moved immediately. He shifted forward slightly, and she wrapped her arms around him from behind, her cheek brushing his back. His skin radiated heat so intense it felt like pressing against a sun-warmed forge. His breath came in short, uneven bursts.

"This will hurt," the healer warned.

The ash hit his skin with a hiss.

Erabor arched violently, a broken sound tearing from his throat. Nilsa tightened her grip, her body trembling as he tensed like a bow drawn past its limit. The violet light flared bright and jagged beneath his skin, coursing in frantic pulses. He bowed his head, hair dampening with sweat, and she whispered a steady stream of his name, trying to anchor him to something beyond the pain.

"It's almost out," the healer said through clenched teeth, working the mixture into the spreading lines. "He fights it. Good. That will keep it from taking root in the blood."

Erabor's voice cracked in a near-growl. "Nilsa—don't—let go."

"I'm right here," she whispered fiercely. "I'm not going anywhere."

His forehead lowered against her forearm, breath ragged and uneven. She felt every tremor roll through him, each one like a blade scraping through sinew.

Finally, the healer stepped back, shoulders sagging. The markings had dimmed considerably; the darkest branches had receded almost entirely, though faint lines still crawled like embers beneath Erabor's skin. "All I can do is slow it," she said. "The root cause—whatever touched him—must be faced, or it will return."

Nilsa swallowed hard. "But he will live?"

After a moment's pause, the healer nodded. "He will live. Though he may wish he hadn't for the next few days."

Relief broke over Nilsa in a wave so profound it nearly robbed her of breath. She sagged forward, resting her forehead against Erabor's shoulder. His breathing had settled into something steadier, though faint shudders lingered in the muscles beneath her hands. He tilted subtly into her touch, as if her presence soothed the ache burning through him.

The healer poured steaming liquid into two clay cups, the scent of pine sap, mint, and bitterroot curling upward in herbal tendrils. She handed one to Nilsa with a pointed look. "You both carry burdens older than you realize. But tonight you rest. The forest will keep watch."

Nilsa accepted the cup but could not tear her gaze from Erabor. His eyes were half-lidded, his breath still uneven, but he remained grounded—because she was touching him, because she refused to let go. She brushed her fingers lightly along his arm, careful to avoid the mark. He leaned into the warmth with a soft, unguarded sound that cut straight through her.

He was still hiding so much. Still burying entire truths beneath silence and pain.

But not tonight.

Not while she sat beside him in this cedar-scented refuge beneath the whispering pine boughs.

Tonight, she would not let him face the darkness alone.

CHAPTER SIXTEEN

Embers and Echoes

Night settled thick and softly over the healer's hut, muting the forest outside and drawing a warm, amber cocoon over the single-room cottage. The hearth crackled with gentle persistence, its glow spilling across shelves of hanging herbs and glass vials, softening the sharp lines of exhaustion carved into Erabor's face. Cedar smoke and crushed lavender thickened the air, warm and soothing, settling over Nilsa's shoulders as she rose from the fire and pulled a wool blanket from the back of a wooden chair.

Maelra—the healer who had finally offered her name like a guarded secret—moved quietly around the hearth, her worn hands measuring herbs and powders with the certainty of someone who had lived long enough to see remedies fail and miracles surprise her. Every so often her sharp, pale-blue eyes flicked toward Erabor, not with curiosity, but with a wary appraisal that sent a cold knot of worry coiling in Nilsa's stomach.

Carrying the blanket, Nilsa approached him carefully, afraid even the shift of air might pull pain from him. Erabor sat propped against the wall near the hearth, one knee bent and the other stretched along the floorboards. His storm-gray eyes, usually alert and watchful, had dulled to a heavy, unfocused haze; the shadow-poison made his pupils slow and his breaths shallow. His face—always a study in discipline—looked softer now, the mask cracked by strain.

"You should lie back," she murmured, draping the blanket over him.

"I'm fine," he answered, but the words slurred faintly, softened by exhaustion rather than pride.

"You're not." She touched his forehead lightly and pulled her hand back as if startled by the warmth there—still too hot, but no longer the feverish burn from before.

He blinked up at her, lids heavy. "You worry too much."

"And you don't worry enough."

A faint, tired smile tugged at his lips, not quite reaching his eyes. "Maybe one of us balances the other."

Something warm shivered through her chest at that—the gentleness in his voice, the unguarded softness. For all his secrecy, all his rigid distance, she saw the man beneath the armor tonight. Not the weapon he kept claiming to be, not the danger Maelra clearly feared—just a wounded, weary man fighting more battles inside himself than he would ever admit.

Maelra cleared her throat sharply and beckoned Nilsa to sit near the hearth. "Come. There are things I must speak, and you must listen."

Nilsa obeyed, but her eyes flicked constantly to Erabor, noting every drift of his gaze and every wince he failed to hide. At first he watched her back—he always did—but as Maelra stirred the simmering pot with a carved wooden spoon, his eyelids sagged lower, his focus slipping.

"Your companion," Maelra said softly, keeping her voice just above the crackle of the fire, "has survived something that kills most men. You know this."

Nilsa nodded. "I've seen enough death these past years to know when someone shouldn't still be breathing."

"Then understand this," Maelra continued, ladling steaming liquid into a clay cup, "his strength is not born of training or stubbornness alone."

Nilsa's heart thumped hard. "Magic?"

Maelra nodded once. "Old magic. Buried magic. Roots laid deep before your kingdom even had a name. Magic that only shows when threatened."

Nilsa swallowed. "Do you know… what he is?"

The healer's gaze sharpened. "Child, if I knew that, I might have barred my door entirely."

Nilsa stiffened. "He's not dangerous."

"Anything bearing that mark on his skin is dangerous," Maelra replied calmly, "and so is the one who shares your visions."

A chill slid down Nilsa's spine. "You mean—him."

Maelra looked toward the shuttered window, where the wind pressed against the wood with a hollow sigh. "My woods whisper when creatures cross through them. They whispered loudly last night. You carry shadows behind you, Princess—whether or not you meant to."

Nilsa lowered her gaze. "I didn't choose it."

"Few do," Maelra murmured. She reached into a drawer and withdrew a tarnished bronze disk etched with a hollow-centered star—familiar and terrible. "You know this mark."

Nilsa's breath hitched. "Yes."

"The erased kingdom," Maelra said, her voice a hush of awe and fear. "A line the world swore never to speak of again. Blood from that house breeds trouble—hope and ruin in equal measure."

Nilsa leaned closer, heart pounding. "My blood?"

The healer's expression softened. "Did you truly believe your family's tragedy was simple misfortune? Magic does not fray by accident. Lineages do not crumble without design. Something—or someone—wants your line severed."

Nilsa felt the room tilt. "Why?"

"That," Maelra murmured, "is a question even the gods pretend not to hear."

Behind them, Erabor shifted with a low, unsteady groan; Nilsa rushed to him instantly. "Erabor?"

His head lolled toward her, eyes half-open but not quite seeing. He blinked hard, as though trying to recall how to stay awake, then slumped back against the wall.

"Is he in danger?" Nilsa asked, panic tightening her throat.

"For now, no," Maelra said, stepping closer. "The shadow-poison recedes. The boy is only exhausted."

"He hasn't slept in days."

"Then let him sleep." Maelra brushed a hand gently over his brow—a touch he would never have tolerated awake—and nodded. "Deep sleep. Healing sleep. He will wake."

Nilsa let out a slow, shaking breath, warmth spreading through her bones. She pulled the blanket higher around him, tucking it close, as his breathing eased into something quiet and even. For the first time since she'd known him, he slept without jerking awake, without searching the dark corners for threats, without holding his breath as if waiting for an attack. His face softened, the tension melting into something almost peaceful—almost boyish. The severity of his features eased, leaving behind only weariness and the fragile beauty of rest.

He looked heartbreakingly young. Too young for the burdens he carried.

Tears stung Nilsa's eyes—not from fear, but from an overwhelming tenderness she couldn't swallow down. "I thought… I thought he never slept."

"Some beings don't," Maelra replied, stirring her herbs. "Not unless they feel safe."

Nilsa's breath caught. "Safe," she whispered.

Maelra offered no further explanation. She didn't need to.

Nilsa sat beside Erabor, studying the slow rise and fall of his chest, the fading tremor in his fingers, the warmth radiating from him in steady waves. If he were some monstrous thing, as the world seemed to suggest, wouldn't sleep reveal it? Wouldn't the darkness beneath his skin rise to the surface when he finally let go? Yet he looked human—achingly, vulnerably human.

She brushed a lock of hair from his forehead, her fingertips barely grazing his skin. "You're just a man," she whispered, "a man with secrets and strange magic… but still just a man."

Maelra made a quiet sound of dissent from across the room, but Nilsa ignored it, letting herself believe—if only for this single night—that Erabor's mystery was a matter of strength, not some lurking truth waiting to swallow them whole.

She remained at his side until her body leaned naturally against his, shoulder to shoulder, warmth blending into warmth. With his steady breathing beside her, the fear in her chest loosened into something softer, something quiet and safe.

For the first time since leaving Orlanthia, the weight on her shoulders eased. Outside, the forest whispered its secrets, the wind slipping through needles and branches like distant warnings, but inside the healer's hut she found a stillness she hadn't realized she had been starving for.

If only it could last.

CHAPTER SEVENTEEN

The Map of Forgotten Roads

Dawn filtered into the healer's hut in muted gold, soft enough that the firelight still glowed against the wooden walls. The scent of cedar smoke and simmering herbs hung in the air, warm and grounding. Nilsa woke not to noise, but to the profound quiet of a place holding its breath. Erabor still slept beside the hearth, his face turned slightly toward her, his lashes resting against his cheek in a way she never thought she'd see — peaceful, unguarded, unmistakably human.

Maelra was already awake, though her movements were quieter than the settling logs in the fire. She stood at a long, scarred table on the far wall, sorting bundles of dried leaves into neat rows. The morning light caught strands of silver in her hair as she glanced sharply toward Nilsa.

"Up, are you?" she murmured. "Good. Come."

Nilsa rose, careful not to disturb Erabor, and joined the healer by the table. Maelra's long fingers moved with ritual precision, tying herbs in tight knots.

"Walk with me," she said. "Just beyond the door. There is something I must show you before he wakes."

Nilsa hesitated, glancing back at Erabor. His chest rose and fell rhythmically beneath the blanket she'd wrapped around him, his brow relaxed, his body finally resting instead of resisting.

"He will not wake soon," Maelra assured her quietly. "The sleep I gave him is deep. It will heal what it can."

Nilsa nodded and stepped outside with the healer into the crisp morning air. The forest welcomed them with the scent of pine sap and frost. A gentle wind stirred through the treetops, whispering like distant voices.

Maelra led her only a few steps from the hut before stopping beside a moss-covered stump. With a grunt, she knelt, retrieving something wrapped in oilskin from beneath a pile of dried leaves. When she stood, she held the bundle with both hands, as if it carried weight beyond the physical.

"You are traveling east," she said.

"Yes."

"Into Morrivan."

Nilsa frowned. "Morrivan? The kingdom of whispering shadows?"

"The same." Maelra unwrapped the oilskin slowly, revealing a thick sheet of parchment, edges darkened with age. "It's the closest border from here. And the most dangerous for a girl with your blood."

Nilsa felt a cold ripple along her spine. "Why?"

"Because Morrivan does not hide truth." Maelra looked at her sharply, eyes sharp as splintered ice. "And truth clings to you like scent to fur."

Nilsa swallowed hard, unsure how to respond. Maelra pressed the folded parchment into her hands.

"This," she said softly, "is a map drawn before the Sundering. Before kingdoms forgot who they were. Before truths were buried in ash."

Nilsa unfolded it cautiously. The parchment crackled, stiff with age. Dark ink traced ancient roads across territories she barely recognized. Strange runes curved around river bends. Forests were marked with symbols she couldn't decipher. And at the far end — deep in the lands marked as Morrivan — was a sigil she knew too well: twelve stars circling an empty center.

Her heart stuttered.

"This symbol—"

"The Thirteenth Kingdom," Maelra finished. "What remains of its traces, anyway."

Nilsa traced her fingers over the ink, feeling something there beneath the surface. A hum. A pulse. A memory she did not possess.

"I can't read these runes," Nilsa murmured.

"No," Maelra said. "But he can."

Nilsa stiffened, lifting her gaze. "Erabor?"

The healer nodded once, sharply. "When he came through my door yesterday, the shadows in the rafters stirred. They know him. The old magic knows him." Maelra's voice lowered to a warning whisper. "Whatever he is — whatever he hides — he will be able to read this map."

Nilsa felt her breath catch, torn between disbelief and the memory of Erabor's quiet, peaceful sleep. The way he'd leaned into her hands. The way his breathing had softened against her shoulder. The vulnerability she'd witnessed in the firelight.

"He's just a man," she whispered.

Maelra's expression softened with something like pity. "Child… no man sleeps like that unless he is exhausted beyond the mortal body's limits. And no mortal body endures shadow-poison without revealing its true nature."

Nilsa shook her head. "He slept deeply. Quietly. Peacefully. I watched him. Whatever he's hiding, it isn't monstrous."

Maelra hummed, neither agreeing nor arguing. "Perhaps not monstrous. But not simple, either." She touched the edge of the map. "Give this to him when he wakes. See how his eyes change when he looks at it. That will tell you more than anything I could say."

Nilsa folded the map carefully, her fingers trembling just a little. When she turned back toward the hut, a faint sound reached her — the quiet rustle of shifting blankets, the soft exhale of someone waking slowly from deep rest.

Erabor.

Nilsa took a steadying breath.

"Why do I feel like this map is a turning point?" she asked.

Maelra's voice was low, somber, certain. "Because it is."

CHAPTER EIGHTEEN

The Map That Remembered Him

The air inside the healer's hut was warm enough that Nilsa's breath no longer fogged when she exhaled, though the cold outside clung faintly to her cloak as she stepped inside. The smell of simmering herbs and cedar smoke lingered in gentle waves, mingling with the earthy scent of pine needles Maelra had tracked in at dawn. The room felt contained, protected — like the world had decided not to intrude for a few more hours.

Erabor still slept when she entered.

He lay where she'd left him, half-slumped against a cushion Maelra had wedged between his shoulder and the wall. His face was bathed in soft firelight, highlighting the curve of his cheekbone, the faint shadows beneath his eyes, the loosened set of his jaw. The fever-flush was gone now, replaced by a quiet stillness that made her chest tighten.

Sleep softened him.
Made him look almost fragile.
Made it almost easy to believe he was just a wounded young man in a stranger's home, not someone carrying ancient echoes in his blood.

Nilsa approached slowly, her boots silent on the wooden floor. The map weighed heavily in her hands — not from its mass, but from everything Maelra had said beneath the dawn light. She traced her thumb along the folded edge, feeling the slight tremble in her own fingers.

She'd thought bringing it to him would steady her.
Instead, it made her anxious in ways she didn't know how to name.

Outside, the forest shifted — a sigh of wind through pine needles, a whisper against the shutters that sounded almost deliberate. She paused, letting her eyes travel to the window.

Frost feathered its edges, but the movement beyond was real. The trees were watching. She felt it the same way she felt her own heartbeat — quiet, but undeniable.

Maelra's voice drifted from the hearth, low and matter-of-fact. "The forest knows old things, girl. Some trees remember more truths than men."

Nilsa turned her head slightly. "Is it reacting to me… or to him?"

Maelra's silence stretched long enough that Nilsa knew the answer wasn't simple.

"Both," the healer finally murmured. "But differently. The land listens for your pulse. It listens to him for something older."

Nilsa felt a faint chill crawl down her spine. She looked back at Erabor — his peaceful breathing, the faint twitch in his fingers as the last remnants of pain ebbed from his body. He didn't look like something that would stir an entire forest.

He looked… human.

She knelt beside him, the hem of her cloak brushing the floorboards in a soft sigh. The movement must have disturbed the air, because Erabor's brow twitched, and his breath shifted — deeper, then lighter. Nilsa held her breath, watching as his eyelids fluttered, slow and reluctant, before lifting.

His gaze was unfocused for a moment, gray eyes clouded with sleep, the world still blurred around the edges. He blinked several times before recognition dawned — first in the soft widening of his eyes, then in the subtle tension that returned to his shoulders as memory caught up with consciousness.

"Nilsa," he murmured, her name shaped gently, as if speaking it helped anchor him to waking.

"You're awake," she whispered, allowing herself a small, relieved smile. "How do you feel?"

Erabor exhaled slowly, rolling his stiff shoulder back against the cushion. "Like I fought a mountain and the mountain won. But not as badly as last night." His eyes drifted downward, scanning her face carefully. "Did you sleep?"

"Some," she admitted, "but I was waiting for you to wake."

Something tender flickered in his expression — gratitude, guilt, something painfully human.

"Nilsa… you shouldn't lose rest over me."

"And you shouldn't bleed shadows for my sake," she answered quietly. "Yet here we are."

A faint smile ghosted across his lips, but it didn't reach his eyes. They held too much weight.

She unfolded the map in her hands, the parchment crackling softly. Erabor's gaze snapped to it instantly, his entire posture sharpening as if some instinct awoke the moment he saw its edges.

"Maelra gave me this," Nilsa said gently. "She thought… she thought you might be able to read it."

He went still.

She placed it carefully across his lap, smoothing the folds so none of the delicate parchment tore. As the map unrolled, the old runes — symbols shaped like entwined stars and twisting branches — shimmered faintly in the firelight. Roads long vanished gleamed in ink that had no right to survive the centuries.

Erabor stared at it without breathing.

Nilsa watched the change in him — subtle, almost imperceptible, but unmistakable. His pupils flinched, dilating slightly. His brow furrowed as if something deep inside him tugged, pulling him toward memory he didn't want or didn't expect.

His fingertips trembled when they hovered above the ink — not touching it, simply near it. As though the map was radiating heat.

"Erabor?" she whispered.

Outside, the forest shifted.

Pine needles rattled though the wind had gone still.

The shutters creaked softly, wood bending with a sound like a sigh.

And the shadow beneath Erabor's hand changed shape — stretching just a little, narrowing, as if reaching toward the map before collapsing back into its usual silhouette.

Nilsa gasped, barely in time to stop herself from recoiling. Erabor's head snapped up as if he'd sensed her jolt, his eyes wide, confused.

"What happened?" His voice was thin, breathless.

Nilsa shook her head quickly, masking her reaction. "The forest moved. Or... the wind." A lie, half-truth, something to keep him from withdrawing again. "But the map—Erabor, do you recognize it?"

He lowered his gaze slowly, reluctantly, back toward the parchment.

His fingers finally touched it.

And the map reacted.

Ink lines shimmered, glowing faintly with silver light, tracing themselves clearer beneath his touch. Runes that had been dull brightened, as though awakening. One symbol — a star with a hollow center — pulsed once beneath his fingertip like a heartbeat.

Erabor inhaled sharply, his entire body tensing.

Nilsa felt cold spread through her limbs. "You do know it."

"I…" His throat bobbed, eyes darkening with something she had never seen in him before — not fear, not pain, but recognition. "…I shouldn't."

"But you do," she said softly.

He tore his gaze from the map, looking at her with something like desperation. "Nilsa, I have never seen this map in my life. But I know what these symbols say. I can read them."

Outside, the forest reacted again — pine needles falling upward, frost melting in tendrils across the ground, shadows leaning subtly toward the hut like listening children.

"Erabor," Nilsa whispered, her voice trembling, "how?"

He opened his mouth.

Then closed it.

And his shoulders shook, just once — barely noticeable, but real.

"I don't know," he said, but it wasn't a lie. It was something worse.

It was the truth of someone whose memories had holes in them.

Nilsa reached out, laying her hand gently over his.

He froze — not pulling away, not leaning in, just… breathing.

And for the briefest heartbeat, she felt something pulse beneath his skin — not magic, not heat — but a quiet, terrified question.

Whatever this map meant,
whatever Morrivan would force them to confront,
whatever truths lay in the shadowed folds of Erabor's past…

It had already begun.

CHAPTER NINETEEN

The Forest of Listening Pines

The morning they left Maelra's hut broke cold and pale, with a thin veil of frost silvering the needles of the pines. The healer's cottage stood quietly in the dim light, smoke curling lazily from the chimney as if reluctant to let them go. Nilsa tightened the straps on the last pack horse while Erabor saddled Flint with careful, deliberate movements. She watched him subtly—his left arm still stiff, his jaw set with a tension he was trying to hide—but the map safely folded in his inner pocket seemed to lend him a strange, steady focus.

When they were finally mounted and ready, Maelra stepped into the doorway, leaning heavily on her cane. Her gaze swept over them with a somber weight that made the hairs on Nilsa's arms rise. "Follow the old hunter's trail until the ground begins to slope," she said. "Then bear northeast. Morrivan's wardlines begin where the pines shift color."

Nilsa frowned. "Shift color?"

"You'll see." Maelra's eyes softened only slightly when they fell on Nilsa. "The forest will watch you. Do not lie to it."

Nilsa nodded, though the instruction sat uneasily in her stomach.

Maelra's attention turned to Erabor, and the healer's sharp voice gentled. "You should not have survived the shadows. The fact that you did means the forest will see you before it sees her." She pointed her cane toward his chest. "So mind your thoughts. Morrivan listens."

Erabor stiffened, grey eyes flashing with a discomfort Nilsa sensed more than saw. "I'll be careful."

"You'll need to be," Maelra murmured.

Nilsa guided Starwind forward and leaned down to offer the healer a respectful nod. "Thank you. For everything."

"Bring your truths with you," Maelra replied. "And hold your lies close."

With that, she stepped back inside, closing the door with finality. Nilsa felt the shift immediately—like stepping out from under a roof into open air, the world expanding around her.

She glanced at Erabor. "Are you ready?"

He exhaled slowly, eyes flicking once toward the line of trees ahead. "As I'll ever be."

They began to ride.

The forest greeted them with stillness—no birdsong, no rustling of small creatures, just the soft crunch of frosted earth beneath hooves. Sunlight filtered through the tall pines in cold, slanted beams, catching on drifting needles and tiny sparks of ice. In the quiet, every sound seemed amplified: the creak of leather saddles, the soft jingle of buckles, the rhythmic breath of horses.

After a time, Nilsa spoke softly, as if trying not to disturb the hush. "It feels different. Like the air is… thicker."

Erabor nodded, though his expression was distant. "Magic pools differently here. Slower. Older."

"Does that happen everywhere?"

"No," he replied, his voice dropping. "Only in places where the land remembers."

Nilsa shivered, unsure why those words unsettled her so deeply. She tried to focus on the trail, guiding Starwind along the narrow strip of packed earth winding between ancient trunks.

The farther they rode, the stranger the forest became.

The light shifted first—subtle, almost imperceptible. Golden morning sunlight dimmed to a cooler, bluer hue as if filtered through colored glass. The trees grew taller, their trunks thicker, their shadows stretching longer than they should. The pine needles above changed too, darkening from deep green to a muted blue-gray, forming a canopy that rustled in a language she could not decipher.

Then came the whispers.

Faint. Soft. Like the hush of cloth brushing stone.

Nilsa slowed Starwind. "Do you hear that?"

Erabor's posture stiffened, and he angled Flint closer to her. "Shadows," he murmured. "Only whispers. No intent."

"Intent?"

"They speak when they feel truth," he said, scanning the branches above. "Or lies."

Nilsa swallowed hard. "What are they saying?"

He shook his head. "It's not a language we can hear fully. It's more... a feeling."

"A feeling of what?"

Erabor hesitated, brow furrowing slightly. "Recognition."

Nilsa's pulse quickened. "Of me?"

He shook his head again, though his answer wasn't reassuring. "Of us."

They continued on, and the forest leaned closer, curious. The path narrowed, roots coiling across the ground like veins. Shafts of cold light formed columns between ancient trunks. Every now and then, a drifting pine needle would fall upward, spiraling gently toward the canopy instead of down. Nilsa watched, captivated and uneasy.

"Is that normal?" she whispered.

"For Morrivan? Yes," Erabor said. "Gravity is a suggestion here."

She let out a nervous laugh, and he glanced at her with a faint, warm smile—fleeting but real. The kind of smile he rarely gave willingly.

A few minutes later, the ground sloped sharply, just as Maelra had said. And at the crest of the rise, Nilsa saw it:

The forest changed color in a single, breathtaking sweep.

The trees before them were silver.

Not frosted. Not moonlit.
Silver-barked. Silver-veined. Silver-shadowed.

Their branches rose like skeletal fingers, and their leaves—still pine needles, but elongated—gleamed with soft metallic sheen. When the breeze passed through them, they chimed faintly, like distant bells.

Nilsa stared, mesmerized. "Gods… it's beautiful."

Erabor's expression shifted—wonder and worry tangled in equal measure. "This is the border. Once we pass those trees, we are in Morrivan."

Nilsa nudged Starwind forward, unable to tear her eyes from the silver glow. "Are you afraid?"

"Yes," he said quietly. "But not of this."

She slowed, looking back at him. "Then what?"

He hesitated, gaze flicking toward the silver woods. The faint wind carried a ripple through the metallic needles, and the forest's whispers grew just a little louder—gentle, curious, and chilling.

"A place that whispers truth," he said softly, "will try to whisper mine."

Nilsa's breath caught. "And your truth is something you fear?"

Erabor's eyes met hers—haunted, vulnerable, unbearably guarded. "My truth is something that could destroy everything."

A hush fell between them, heavy and intimate as snowfall.

Nilsa reached across the space between their horses, brushing her fingertips against his wrist. "Then I'll listen with you."

His breath hitched—only slightly, but she felt the tremor under her fingers. He didn't pull away. Not this time.

The silver forest chimes swelled softly, as if echoing her promise.

And together, side by side beneath shimmering branches, they rode into Morrivan.

CHAPTER TWENTY

Under the Silver Pines

The deeper they rode into Morrivan, the quieter the world became — not in the way of still forests, but in the way of sacred places that demanded silence. The silver pines rose tall around them, their metallic needles shimmering faintly in the shifting light. Every breeze sent a soft, chiming whisper through the branches, a music that felt both beautiful and unsettling. Nilsa felt those whispers along her skin, a prickling awareness as if the forest had taken note of her presence and was debating her worth.

Erabor rode beside her with unusual stillness, Flint's reins resting loosely in his gloved hand. His gaze roamed the trees with an alertness sharpened by unease. The faint stiffness in his shoulder had eased since the healer's intervention, but the shadow-poison had left exhaustion clinging to his bones. Even now, beneath the glow of the silver canopy, Nilsa saw the pallor in his complexion — a tiredness he tried to hide behind steady breath.

They traveled in silence until the trail began to widen into a narrow glade carpeted with dew-soaked moss. The light filtered down in shifting bands, catching the silver needles above and casting pale reflections on the forest floor. Nilsa slowed Starwind, letting the mare's hooves sink softly into the moss.

"We should rest," she said gently.

Erabor didn't object — which worried her more than any argument might have. He dismounted with controlled precision, but when his boots met the soft ground, he wavered for half a breath. Nilsa saw it. He pretended he didn't.

They led the horses to the edge of the glade. As Nilsa loosened Starwind's girth and ran her hand along the mare's warm neck, a faint sound drew her attention.

Not wind.
Not the chime of needles.
Something else — a footstep, soft and deliberate, on the moss.

She turned sharply.

A figure stood at the edge of the trees.

Nilsa's breath caught.

The stranger was tall and lean, wrapped in a long cloak of pale woven reeds that shifted like liquid silver when he moved. His face was half-hidden beneath a hood, but the lower half was youthful, sharp-jawed, and distinctly Morrivani — high cheekbones, skin tinted with the faintest cool blue undertone. His hands were ungloved, long fingers tipped with faintly inked glyphs that spiraled up the wrists in intricate patterns.

But what struck her most was the silence.

He didn't speak.
Didn't signal greeting.
Didn't move toward them.

He simply watched.

A Morrivan forest guide.

Erabor stepped beside Nilsa, quiet as a shadow. "Do not startle him," he said in a whisper that barely stirred the air. "Guides of Morrivan speak little, if at all. They communicate with gesture, and they appear only for those the forest permits."

Nilsa swallowed, forcing her breath to steady. "And if the forest doesn't permit us?"

"Then he wouldn't be here." Erabor's voice held a tremor — not of fear, but of another emotion she couldn't name. "Or... we wouldn't."

The guide lifted one hand — slow, fluid — and pressed two fingers to his chest before extending them toward Nilsa. A gesture of acknowledgment. Of welcome. His pale eyes flicked briefly to Erabor, then back to her.

"He recognized you," Nilsa murmured.

"No," Erabor said softly. "He recognized *your bloodline*."

The guide moved silently across the moss until he stood closer, though still cautious, his presence calm and strangely comforting. He lifted his hand again and traced a careful pattern in the air — a downward arc, a flick to the left, then a slow curl like a winding road.

Erabor inhaled sharply. "He's offering safe passage."

Nilsa blinked. "Just like that?"

"Not just like that," Erabor murmured. "Guides of Morrivan see truth as shadows see shape. They don't offer anything unless they sense purpose. Or danger."

The guide pivoted slightly, stepping beyond the glade toward a narrow, barely-visible path that wound deeper into the glowing trees. He paused, looking back with the smallest tilt of his head — urging them to follow.

Nilsa's pulse quickened. "Should we?"

"That depends," Erabor said, watching the guide with quiet intensity. "Do you trust him?"

Nilsa looked into the silver forest, into the strange, shifting light. She felt the press of magic all around her — old, rooted, wary — yet there was no malice in the air. Only… curiosity.

"Yes," she said. "I do."

Erabor exhaled slowly, something softening in his posture. "Then so do I."

But before they followed, the guide lifted his hand again — palm outward — and made a gesture like lowering a weight. Rest.

Nilsa turned to Erabor, understanding. "He wants us to pause before continuing."

Erabor gave a faint huff of breath that wasn't quite a laugh. "Even the forest thinks I'm about to fall over."

Nilsa smiled gently. "Maybe it listens better than you."

They settled beneath one of the silver pines, whose roots created a natural cradle in the moss. The air beneath its branches was cool but soothing, infused with the scent of crushed pine and faint metallic sweetness. Nilsa sat close enough that their shoulders nearly brushed, but not quite touching. The nearness felt warm, grounding.

Erabor leaned back against the trunk, tilting his head until it rested lightly against the bark. He closed his eyes, breath steadying. "I didn't realize how much the sleep helped until now," he murmured, voice low and rough. "It feels like parts of me finally stopped fighting."

Nilsa looked at him—really looked. "You're still fighting," she said softly. "Just not alone this time."

His eyes opened slightly, turning toward her. "You always say things like that."

"And you always act like you don't need to hear them."

A long breath left him, something between a sigh and surrender. "Maybe I do."

The guide watched from a respectful distance, cloak blending with the silver trunks, patient and unmoving as if he, too, understood the necessity of this moment. Above them, the needles chimed faintly, their sound eerily beautiful — like tiny bells carried on the wind.

Nilsa brushed a stray lock of hair from her face. "Erabor… when the map reacted to you—"

He tensed.

"I didn't mean to upset you," she said. "But you looked at it like you'd found something you'd lost."

Erabor's voice was barely above a whisper. "Maybe I did."

Nilsa felt a faint shiver run through her. "Do you ever wonder who you were before all of this?"

He closed his eyes again, as though the question hurt. "Every day."

"And do you want the answers?" she asked gently.

Slowly, he turned his head toward her. His grey eyes were storm-dark beneath the silver canopy. "Only if they lead me to the truth without hurting you."

Her throat tightened. "I trust you."

His breath hitched, barely audible. "Then I'll try to trust myself."

The guide stepped forward again, a soft, nearly silent movement in the moss. He lifted his hand, drawing a slow spiral — continuation.

Their rest was over.

But the softness lingered in the air, warm and fragile, clinging to them like the silver light.

Nilsa rose first. Erabor followed, slower but steadier, and when their eyes met beneath the shimmering branches, an unspoken promise passed between them:

Whatever truths waited in Morrivan's whispering shadows, they would face them together.

CHAPTER TWENTY-ONE

The Watchtower of Listening Stone

The Morrivan guide moved with a fluidity that made him seem less like a man and more like a part of the forest itself. His reed-woven cloak shifted without sound, catching glimmers of silver light as he slipped between the towering pines. Nilsa and Erabor followed closely, horses picking their way over moss-softened roots and patches of frost that glimmered beneath the filtered light.

Nilsa felt the strangeness around them like a tangible presence. Shadows clung to the trees more loosely here, as if drifting, unanchored, drawn toward the trio but never daring to touch them. The guide did not look back, but his gestures were precise—small flicks of his hand, nods of his head, fluid sweeps that indicated where the trail narrowed or where the earth dipped suddenly beneath the moss.

The forest shifted subtly as they went. Pines grew farther apart, their silver needles thinning into curtains that swayed gently in a breeze Nilsa could not feel. The air deepened into a cool blue-gray tone, carrying a quiet hum that settled beneath her skin. And somewhere beneath that hum was another rhythm… something like a pulse.

"Are you sensing it too?" she whispered to Erabor.

His jaw tightened, gaze locked ahead. "Not the forest. Something else." His fingers tightened briefly on Flint's reins. "Someone is following."

Nilsa's chest constricted. "Not the guide?"

"No." Erabor shook his head minutely, eyes flicking to the side where the trees thickened into an unbroken wall of silver and shadow. "He doesn't feel it—can't, maybe. Morrivan guides see truth when it stands before them, but they don't sense what hides behind."

Nilsa swallowed hard. "Do you know what it is?"

A long silence stretched before he answered. "No. And that is what troubles me."

The guide halted suddenly, raising his hand. Nilsa followed his gesture toward a break in the trees ahead. A clearing opened like a small valley, sun piercing through in cold, sharp beams. At its center rose a stone watchtower, half-overgrown with moss and creeping vines that glimmered faintly with silver dust. The structure leaned slightly, but its foundation looked carved from a single piece of old-world stone—smooth, dark, ancient.

Nilsa felt a chill when she saw it.

Erabor felt something else entirely. His breath hitched, faint but noticeable, as if the sight of it tugged at something buried deep in him.

The guide beckoned them forward, touching his hand lightly to the ground in a gesture of permission, then leading them down a gentle slope toward the abandoned tower.

As they approached, a soft vibration hummed beneath Starwind's hooves. Nilsa stiffened, leaning forward instinctively. "Do you feel that?"

Erabor nodded. "Yes. That's wardline magic."

"From the tower?"

"No," he said, scanning the clearing. "From below it."

The guide stopped at the base of the tower, pressing his palm to a large stone set upright at the entrance. It was a ward stone—Nilsa recognized it at once. Every kingdom had their own form of protection, but Morrivan's ward stones were uniquely shaped:

tall, narrow pillars carved with runes that spiraled downward in looping patterns like falling leaves.

This one was cracked down the middle.

Nilsa dismounted carefully, Starwind snorting uneasily as if the very air around the stone vibrated with invisible pressure. Erabor stayed mounted for a moment longer, scanning the tree line with a strange, rigid intensity.

The guide reached out toward Nilsa, tapping his own chest once, then gesturing toward the ward stone. An invitation. Or a warning.

Nilsa approached slowly.

As she drew near, the runes carved in the stone shimmered faintly—a soft glow that brightened with each step she took. A prickle raced up her spine, heat pooling beneath her skin like an awakening, like something stirring inside her blood.

"Nilsa…" Erabor's voice cut sharply across the clearing. "Stop."

But it was too late.

The ward stone pulsed.

Light—cold and silver-bright—rippling through the runes like veins of lightning.

Nilsa froze in place. Her breath caught, trapped in a chest that suddenly felt too tight. The air around her twisted, pulling inward, forming a soft vortex that tugged at her cloak.

Erabor slid off Flint in one fluid motion, nearly stumbling as his boots hit the ground. He reached her in a heartbeat, his hand going instinctively to her arm.

And that's when the stone reacted again.

This time it wasn't a pulse.
It was recognition.

A deep, resonant **tone** thrummed through the clearing, spreading through Nilsa's bones like sound underwater. The runes brightened until the entire ward stone glowed with piercing clarity.

The guide stumbled back, cloak rustling as he dropped to one knee. Shadows along the tree trunks flattened and twisted, whispering furiously in a language Nilsa couldn't decipher.

Erabor swore under his breath—something sharp, ancient, unutterably afraid.

"Nilsa," he said, gripping her shoulder tightly, "pull back. The stone is reading your blood. You have to step away—now."

"I'm trying," she managed, breath shaking. "It's… holding me."

And it was. The air felt thick around her legs, like invisible threads anchoring her to the stone.

The ward stone flared again.

This time the light was not soft.
It was blinding.

Nilsa cried out as brightness swallowed her vision. She felt Erabor's arm wrap around her waist, pulling, anchoring, protecting. His grip trembled—not from weakness, but from fury. Determination. Fear.

The guide rose abruptly, moving toward them with outstretched hands and frantic gestures, but Erabor snarled a warning sound—not quite human, not quite mortal—forcing him back.

Nilsa's heartbeat thundered as images flickered through her mind—flashes she couldn't fully grasp: a crown of stars, a circle of twelve flames, a throne carved from shadow and silver, and one name whispered like a memory she had tried to forget.

Then—

As abruptly as it began, the light died.

Nilsa collapsed backward into Erabor's arms, her breath coming in sharp, desperate pulls. The forest stilled. The humming faded. The runes dimmed to a dull, harmless glow.

Erabor held her tightly, one hand at the back of her head, the other braced at her waist, grounding her with his warmth and steadiness. "Are you hurt?" His voice cracked with the strain of holding himself together.

"No," she whispered, leaning into him. "Just shaken."

He exhaled shakily, forehead pressed briefly to her temple. "The stone recognized you. That shouldn't be possible."

Nilsa swallowed, voice unsteady. "What does that mean?"

He hesitated.

Before he could answer, the guide moved between them and the ward stone, lifting both hands in a gesture that was unmistakable.

Fear.
Warning.
Proceed with caution.

The tower had not just seen her.

It had **known** her.

And somewhere beyond the clearing, deeper in the silver woods, something stirred in response.

CHAPTER TWENTY-TWO

The Stone That Remembered

The echoes of the ward stone still thrummed in Nilsa's bones long after its light had faded. Even as Erabor helped her step away from it, the world seemed to pulse faintly, like her heartbeat had been synced to some deeper rhythm beneath the forest floor. Her breath came unevenly, and each inhale carried the metallic taste of silver needles and old magic.

Erabor kept one steadying hand on her elbow until she regained her balance. His touch was warm, grounding, and she lowered her gaze for only a moment before he gently tipped her chin upward. "Nilsa," he murmured, voice low with alarm, "your eyes."

She blinked, disoriented. "What about them?"

"Just for a moment—" His voice tightened. "They weren't the same color."

A faint shudder coursed through her. "What did you see?"

"Light," he said softly, his thumb brushing her cheekbone as if to erase the memory. "Silver. Too bright to be natural."

The guide watched them with unnerving stillness. His reed cloak rustled faintly as he lowered himself to one knee beside the ward stone, pressing his palm to the cracked surface with reverence and dread. The runes glimmered weakly beneath his touch, as if drained of the immense force they had roused moments before.

Nilsa drew a slow breath and stepped closer, though her legs trembled. "The stone… did it show me something? Or did I imagine that?"

Erabor was already shaking his head. "Ward stones never imagine. They reflect truths they recognize."

"But I don't know what it recognized."

"Not yet," he said quietly. "But the tower might."

Nilsa followed his gaze upward.

The watchtower rose like a spine of old stone against the pale sky. Its surface bore the scars of centuries—cracks and missing chunks of dark rock—yet it stood tall, stubbornly refusing collapse. Vines spiraled up its sides in delicate silver threads, weaving patterns that echoed the runes carved into the ward stone.

Erabor retrieved a lantern from one of the pack horses and ignited it with a strike of flint. The warm flame pooled amber light across the moss before narrowing into a focused glow. "Stay close," he said softly. "And step where I step."

The guide lifted a hand in a brief, silent blessing before drifting back into the tree line, as if the tower itself was no place for him.

Nilsa moved beside Erabor toward the entrance, her fingers brushing Starwind's mane as she passed. The mare pressed her warm nose briefly to Nilsa's shoulder, sensing unease. Nilsa whispered a gentle reassurance, then stepped into the tower's shadow.

The doorway was tall but narrow, framed by two stone pillars carved with spiraling symbols. They flickered faintly at the lantern's approach, as though waking from an old slumber.

A chill swept over her.

"Erabor…" her voice faltered. "These runes—do you recognize them?"

His jaw clenched as he traced one with the tip of his glove. "Yes," he said reluctantly. "The same symbols from the map."

Nilsa's breath caught. "So this tower was built by—?"

"I don't know." He swallowed hard. "But it wasn't built by Morrivan."

Inside, the air changed. It grew warmer, then colder, then settled into a distant echo of warmth again, like weather shifting in a single breath. Dust motes drifted through the lanternlight, shimmering faintly with flecks of silver.

The interior chamber was round, its stone walls carved with twisting reliefs—flowing lines that spiraled and knotted, forming shapes she didn't recognize. A staircase wound upward around the edge, narrow and steep, curving into darkness.

Nilsa swallowed uneasily. "What is this place?"

"A waystation," Erabor murmured. "A place for travelers. Messengers. Seers. Anyone passing between the old kingdoms." His palm grazed the stone wall, pausing over a cluster of symbols. "This tower predates the Sundering."

Nilsa felt her stomach drop.

"That makes it at least three hundred years old."

"More," he whispered.

They climbed slowly. The stairwell echoed with the faint drip of melting frost and the hollow sound of their steps. Erabor's lantern cast shadows along the walls — shadows that moved in ways that made Nilsa want to hold her breath.

At the top, they emerged onto a half-ruined platform open to the sky.

The view struck her breathless.

Morrivan stretched before them.

Not the border forest they had been traversing — but the true kingdom beyond. The land unfolded in shimmering layers: silver pines that glowed like frost-lit glass, rolling hills washed in pale blue light, and deeper still, valleys veiled in drifting shadow-mist. The air hummed with energy, as if every blade of grass, every root, every stone was listening.

Nilsa leaned forward, gripping the broken parapet.

"It's beautiful," she whispered.

"And dangerous," Erabor said quietly, though his voice held awe he couldn't hide.

The lanternlight pooled across the floor, revealing a large circular carving at the tower's center. The design was unmistakable.

Twelve sigils
surrounding an empty center.

Nilsa's throat tightened. "The missing kingdom."

Erabor crouched beside the carving, running his fingers along the outer symbols. His hand trembled, but not from weakness. From recognition.

"When the ward stone reacted to you," he murmured, "this is what it saw."

Nilsa touched the empty center. "Why is it blank?"

"Because the world erased it," Erabor whispered. "Because something—or someone—wanted it forgotten."

Nilsa's pulse hammered. Her fingers pressed more firmly to the stone, and a faint warmth blossomed beneath her palm.

At first, she thought she imagined it.
But then—

Light.
Soft, silver.
Blooming from the center like a heartbeat.

She jerked back with a gasp.

Erabor reached her instantly, steadying her, lantern swinging wildly in his other hand. "What did you see?"

"Nothing," she whispered, trembling. "Everything. I don't know."

The warmth faded as quickly as it came. The carving fell silent again, patient and ominous.

Erabor exhaled slowly. "This tower recognized you… just like the ward stone."

"And we still don't know why."

"No," he said softly, "but Morrivan will not let us question blindly much longer."

Nilsa turned back toward the kingdom stretching before them. The wind brushed her cheek, cool and soft, carrying with it a faint, whispering sound — not words, not quite, but something close enough to stir the hairs at the back of her neck.

A welcome.
Or a warning.

Erabor rested his hand lightly on her back, guiding her gently away from the carving. "Come," he said quietly. "We need to descend. The guide will take us into the true heart of the kingdom."

Nilsa nodded, allowing herself one last lingering look at the vast silver lands ahead.

They were close.
Closer than they'd ever been.

Tomorrow—
they would enter Morrivan.

And whatever truth had been waiting for her in the shadows…
it would no longer hide.

CHAPTER TWENTY-THREE

The Kingdom That Listens

By the time they descended from the tower, dusk had begun to seep between the silver pines, filling the forest with a muted blue glow that softened every shadow while somehow making them feel deeper. The Morrivan guide waited at the bottom of the slope, still as carved stone, watching them with that quiet intensity that revealed nothing and suggested everything.

Nilsa's pulse had steadied since the ward stone's vision, but a faint tremor lingered beneath her skin, like a memory she wasn't supposed to hold. Erabor kept a steadying hand at her back until she found her footing. When she looked at him, he didn't hide the worry in his eyes.

"Are you sure you're ready?" he asked quietly.

"No," she said. "But we can't wait."

He nodded once, accepting the truth without argument.

The guide raised one hand in a sweeping gesture—forward, deeper—and they followed him into the darkening forest. As they moved, the trees leaned inward, their branches arching overhead to form a vaulted canopy. Silver needles glimmered like frost-lit stars. The air hummed faintly, charged with magic that prickled across Nilsa's arms.

They had been walking only minutes when Nilsa heard it.

A whisper.
Soft.
Fleeting.
Almost imagined.

She turned her head sharply.

Erabor stiffened immediately. "What is it?"

She swallowed. "I... thought I heard something."

"Your name?" he asked, too quietly.

Her breath caught. "Yes."

He exhaled through his teeth, gaze sweeping the tree line. "We're past the border wards now. The forest sees more than it should. Stay close."

The guide continued without looking back, but when Nilsa listened carefully, she realized there were two sets of whispers in the air.

One—soft, curious, brushing her mind like featherlight fingertips.

Nilsa…
Nilsaaa…

Airy. Echoing. Almost tender.

The other—farther off.
Sharper.
Hungrier.

Erabor felt that second one immediately. His posture shifted, instinctive and protective, his hand brushing the hilt of his knife. "We're not alone."

Nilsa's heart lurched. "The thing that's been following us?"

"Yes." His voice lowered into something guttural, almost inhuman for a heartbeat. "And it's closer than before."

The forest responded.

Silver branches shivered overhead. The ground beneath their feet seemed to pulse once, twice, as if the land itself inhaled.

The guide halted so abruptly that Flint snorted behind him. He lifted both hands, palms outward—**Stop. Danger. Do not move.**

Erabor shifted in front of Nilsa instinctively, every muscle in his body coiled and ready.

The forest changed.

Not gradually.
Not politely.

A ripple passed through the trees like a wave of windless motion. Trunks elongated in a single breath. Branches twisted, curling into new shapes. Pathways closed. New ones opened. The air thickened, humming with old magic.

The forest was shifting.
Rearranging.
Choosing.

Nilsa inhaled sharply. "It's guiding us."

"No," Erabor murmured. "It's hiding us."

From behind them, something moved through the silver pines with heavy, dragging steps. A wrongness radiated from it—low, cold, crawling against the skin like an icy breath. The light dimmed noticeably. Even the silver needles seemed to dull their shine.

The Morrivan guide made a slicing gesture—**Down. Now.**

Erabor pulled Nilsa beside him and dropped behind a fallen trunk, where the shadows grew thick and strangely warm. The guide flattened himself against a tree, cloak blending seamlessly into the bark.

The forest held its breath.

Nilsa did too.

Through the densely shifting pines, she glimpsed movement—just a flicker, a silhouette gliding between the trees. Tall. Thin. Wrongly jointed. Its shape seemed to bend in ways flesh shouldn't bend.

It paused.

Nilsa couldn't see its face, but she felt its attention sweep across the clearing—a cold, probing pressure against her mind. Her heartbeat stuttered violently.

Erabor's hand found hers in the cover of the shadows. His grip was firm, almost too tight, but she clung back just as fiercely.

He whispered, barely audible. "Don't let it hear your fear."

She tried. Gods, she tried.

The creature tilted its head. The shadow of its form stretched, unfurling like tattered wings dragging along the forest floor. A faint rasping sound followed:

…not yet…

Nilsa's blood iced.

Then, just as abruptly as it had arrived, the creature turned. Its body dissolved into the trees, as if sliding between the seams of reality. The cold presence lifted. The forest's glow returned, soft and steady.

The guide rose first, tapping the bark twice—**Safe. Move. Now.**

Nilsa exhaled shakily. Erabor pulled her up, his hand lingering a moment longer than necessary, ensuring her legs were steady.

"What was that?" she whispered.

"I don't know." Erabor's voice was rigid. "And I've dreaded this entire journey that I might someday recognize it."

"But you didn't."

"No." He cut his gaze toward the direction the creature vanished. "Which frightens me more."

The forest opened ahead into a long, gradual slope. The ground glowed faintly beneath the silver trees, illuminating a path that had not been there moments before.

The guide stood at its entrance, lifting one hand in a gesture that held no ambiguity.

Welcome.
Proceed.
You are seen.

Nilsa felt the words settle into her bones.

Morrivan awaited them.

Erabor stepped beside her, face taut with lingering tension, but his voice steadied as he asked, "Are you ready?"

No.
Yes.
She didn't know.

But the forest had chosen them.
And something had nearly reached them first.

Nilsa squared her shoulders, breath firming. "Let's go."

Together—with the guide ahead, the forest shifting around them, and something dangerous hunting the trail behind—they walked down the glowing path.

Toward the kingdom that whispered her name.

CHAPTER TWENTY-FOUR

The Oracle of Shadows and Silver

The forest shifted with every step they took, not in abrupt or dramatic motions but in small, unnervingly organic ways, as though the land itself had a pulse they had slowly begun to sync with. The Morrivan guide moved ahead of them in that fluid, gliding walk that disturbed neither moss nor needle. His cloak—woven from reeds, mist, and something unmistakably magical—caught faint glimmers of silver light with each motion, reflecting the soft glow filtering through the pines overhead.

Nilsa rode slowly, one hand resting lightly on Starwind's mane, the other adjusting the pack slung behind her saddle. The mare's ears flicked constantly, reacting to sounds Nilsa could not hear—whispers too faint for human ears, or perhaps meant only for animal instincts. The cold-blue dusk had begun its descent through the branches, casting long shadows across the path and staining the air with a muted, ethereal glow that made every breath feel simultaneously heavy and delicate.

There was something about Morrivan that carried weight but also lightness—like being inside a dream where the rules of the waking world were temporarily suspended. The pine scent was sharp, clean, but layered beneath it was the faintest metallic tone, almost like tasting silver on the tongue. Every exhale rose like mist, only to fade unnaturally fast. Nilsa wasn't certain what part belonged to the forest's magic and what part belonged to the fear rising slowly from her chest.

Erabor moved beside her, his steps uneven but masked beneath practiced composure. Even while walking, he kept a subtle perimeter—positioning himself between Nilsa and the tree line, always slightly ahead or slightly to the side, never leaving an angle unprotected. He had been doing it since they crossed the border, the protective instinct becoming more pronounced with every passing hour.

He was struggling, though. Morrivan's magic wasn't just affecting him; it was **stripping** him, peeling away layers of whatever he used to hide who—or what—he was. His breathing had grown labored, shallow enough that Nilsa noticed even with the forest's hush around them. Sweat dampened the collar of his tunic despite the cold. His eyes flicked continually to shadows only he seemed to sense, and when her hand brushed his, she felt the tremor in his fingers.

"Erabor," she murmured softly, leaning closer from her saddle, "tell me how bad it is."

He didn't look up right away. His eyes were locked on a patch of forest where the trees bent inward, their trunks unnaturally smooth, their branches curling like skeletal fingers. When he finally answered, his voice was too even.

"I'm fine."

She gave him a look that would have cut through armor, much less that stubborn veil he wore around himself. "You're lying."

His jaw tightened, a muscle feathering beneath his skin. "I can hold until we find shelter."

"That wasn't what I asked."

"I know," he whispered.

The guide raised a hand then—a gesture Nilsa had learned quickly. **Stop. Silence. Listen.**

The three of them halted. The horses shifted uneasily. Starwind tossed her head, snorting, and the pack horses pressed closer to Flint's sturdy presence.

Nilsa strained her ears.

At first she heard nothing.

Then the forest exhaled.

A slow, rolling shiver traveled through the pines. The silver needles chimed faintly, each note soft as a sigh. The ground felt as if it dipped or shifted beneath them—not physically, but perceptually, as though the forest was adjusting its lens and the travelers were being refocused inside it.

Erabor inhaled sharply. "It's watching us."

Nilsa frowned. "The forest?"

"Yes. And… something else."

Before she could ask what he meant, the guide stepped aside with a graceful motion and pointed to the trees ahead where the canopy grew thick enough to swallow the sky.

And then Nilsa saw it—

A soft glow spreading across the forest floor like moonlight poured from a bowl.

The clearing revealed itself gradually, like a shy creature revealing its face. The trees didn't part all at once—they shifted with slow, swaying motion, pulling their branches aside in overlapping waves until the sky appeared as a massive dome overhead. The air widened around them, the pine needles drifting more sparsely, the ground leveling into a broad circular expanse of moss that glowed faintly blue-green beneath the descending twilight.

Nilsa's breath caught as the clearing finally opened fully.

It looked like the inside of a cathedral carved from living wood and moonlight.

The silver pines formed an arching canopy overhead, their branches weaving into lattice patterns that glimmered with threads of natural light. Faint runic patterns glowed along the trunks—some vertical, some spiraling, some crossing like intersecting constellations. The breeze stirred them into soft shimmers, and the resulting light patterns danced across the mossed earth in fluid shapes that seemed to respond to breath and movement.

But it wasn't the canopy that froze her heart.

It was the sight at the clearing's center.

A perfect ring of twelve ward stones—each standing taller than a grown man, carved from obsidian dark-stone threaded with veins of silver that pulsed like slow-moving rivers of starlight. They hummed faintly, as though murmuring to one another. They were ancient—weathered by centuries, perhaps millennia—and yet the energy radiating from them filled the clearing with warmth, tension, and a presence that felt awake.

Within the ring sat a sunken shrine, its stones half-swallowed by roots and vines of silver fire-plant. The vines pulsed softly like veins beneath skin, as though alive. The center of the shrine emitted a faint heat, subtle and rhythmic, like a heartbeat buried beneath stone.

Nilsa felt it the moment her eyes touched it.

Recognition.
Bone-deep.
Terrifying.
Beautiful.
Wrong.

Not déjà vu—something older.

Erabor's fingers brushed her elbow. She hadn't meant to take a step forward, but she had. The shrine had drawn her like a tether.

He steadied her gently, but she felt the tremor beneath his grip. His skin was fever-warm.

She whispered, "Do you feel it?"

His jaw clenched. "I feel everything."

The Morrivan guide lifted both hands—

Stay. Don't enter the circle. Danger.

Nilsa obeyed.

The forest inhaled again.

Shadows deepened.

And then—

They appeared.

Tall figures slipped from between the silver trunks like phantoms given mass. Their cloaks were deep midnight blue, almost black, embroidered with subtle sigils that caught faint light in starlike threads. They glided in perfect unity across the moss, moving without a single sound—neither footstep nor breath nor rustle of fabric. Their faces were concealed behind elongated, expressionless silver masks that caught the reflection of the ward stones' glow.

Morrivan Wardens.

Nilsa felt her heart hammer. Not fear—not exactly—but respect mixed with unease. They radiated a presence so commanding that the moss seemed to retreat beneath their feet.

Erabor stepped subtly in front of her, shoulder brushing her knee where she sat on Starwind—protective, instinctive, a shadow ready to shield a burning star. The guide stepped aside as if yielding to a higher authority.

The lead warden reached the edge of the stone circle and lifted her staff. The mora-crystal at its tip lit with a swirl of stormlight.

"We felt the tremor," she said, voice layered with two tonalities—one mortal, one otherworldly. "The border stirred."

Nilsa drew a steadying breath. "Something followed us from the woods."

"That is not what disturbed the stones," the warden said, turning her masked face directly toward Nilsa. "It was you."

Erabor tensed sharply.

Nilsa's pulse stumbled. "What—?"

Before she could finish, a harsh, low tremor rippled through the earth.

Erabor's head snapped toward the tree line. "It's here."

The ward stones ignited with blinding white-silver light.

All twelve burst upward like columns of pure magic, shooting through the canopy with tearing force that set the branches shaking violently. The air thickened, vibrating as though struck by a massive bell.

The creature lurched from the shadows in the next breath.

It staggered into the clearing, its form flickering between mass and nothingness. Its limbs stretched in impossible angles, bent backward, forward, sideways like broken marionette joints. Its skin—if it could be called that—shifted like smoke rippling over bone. When it opened its mouth to hiss, the sound came not from lungs but from the shadows clinging to its ribs.

Nilsa choked on a gasp. Erabor's hand found her ankle and squeezed—hard—grounding her.

The creature lunged.

And the ward stones *screamed*.

Light snapped outward in a deafening wave. The force struck the creature with explosive violence. Its body convulsed, shadows peeling away in strips that dissolved into the air. The ground shook beneath their feet, tremors echoing through Nilsa's bones. Starwind reared back, Flint bellowed, and the pack horses kicked wildly, panic flooding their movements.

Erabor threw his arms around Starwind's reins, wrestling her back under control with a strength that defied the trembling in his body.

The light surged again—brighter, harsher—and the creature shrieked with a sound that split Nilsa's skull. It clawed futilely at the wardline barrier, its fingers leaving streaks of darkness across the glowing surface.

The ward stones pulsed one final time—

An explosion of silver consumed the creature.

When the smoke cleared, nothing remained but fading wisps of shadow, dissolving like dying embers into the twilight.

Silence fell.

Not gentle silence.
Heavy.

Tense.
Observing.

Erabor sagged slightly, catching himself on Starwind's saddle. Nilsa leaned down instantly.

"Erabor—"

"I'm fine," he rasped, but his eyes betrayed him.

One of the wardens stepped forward. "The creature was not the greatest disturbance tonight."

Her mask tilted toward Nilsa again. "You were."

Nilsa's chest tightened. "I—don't understand."

"You will," said a new voice—a voice that seemed to reverberate through bone and shadow.

The moss behind the shrine stirred.

And the Oracle emerged.

She glided into the clearing with a motion so smooth it defied natural law. Her veils—black, layered, weightless—fluttered behind her like ink suspended in water. Her hair, silver-white, moved with a breeze that did not reach anyone else. Her skin held a faint glow, as though moonlight lived beneath it. And her eyes—

Eyes like polished amethyst aflame with deep violet light.

The wardens bowed.

The Morrivan guide pressed his hand to his chest.

Nilsa's breath caught.

The Oracle approached her like someone approaching an altar—each step precise, weighted, reverent.

When she stopped before Nilsa, the clearing seemed to hold its breath.

Slowly, the Oracle lifted her hand. She didn't touch Nilsa, but swept her fingers in a circular motion around her face. Faint silver light rose from Nilsa's skin like mist drawn upward by some unseen force.

Nilsa gasped sharply as the air thickened.

The Oracle inhaled as though she had expected something extraordinary—yet the look in her eyes suggested even she was shaken.

"It is true," she whispered. "The blood that vanished returns."

Nilsa shivered. "What blood?"

"The blood of the erased kingdom," the Oracle murmured. "Of the star that was written out of the sky."

Nilsa felt her heart stop. Erabor's grip tightened on her arm—not restraining, but bracing.

The Oracle turned her luminous eyes toward him.

"You," she whispered, her voice trembling with layered meanings, "walk in two shadows."

Erabor froze as if struck.

Nilsa stepped between them. "Leave him alone."

The Oracle blinked, and something like respect softened her expression.

"You defend him," she murmured. "He is fated to you, then. Dangerous. But necessary."

Nilsa swallowed hard. "What does that mean?"

"Come to the shrine," the Oracle said softly. "Its truth calls for you both."

She extended her hand toward the sunken stone circle, and the vines parted, peeling away from the stone like living tendrils obeying a forgotten command.

The ward stones glowed steadily.

The forest trembled.

Erabor reached for Nilsa's hand, fingers sliding between hers with a trembling warmth that steadied them both.

Together, they stepped toward the shrine—

—and Morrivan whispered her name like a prophecy awakening.

The air thickened as Nilsa and Erabor stepped deeper into the clearing, the moss soft beneath their boots and glowing faintly with each footfall as though responding to their weight. The twelve ward stones surrounding the sunken shrine vibrated with a low hum—no longer the violent pulse that destroyed the creature at the border, but a quieter resonance that settled beneath Nilsa's skin like a second heartbeat, one that didn't belong to her. Starwind pawed at the ground behind her, ears pinned back, breath coming in quick bursts that fogged the air. Even the horses sensed the tension, the ancient magic threading through the ground.

The Morrivan wardens—six of them—shifted subtly as Nilsa moved forward, their long silver masks reflecting the faint shimmering light from the ward stones. They formed a symmetrical half circle, staffs planted lightly on the ground, crystals flickering with inner storms. Their cloaks barely stirred in the breeze, and yet Nilsa swore she felt their attention like the weight of a dozen unseen hands pressing lightly against her shoulders.

One warden stepped forward, her cloak brushing the moss in whispering motions that sent ripples of faint glowing dust into the air. Her mask caught the dim light, creating the illusion of shifting expressions though it held none. She raised her staff and touched its crystal tip to the ground. Silver lines spiraled outward like cracks in glass—no, runes, forming and fading almost too quickly to decipher.

"Princess of Orlanthia," the warden said, her voice layered with ethereal tonality. "You stand upon sacred ground. The twelve see you."

Nilsa's chest tightened.

Erabor stepped subtly in front of her—not fully blocking her, but angled just enough to show the wardens that she was not alone. His stance was protective, yes, but also strained. Morrivan's magic gripped him like invisible hands pressing at the edges of his ribs. Nilsa watched a tremor run through his fingers before he steadied them.

The warden's masked face shifted to him. "And you… your shadow moves strangely."

Erabor didn't move a muscle. "Strange isn't always dangerous."

"In Morrivan, it is."

The guide stepped forward, raising both palms in a gesture Nilsa recognized now as respectful intercession. The wardens stilled. The guide lowered his hands, then pointed to Nilsa and swept his arm toward the shrine—**She must approach. It calls to her.**

Nilsa felt it again then—a pull, not physical but magnetic, drawing her toward the center of the ward stone ring. The shrine pulsed like a heart of buried fire. The vines that encased it lifted ever so slightly, as though awakened by the Oracle's presence.

And the Oracle…
She glided forward now, her veil trailing behind her like flowing ink spilled across the moss. Her violet eyes glowed with soft luminescence as she lifted a hand and traced a sigil in the air that shimmered faintly, then dissolved like dust in sunlight.

"Do not fear, Princess," the Oracle said. "That which stirs in you is older than fear."

Nilsa swallowed thickly. "I don't understand any of this."

"You will," the Oracle said gently. "Truth reveals itself in the order it must—never sooner, never later. Now come."

The wardens parted in silent unison, making a path toward the shrine. Nilsa stepped forward, her hand tightening around Erabor's. He exhaled sharply at the contact—whether in pain or relief she couldn't tell—but he didn't loosen his grip.

As they approached the ward stones, the ground trembled faintly beneath their boots. A swirling mist curled around the base of the stones, rising and responding as Nilsa passed. The runes on the stones brightened, glowing with the brilliance of softly lit moons.

The Oracle's voice followed her as she entered the ring. "You feel the heartbeat," she murmured.

"I do," Nilsa admitted, breath unsteady. "It's alive."

"It remembers," the Oracle corrected.

Erabor remained close, though each step weighed heavily on him. His breaths grew shallow, and the muscles in his neck tightened with the effort of controlling the pain or pressure he was feeling. Nilsa squeezed his hand again.

"Are you sure you can do this?" she whispered.

"No," he whispered back. "But I'm not leaving you."

The wardens observed them, unmoving and silent. The air around the shrine thickened again. Nilsa inhaled—and the scent hit her like a storm. Warmth. Ages. Magic. Something like burning cedar mixed with cold moonlight and sweet crushed petals of some night-blooming flower.

Then—

The shadows moved.

The pines shifted.

Something—someone—watched.

Nilsa froze.

"Erabor... did you feel that?"

His fingers tightened around hers. "Yes."

"Behind us?"

"No."

She turned her head, slowly.

The forest behind the ward stones was darker than it had been. The silver needles overhead dimmed slightly, catching less light.

The shadows beneath the pines stretched longer, reaching toward the circle.

Nilsa saw a flicker of movement.

A silhouette standing perfectly still between two trees.

A human shape—tall, slender, motionless.

Her breath stuttered. "Erabor."

"I see it."

The wardens turned simultaneously, their crystals flaring with inner stormlight.

The silhouette stepped forward—

—and vanished.

Nilsa's heart jumped. "What—?"

"Not now," Erabor muttered, voice low and urgent. "Focus on the shrine. That thing won't challenge Morrivan's circle."

Nilsa tried to steady her racing heart.

The Oracle extended her hand again, this time sweeping a gesture toward the sunken shrine. The vines shifted, pulling back like living tendrils responding to her command.

"Enter, Nilsa," the Oracle whispered. "Let the shrine see you."

Nilsa stepped forward.

But before her foot touched the first stone, Erabor jerked suddenly, hand flying to his chest as if struck. His knees buckled. Nilsa caught him with both arms, her heart lurching.

"Erabor!"

His breath came in ragged bursts. The shadows at his feet twisted into strange shapes, stretching outward like elongated wings and then shrinking violently, as though fighting an unseen force. His pupils dilated, and for a moment, something flickered behind his eyes—something dark, ancient, almost luminous.

Nilsa felt his grip falter.

"It's pressing on me," he gasped. "The magic—Morrivan—it's trying to strip me open."

She turned desperately toward the Oracle. "Help him!"

The Oracle stepped forward, her expression grave but composed. "He is holding two truths at once," she murmured. "Two shadows. One belongs to Morrivan's recognition. One… does not."

"What does that mean?" Nilsa demanded.

"That he is more than he appears," the Oracle said softly.

Nilsa shoved back tears. "Then help him!"

The Oracle's gaze softened. "I will. But first, the shrine must receive you."

Nilsa stared at her, stunned. "We can't—he's hurting—"

"Nilsa," Erabor whispered hoarsely, gripping her arm. "Go. Please. I can hold a little longer."

"No—"

"Yes." He forced a small, strained smile. "This kingdom wants you, not me. Don't make it angry."

The ward stones pulsed again—once, twice, three times—each vibration running through Nilsa's bones and urging her forward like a magnetic pull.

Nilsa lowered Erabor carefully to his knees, steadying him against her thigh for a moment.

"I am coming back," she whispered fiercely.

"I know," he rasped.

With trembling breath, Nilsa stepped toward the shrine.

The vines parted entirely now, revealing the stone circle's inner chamber—glowing from within as though lit by fire that did not burn.

Nilsa took her first step into the shrine.

The ground breathed beneath her.

The stones awakened.

And every shadow in Morrivan leaned closer.

The moment Nilsa stepped into the shrine's inner ring, the air changed.

Not gradually, not gently—
immediately.

The temperature dropped first. A crisp bite slid across her skin, sharp and metallic, like the edge of a blade that had been dipped in winter meltwater. Her breath left her in a soft mist, dissipating faster than natural. The hairs on her arms rose despite her cloak. The ground beneath her boots—smooth, circular stone veined with faintly glowing sigils—hummed like a dormant creature suddenly stirred awake.

She took another step.

The hum deepened into something low and resonant, vibrating in her bones. The shrine lit from within as if fired by an inner glow. Runes carved into the stone—some broken, some half-erased by age—flared to life with pale silver light, then dimmed, then flared again, as though trying to find the right rhythm in response to her presence.

Nilsa felt her pulse synchronize with it.

Her heart beat.
The shrine answered.

Her breath caught sharply. "Erabor…"

She didn't expect an answer and didn't get one.

He was kneeling at the edge of the shrine, one hand braced against the ground, body trembling with effort. His shadow was wrong—almost pulsating, stretching and shrinking with each tremor in the ground. Sweat beaded on his brow despite the chill. Nilsa had seen him injured, exhausted, and poisoned before—but never like this.

This wasn't physical strain.
This was identity strain.

Morrivan was trying to tear pieces of truth out of him.

Nilsa took a step toward him—

But the shrine's light snapped sharply, almost scolding, and a thin band of shimmering air rose between her and Erabor like an invisible wall.

Nilsa gasped and pulled back, her hand tingling where the barrier had repelled her. "No—let me go to him!"

The Oracle stepped closer, her veils whispering across the moss. "Not until the shrine sees you."

Nilsa's chest tightened until she thought it might shatter. "He's in pain!"

"He is," the Oracle agreed softly, "and he will bear it. His truth resists Morrivan. That is why the magic crushes him. But the shrine calls for you." Her violet gaze flicked to the glowing circle under Nilsa's feet. "Answer it, and he will stabilize."

Erabor groaned softly, clutching at his ribs. Nilsa met his eyes—flickering, wild, frightened.

He rasped, "Nilsa—do it. Please."

Her throat tightened. Fear and fury warred inside her chest, but she nodded once, then turned fully to face the shrine's center.

The air thickened with expectation.

Nilsa stepped closer.

THE HEART OF THE SHRINE

The center of the shrine was a shallow depression—circular, smooth, veined with sigils so worn they resembled water stains until the light flickered beneath them. Runes spiraled outward from the center point, forming concentric loops that intersected like constellations carved into stone.

As Nilsa approached, the inner loop began to glow faintly.

Soft silver radiance seeped from the cracks—thin at first, then growing until the entire chamber breathed in slow pulses of light.

The sound—the hum—deepened again.

A low, melodic vibration…

Like a voice singing from beneath the stone.

Nilsa felt the resonance in her chest. Her heartbeat matched it. Her breaths aligned with it.

The light intensified.

The runes brightened.

And every hair on her body lifted as something unseen brushed against her mind like cool fingers.

Nilsa.

Her breath stopped.

That whisper wasn't imagined.

It wasn't the forest.

It wasn't the Oracle.

It was the shrine itself.

Nilsa swallowed, voice trembling. "You… know me."

A pulse of light answered.

Nilsa stepped into the exact center.

The world **ignited.**

THE SHATTERING VISION

A burst of silver-white brilliance surged upward—so bright the wardens shielded their masked faces. The Oracle's veils whipped in a sudden wind. Erabor cried out, clutching his chest as if something inside him snapped taut.

Nilsa's world went blank—

Then filled with images not her own.

Not fully formed visions.

Fragments.
Memories.
Echoes.

A throne—carved from obsidian and silver, encircled by twelve tall pillars and a thirteenth that had been broken, shattered at its base.

A crown—shaped like a star with twelve points…and one missing.

A child—her hair long and dark, her eyes luminous with silver flame—standing in the center of a glowing circle.

A voice—echoing like thunder wrapped in silk—speaking a single word:

"Eidonrael."

Nilsa's breath seized.

The vision shattered.

She gasped violently as her knees gave out, collapsing to the stone floor. The shrine's glow dimmed sharply, but the humming continued, vibrating beneath her hands.

"Nilsa!" Erabor tried to reach her but the barrier flared again, throwing him back with a spark of silver energy that sent shockwaves through his body. He choked on a breath, doubling over.

The Oracle stepped forward sharply. "Enough!" she commanded the shrine.

Shockingly—it obeyed.

The barrier thinned, allowed Erabor to crawl forward until he reached the edge of the circle. He couldn't stand, but he extended his arm toward her, shaking violently.

Nilsa crawled into his embrace, trembling as much as he was. His fingers found her cheek, her hair, her shoulders, as though grounding himself by ensuring she was real.

"What did you see?" he whispered, voice trembling.

Nilsa swallowed hard. "A kingdom I've never seen… but that knew me."

Erabor's breath hitched.

And then the ground trembled again.

Not softly.
Not subtly.

Deeply.

A rumble rolled beneath the shrine as though something massive shifted below them. The ward stones flickered. The wardens stiffened. The forest went completely still.

Nilsa's blood went cold. "Erabor… something's happening."

He tried to rise but failed, gripping her arm. "Something's waking up."

The Oracle's voice whispered through the growing quake. "It has sensed her."

"What has?" Nilsa cried.

The Oracle pointed at the ground beneath the shrine.

Beneath the runes.

Beneath the stone.

"What the world tried to bury."

Before Nilsa could speak, a shockwave blasted upward through the shrine.

Stone cracked.

Light surged.

And something ancient stirred beneath Morrivan.

THE FIRST CRACK

The stone beneath Nilsa's palms vibrated more violently, shifting with a grinding sound like mountains scraping against one another. Thin fissures skittered outward from the center of the shrine—hairline cracks glowing with pale silver fire, crawling across the carved runes like veins of lightning beneath ice.

Nilsa flinched back as one split open beneath her knee. A ribbon of cold light spilled upward, fluttering like smoke caught in a reversed wind.

Erabor dragged himself toward her—not fully upright, but bracing on one knee, face twisted in pain. "Nilsa, move—"

The ground shook again—

BOOM.

A deep, resonant thud echoed from beneath the shrine. Wind erupted upward, whipping Nilsa's hair around her face, stirring her cloak like a storm's breath. Erabor shielded her with one arm, pulling her against him as debris rattled across the stones.

The ward stones answered immediately.

A surge of power ignited across all twelve, lighting the clearing in stark white brilliance. Runes spiraled upward, swirling like chains of silver flame racing through the air. The wardens gripped their staffs, bracing, the mora crystals flaring violently.

"Oracle!" one warden cried, voice cracking. "Contain it—!"

"I cannot," the Oracle answered, her voice resonating with a dozen tones at once—ancient, human, spirit, storm. "She has awakened what sleeps beneath."

Nilsa trembled. "What *is* beneath—?"

"Silence," the Oracle hissed, not unkindly, but in fear. "Listen."

Nilsa held her breath.

From beneath the shrine—

Through stone
Through runes
Through centuries of buried power—

a sound rose.

Faint at first.
Then stronger.
Then undeniable.

A heartbeat.

Not a literal pulse of flesh and blood.

No.

Something older.
Something deeper.
Something like the echo of a kingdom's dying gasp preserved beneath stone.

THUMM.
THUMM.
THUMM.

Each vibration rattled the earth. Each beat seemed to push the air in concentric waves, bending the light, blurring the trees. The pine branches above trembled violently, shedding silver needles that spiraled downward in a shower of shimmering rain.

Nilsa covered her ears as the humming grew louder, deeper—until it seemed to vibrate inside her ribs.

Erabor roared through clenched teeth, gripping the ground to keep from collapsing. His shadow writhed violently behind him—stretching, contracting, crawling along the stone like something alive and panicked.

One warden stumbled back and knelt, overwhelmed by the rising energy.

The Oracle raised her hands to the sky.

"BE STILL!" she commanded.

The ground stilled—but the heartbeat did not.

Nilsa felt it match her own rhythm.
Felt her breath link to it.
Felt her bones echo it.

She shuddered. "It's connected to me…"

The Oracle's eyes glowed brighter than the ward stones. "Of course it is."

THE SHATTERING OF STONE

The center of the shrine cracked open suddenly.

Not a small crack.
Not a thin fissure.

A **rupture**.

A geyser of white-silver energy burst upward like a spear through the air. Nilsa screamed and threw her arms over her head. Erabor shielded her again—this time with his entire body, wrapping his arms around her shoulders as debris rained down.

The Oracle staggered back. The wardens stumbled. The forest bowed.

When the blast faded, Nilsa blinked through the swirling dust and light.

The shrine's heart was now a jagged pit, glowing as though molten starlight filled it.

And above it—rising like a mirage—

was an image.

Not physical.
Not ghostly.
Something between memory and magic.

A circular emblem floated in the air, drawn in spiraling threads of silver fire:

Twelve stars…
encircling a thirteenth.
The missing one.
The erased one.

Nilsa gasped sharply.

The Oracle exhaled as if punched. "The sigil of Eidonrael."

The name struck Nilsa like a blow. Her breath fled her lungs.

"Eidonrael," she whispered.

Erabor froze, fingers tightening painfully on her arm. His eyes widened—not in surprise, but recognition.

Nilsa's heart hammered. "I—I don't know why I know that word. I've never heard it before."

"That," the Oracle said, stepping toward her with trembling reverence, "is because your kingdom, child, was not merely forgotten."

She raised a hand toward the spiraling sigil.

"It was erased."

Nilsa swallowed, trembling. "By who?"

The Oracle lowered her gaze. For the first time, she looked truly ancient—not ethereal or powerful, but tired. Haunted.

"We do not speak that name," she whispered. "Not in this forest. Not in any living kingdom."

Nilsa's chest constricted painfully. "Why?"

"Because the one who destroyed Eidonrael is not dead."

A shiver slithered down Nilsa's spine.

Erabor's breath stuttered. "Oracle—"

The Oracle cut him off with a single raised hand. "You, shadow-born, will keep your secrets a moment longer. The princess requires truth before you unravel."

Erabor clenched his jaw, shadow writhing faintly behind him. Nilsa felt him tense, his heart racing.

"Princess," the Oracle said, voice softening, "you felt the shrine respond to you. You felt the ward stones flare. You awakened the heartbeat beneath this circle."

Nilsa nodded shakily.

The Oracle stepped closer until she stood directly in front of Nilsa and placed her hand—not on Nilsa's skin, but hovering just above her chest, over her heart.

"What beats beneath Morrivan," she whispered, "is the last remnant of Eidonrael's power. It sleeps in the roots of this forest. It sleeps because someone hid it here—buried it under an oath older than the Sundering."

Nilsa's breath shook. "Why would someone hide it?"

"To protect it," the Oracle said. "To buy the world time."

"Time for what?"

The Oracle's gaze flicked to the forest, to the shadows stretching between the trees, to the place the creature had appeared earlier.

"For the hunt to end," she whispered.

Nilsa's heart hammered faster. "What hunt?"

"The hunt," the Oracle said slowly, "for the last of the erased bloodline."

Nilsa's blood ran cold.

Erabor stepped forward, his pain forgotten, his voice a low growl. "Enough riddles. Stop speaking around her. Tell her what she is."

The Oracle turned to him, violet eyes burning. "You would command a seer of Morrivan?"

"I would protect her from half-truths," Erabor snapped.

The Oracle studied him for a long, tense moment.

And then—

Surprisingly—

She nodded.

Nilsa blinked. "What?"

The Oracle exhaled slowly, her veils trembling as though stirred by an invisible wind.

"Very well," she said softly. "You deserve truth—not prophecy fragments."

She lifted her hand, and the floating sigil expanded—threads of silver fire stretching outward until the emblem hovered above them like a constellation. Nilsa felt warmth sweep over her skin, a presence like unseen hands brushing across her temples.

The Oracle spoke:

"Nilsa Nightstalker, princess of Orlanthia…
you are the last living heir
of the Thirteenth Kingdom."

Nilsa stared, dizzy. "But the thirteenth kingdom—"

"Was burned," the Oracle finished. "Every record destroyed. Every name erased. Every heir hunted."

Her voice darkened.

"But one survived."

Nilsa's pulse stuttered.

"No," she whispered. "No, that can't be— Eidonrael isn't—"

"Orlanthia is where the survivor was hidden," the Oracle said. "Your ancestors did not die of a curse at all."

Nilsa felt the world tilt.

Beside her, Erabor closed his eyes in a long, pained exhale—as though something heavy he'd carried in silence finally made sense.

Nilsa staggered back until she felt Erabor's arm catch her. She grabbed at him, grounding herself in the warmth of his presence.

"I don't understand," she whispered. "I'm Orlanthian. My line—my bloodline—has lived there for centuries."

"No," the Oracle said softly. "They hid there for centuries."

Nilsa's breath trembled.

Erabor whispered into her ear, voice barely audible. "Nilsa…"

His shadow stretched again behind him.

The Oracle's gaze narrowed. "And as for you…"

Erabor stiffened.

The Oracle stepped closer, her violet eyes piercing.

"Shadow-born. Two truths in one body. A creature who should not walk the mortal world. I had thought your kind extinct."

Nilsa jerked her head toward Erabor. "What—?"

The Oracle answered before he could.

"You, Erabor…
are dark fae."

The clearing went dead silent.

Nilsa's breath fled in a violent rush.

Erabor's hand tightened around hers—

—and trembled.

Silence rippled across the clearing like a living thing, expanding outward in slow, suffocating waves. Even the forest stilled. The silver needles on the pines hung motionless, frozen mid-fall. The ward stones pulsed with faint white light, reacting to the tension in the air, each beat syncing eerily with Nilsa's pounding heart.

Nilsa stared at the Oracle, then at Erabor, her thoughts fighting to align with the words she had just heard. The echo of the Oracle's final sentence—*You are dark fae*—hung in her skull like a bell still vibrating after a violent strike.

"No," Nilsa whispered, instinctive, reflexive. "No, he isn't. He can't be." She felt Erabor's hand tighten around hers, painfully tight, as if anchoring himself against the weight of her denial—or bracing for her to pull away. She didn't know which. Her breath hitched. "He's human. He bleeds. He eats. He sleeps. He…" Her voice cracked as the truth she clung to frayed. "He saved me."

Erabor didn't speak.
His silence wasn't calm.
It thrummed with something fierce and wounded, a tension drawn across his shoulders, a tremor in his jaw, a strain around his eyes. His shadow at his feet writhed—not wildly, not aggressively, but like a creature in pain, folding in on itself,

collapsing and stretching as though fighting against invisible chains.

The Oracle watched him with an expression strange in its complexity—part awe, part fear, part sorrow. "Dark fae do bleed. They do eat. They do sleep. They mimic to survive. But their shadows never lie."

Nilsa's gaze dropped despite herself.

Erabor's shadow stretched across the shrine stones in a shape that was undeniably not human—broad where it should be narrow, with edges that curled and flickered like smoke caught in a wind that didn't exist. For a heartbeat—just one—it formed the faint suggestion of wings.

Nilsa sucked in a breath and staggered back.

Erabor's hand slipped from hers as she moved, his fingers trailing against her wrist before falling to his side. His face twisted—not in anger, not in guilt, but in something rawer, quieter, infinitely worse. A kind of helplessness she had never seen in him.

"Nilsa…" he breathed, her name barely formed, barely audible.

Her chest constricted. Not from fear—no, not fear—but from a twisting ache she didn't understand. Her entire world had shifted in a single breath.

She reached for him—instinctively, without thinking—but the Oracle stepped between them with surprising swiftness.

"No," she whispered. "Not yet."

Nilsa glared at her, fury catching in her throat. "Move."

The Oracle shook her head once, slow and mournful. "You cannot touch him while his shadow is unstable. The magic pressing on him will tear both of you apart."

Nilsa's breath faltered. "What does that even mean?"

Erabor answered before the Oracle could.

His voice was low, strained, threaded with anguish he was barely containing. "It means Morrivan is trying to drag the truth out of me. By force."

Nilsa froze.

He forced himself upright—not fully standing, but braced on one knee, determined despite the tremor running through his entire body. His eyes met hers, dark and pained and unbearably vulnerable. "I didn't want you to learn like this."

The Oracle swept her veils back with a single gesture, revealing her full face—sharp, ageless, illuminated by the reflection of the glowing ward stones. "Whether you wished it or not, the truth was always coming. Morrivan is a place of mirrors. No shadow can hide here. No secret can sleep."

Erabor's jaw tightened. His shadow flickered violently.

Nilsa took a shaking breath. "I don't understand. If he's… if he's—" The word stuck in her throat. Dark fae. A creature whispered about in Orlanthian nursery stories with fear and reverence. The beings who had helped break kingdoms during the Sundering. The beings who had vanished before Nilsa was born—slaughtered, hunted, wiped out.

Her voice broke. "If he's one of them, why has he never hurt me?"

The Oracle gave a soft, sad exhale. "Because not all dark fae are monsters."

Erabor flinched as though struck.

"And not all humans," the Oracle continued, "are innocent."

Nilsa's pulse hammered. "Tell me what this has to do with me being—" She couldn't say it. Couldn't make the words leave her tongue.

"Heir of Eidonrael?" the Oracle finished for her gently.

Nilsa's head spun.

Her kingdom—Orlanthia—was not her birthright. Her bloodline was older. Hidden. Hunted. Her ancestors had not broken under a curse—they had fled from something that destroyed their true home. And someone had buried Eidonrael's last heartbeat under Morrivan.

She felt her vision blur. She swayed.

Erabor moved instinctively.

Not with strength.
Not with grace.
With pure, desperate need.

He stumbled forward, reaching for her even as the Oracle snapped, "Do not touch her—your shadow—"

But he ignored her.
He had always ignored danger when it came to Nilsa.

His hand hovered inches from her cheek—shaking, yearning, afraid to make contact. His voice cracked. "I don't care what they call me. I don't care what I am. Nilsa, look at me. Please."

She looked. The moment their eyes met—everything else disappeared.

He didn't look like a monster.
He didn't look like a creature out of bedtime warnings.

He looked like Erabor.

The boy who had bowed in the shadows of her brother's funeral.
The boy who had offered to go with her without hesitation.
The boy who had fought beside her in the woods, who had protected her at the ruins, who had held her as she cried, who had bled for her without second thought.

Her chest ached.

The Oracle stepped closer. "Princess, listen to me carefully. Dark fae have two forms: the physical, and the shadow. When their identity is threatened, their shadow tries to reveal the truth their body hides. Morrivan is forcing his shadow to speak."

Nilsa's breath stopped. "Is he in danger?"

"Yes."

Nilsa's stomach dropped.

The Oracle's voice softened. "He has held his truth suppressed for too long. Morrivan's magic is tearing at the seam. If he does not stabilize soon… his shadow will split from him."

Nilsa's voice trembled. "What happens if it splits?"

The Oracle hesitated.

Erabor answered instead.

"I die."

Nilsa's heart shattered. "No—no, you won't—"

He smiled. A weak, pained smile, but a smile all the same. "I promised you I'd come with you. I didn't promise it would be easy."

Her eyes burned. Tears threatened.

The Oracle raised a hand. "There is a way."

Nilsa snapped toward her. "Tell me."

Erabor groaned softly as the ground trembled again. His shadow flared outward abruptly—stretching into a wide, wing-shaped silhouette before collapsing back into a single distorted form. Nilsa gasped and moved toward him, but the Oracle's arm blocked her again.

"Harm her, and the prophecy fractures," the Oracle warned him.

"I won't touch her," he rasped. "I just—" He looked at Nilsa, pain etched into every line of his face. "I need to know she's safe."

Nilsa felt her throat close. "I'm not leaving you."

"Princess," the Oracle said softly, "if his shadow breaks free, it will attack the nearest source of power to anchor itself. That source is you."

Nilsa froze.
Her heart stuttered.
Her breath caught in her chest.

Erabor's shadow—wild, unstable, trying to survive—would latch onto her magic like a starving creature.

She forced her voice out. "What do I do?"

The Oracle lifted her staff. The crystal at its tip flared with white fire. The ward stones echoed the light, creating a circle of silver flame around the shrine.

"You step away," the Oracle said. "You distance yourself until his shadow recedes."

Nilsa's eyes widened in horror. "No. No, I can't leave him—"

"You must," the Oracle said, suddenly fierce. "If you stay too close while his truth unravels, the magic will tear him in two."

Nilsa looked at Erabor—breathing hard, hair plastered to his forehead, jaw clenched so tightly it trembled. His eyes searched hers with raw, unfiltered fear—not for himself, but for what she would do.

"Nilsa," he whispered, "please—listen to her. Go."

Her heart broke. She shook her head violently. "I'm not abandoning you."

"I know." His voice cracked. "But if you stay—I won't survive. And I won't survive if you run either. So whatever you do, do it carefully. Do it with intention." His eyes softened. "You always do."

Her tears spilled then. She didn't wipe them.

The ground trembled again.

His shadow surged—

And the Oracle's eyes widened.

"Now," she whispered, urgent. "Princess—move."

Nilsa hesitated one single breath.

Then—

She stepped back.

Erabor released a choked sound—as though her distance physically hurt him—but he didn't reach for her. He curled inward instead, bracing both hands on the stone as his shadow convulsed violently.

Nilsa's heart cracked with every step she took.

The Oracle lifted her staff. "He must stabilize with *his* will, not yours."

Nilsa stopped just beyond the ward stone circle. Her hands curled into fists at her sides. Her breath heaved. Her pulse raced. But she did not move forward.

She stayed.

For him.

The clearing filled with a violent surge of shadow—pain, identity, truth unraveling like torn silk. The Oracle's voice layered over it, chanting in a tongue older than kingdoms.

The ward stones flared.
The shrine pulsed.
Erabor's shadow screamed—silent yet deafening.

Nilsa trembled so hard her knees nearly buckled.

She whispered, voice breaking, "Come back to me."

Erabor lifted his head then—eyes locking with hers through the storm of unraveling magic. Even in pain, even in near collapse, there was fierce resolve in his gaze.

"I always will."

The ward stones blazed white—
The shrine roared—
Erabor's shadow exploded outward—

And then—

Silence.

The light receded.
The wind stilled.
The tremor faded.

Erabor collapsed forward, unconscious but breathing.

Nilsa sprinted to him before the Oracle could stop her—dropping to her knees, gathering him against her body, trembling as she held him.

His shadow lay still.

Faint.
Stable.
Quiet.

Nilsa pressed her forehead to his.

"Don't ever do that again," she whispered, voice shaking. "Please."

The Oracle stepped beside them, her veils falling softly around her face. "He will live. For now."

Nilsa looked up, desperate. "What happens next?"

The Oracle exhaled, long and tired.

"Now," she said softly, "your true journey begins. For Morrivan was only the threshold."

Nilsa swallowed. "What do you mean?"

The Oracle's violet eyes darkened.

"The one who hunts Eidonrael's last heir has already felt you awaken. And he is moving."

Nilsa's blood froze.

Erabor stirred faintly against her.

The Oracle's voice dropped to a whisper.

"You have little time left, Princess of the Erased Kingdom. The world is waking. The shadows are stirring. And the enemy you fear most…"

She glanced into the forest, where the silhouette had stood earlier—watching.

"…has already found your scent."

CHAPTER TWENTY-FIVE

The Stone That Remembers

The night in Morrivan did not fall so much as it unfolded.

By the time the wardens carried Erabor from the shrine, the sky above the silver pines had deepened into a rich, velvety indigo. Threads of faint aurora-light shimmered between the uppermost branches, clinging there like liquid starlight caught in cobwebs. The clearing that had roared with power an hour ago now hummed with a low, exhausted quiet—like a heart still beating after a sprint.

Nilsa walked beside the stretcher the wardens had fashioned, one hand never leaving Erabor's arm. Their magic-light lanterns cast soft halos around them, painting the moss in pale blue and silver, turning his skin a strange, otherworldly color. He looked almost peaceful in the glow, except for the faint line of strain between his brows.

He was breathing.

That, for the moment, was enough.

They moved through the forest in near silence. The trees watched them pass with an unsettling stillness. No rustle of nocturnal birds, no distant call of fox or hare—just the soft whisper of cloaks, the crunch of boots in moss, the almost inaudible chiming of the silver needles when an unseen breeze passed through them.

The Oracle walked ahead, barefoot, veils gliding over roots and stone without catching. Her presence parted the forest like a river stone divides water. Wherever her foot fell, the ground glowed faintly, responding to her touch with shy light.

"Where are we going?" Nilsa asked softly after a while, her voice sounding small in the enormous, breathing hush of Morrivan.

"To the inner sanctum," the Oracle replied without turning. "To the chamber where we keep what the world is not yet ready to remember."

"The Memory Stone," Nilsa guessed.

"Yes."

Nilsa's throat tightened. She looked down at Erabor's face again. His hair had dried in messy dark strands that clung to his temples. Someone—one of the wardens, perhaps—had cleaned the blood from his lip and cheek. It made him look less battered, but no less fragile.

He had almost died.

No, she corrected herself. Morrivan had almost torn him in half. Because of the truth it dragged into the light.
Because of what he was.
Because of what she was.

A faint tremor moved through her fingers. She curled them tighter around his arm to hide it.

"You should rest, Princess," murmured one of the wardens walking behind her—a woman by the pitch of her voice, though the mask veiled everything else. "Your aura is strained. Morrivan presses on those who carry too much."

Nilsa let out a short, humorless breath. "I don't have the luxury of falling apart tonight."

"No one does," the warden replied quietly. "But we sometimes must choose where we break. Better in front of those who can help you stand again."

Nilsa didn't answer. She wasn't sure she could, even if she wanted to. The idea of letting herself splinter right now—of letting her fear and grief and anger flood out—felt like handing her spine to someone else and asking them to set it back correctly.

She had never quite trusted anyone that much.

Except, perhaps, the unconscious boy on the stretcher.

The path changed gradually from wild forest floor to something more deliberate. The pines grew closer together, their trunks curving inward at the base like arches, creating a living colonnade. Moss gave way to smooth stone overlaid with thin roots, as if the forest had grown over an old structure rather than the other way around.

Ahead, between twin trees whose bark spiraled with glowing runes, a dark opening yawned.

Nilsa's heart stuttered at the sight of it—not from fear but from a prickle of recognition. The archway was carved, not natural, though time and ivy tried to pretend otherwise. Symbols ran along its inner curve, shallow and nearly worn away; when the Oracle passed beneath it, they flared briefly with light, then faded.

Beyond lay a tunnel sloping gently downward, lit by soft silver orbs suspended in the air like captive moons.

The sanctum was underground.

The air cooled sharply as they descended, the scent of pine giving way to something older: damp stone, faint minerals, a trace of incense that had seeped into the walls over centuries. The wardens' footsteps echoed now, though only faintly, as if the stone swallowed sound before it could fully form.

At last, the tunnel opened into a high, circular chamber.

Nilsa stopped.

For a moment, she could only stare.

The chamber ceiling rose far above her head in a smooth, domed curve, painted with constellations she did not recognize. Not the star-map taught to Orlanthian children, with its twelve-pointed royal compass and neat lines connecting familiar patterns. This sky was older, messier, wilder. Stars clustered in dense, spiraling shapes. Some constellations were drawn in lines of silver leaf; others in tiny fragments of crystal that caught the light and flung it outward in fractured, dancing patterns.

The walls beneath the dome were carved with reliefs—figures walking through forests of silver pines, kneeling before altars, raising hands to watch as shadows poured from their palms like water. None of the faces had eyes. Where eyes should be, the carver had left smooth blankness.

At the center of the chamber stood a raised stone dais, no taller than Nilsa's knee. It was a simple circle, unadorned, worn by touch and time. Resting atop it was the Memory Stone.

It was not what she expected.

She had imagined something large, something monumental—like the ward stones above, but older. Instead, the Memory Stone was small enough to fit into both hands comfortably. A flattened, egg-shaped piece of translucent mineral, clear as glass in some places and smoky in others, shot through with floating threads of silver. They drifted slowly inside the stone like tiny, luminous rivers, ever moving but never reaching an end.

It pulsed faintly.

Not with light.

With feeling.

The moment Nilsa's eyes landed on it, something in her chest twisted.

She approached it slowly, every step cautious and reverent. The wardens set Erabor gently down near the chamber's edge, on a thick fur laid over smooth stone. One of them knelt beside him to check his breathing, fingers hovering above his skin rather than touching—reading the heat, the rhythm, the lingering magic.

Nilsa wanted to go with him. Her feet almost turned.

Instead, she kept walking toward the Memory Stone.

The Oracle stood at the dais already, veils still, gaze fixed on Nilsa. In the soft light of the chamber, her eyes seemed even more luminous, the violet deepening into something like starlight seen through water.

"This is the oldest thing Morrivan remembers," she said quietly. "Older than the Sundering. Older than the ward stones. Older than the shrines."

Nilsa's voice came out hoarse. "Older than Orlanthia."

"Orlanthia was a child when this was already ancient," the Oracle agreed. "The Memory Stone holds one thing, and one thing only: the moment the Thirteenth Kingdom fell."

Nilsa's legs felt suddenly weak. "Why hasn't anyone shown it before?"

"Because it kills those not meant to see it," the Oracle said, utterly calm. "Mortals whose blood does not answer the stone are crushed beneath the weight of what it holds. Their minds break. Their hearts stop." She held Nilsa's gaze. "We learned this the hard way."

Nilsa swallowed against the nausea rising in her throat. "And you're sure I… won't die?"

"No," the Oracle said softly. "I am not sure."

The room seemed to tilt. "Then why—"

"Because you woke the shrine," the Oracle cut in gently. "You stirred Eidonrael's last heartbeat. If the stone rejects you, we are already lost. If it accepts you, we have a chance."

Nilsa laughed once, a hollow sound. "That's not a choice. That's a cliff."

"Yes," the Oracle said. "And sometimes, to cross a chasm, we do not build a bridge. We jump."

For a brief, dizzy moment, Nilsa wanted to refuse. She wanted to scream, to demand simpler answers, to beg for a smaller destiny. She wanted to be back in Orlanthia's stables, brushing Starwind's coat and listening to Kaelvar complain about sword instructors, not standing in a foreign sanctum about to touch a stone that might kill her.

Then she looked over her shoulder.

Erabor lay where the wardens had placed him, his hair a dark spill against the pale fur, his face almost too still. His chest rose and fell in slow, shallow breaths. Her cloak—unfastened when she had thrown herself across him at the shrine—still lay tangled beneath one of his arms, a stubborn scrap of wine-red fabric refusing to be dislodged.

He had almost died for her.
He had fought shadows for her.
He had offered to follow her before he knew what she was.

If this stone held answers that could end the curse, reveal the hunter, or give them any kind of advantage against the thing that wanted her dead, then she would take the risk.

Even if it shattered her.

She turned back to the Oracle. "What do I do?"

The Oracle gestured to the stone. "You place your hands on it. You let it read you. And then you endure."

"Endure what?"

"The final memory of a dying kingdom," the Oracle said. "We do not know what shape it will take. Only that it will not be kind."

Nilsa almost laughed again. "Kindness hasn't exactly been a theme lately."

The Oracle's lips twitched, the ghost of something like sympathy. "You are allowed to be afraid."

"I am," Nilsa said honestly. "I'm doing it anyway."

She stepped up onto the dais.

The stone seemed to brighten in response, the silver threads inside it swirling faster. As she neared, the temperature around it changed—not warmer, not colder, just different, like standing next to the border between seasons.

Nilsa stopped when her knees pressed lightly against the edge of the dais.

Her hands shook. She flexed her fingers once.

"Can he feel this?" she asked quietly, nodding toward Erabor without looking away from the stone.

The Oracle followed her gaze briefly. "If he wakes while you are inside the memory, he may feel an echo of the strain through your bond."

"We don't have a bond," Nilsa said reflexively.

The Oracle raised a pale brow. "Then why does your aura cling to his like ivy to brick?"

Nilsa flushed, grateful the chamber's light made it hard to see color. She ignored the question she didn't have an answer for and focused on the one thing she could still choose:

She placed her hands on the Memory Stone.

It was not cold.

It was not warm.

It was like touching the surface of deep, still water on a windless night—neither welcoming nor rejecting, simply there. The threads of silver inside it whirled faster at her touch, spiraling inward toward the center of the stone as if pulled.

Nilsa took one breath.

Another.

The Oracle's voice drifted to her, distant already. "Do not fight it. Let it in, or it will tear through you instead of passing through you."

"Encouraging," Nilsa muttered.

Then the stone pulsed beneath her palms.

Light surged upward, blinding, and the sanctum vanished.

Morrivan.
The Oracle.
Erabor.
The wardens.
The chamber of quiet stars.

Everything fell away.

Nilsa's breath vanished—not exhaled, not stolen, simply *gone*, snuffed out like a candle in the dark. Sound dissolved. Sight fractured. Her body became weightless. For an infinite moment, she floated in a cold, perfect void where even thought struggled to form.

Then—

Light.

Not bright.
Not blinding.
Growing.

A soft glow swelled at the edges of the darkness, blooming like dawn seen through fog. It grew warm and warm again, pushing shadows back until Nilsa felt the sensation of *falling*—not downward, but *forward*, drawn toward the light like gravity had reversed its direction.

Somewhere in the distance, a voice whispered her name, not with breath but with memory.

nil-sa…

The whisper curled around her spine, brushing against her ribs like gentle fingers. She wanted to ask whose voice it was—why it sounded familiar, ancient—but the world around her was rebuilding itself too quickly.

Fog thinned.

Shapes formed.

A skyline emerged.

Nilsa blinked—and the world snapped into focus.

She stood in a city she had never seen yet immediately recognized.

A city of silver spires and black stone, built on wide, circular terraces that rose above one another like steps to the heavens. Bridges arched between towers. Crystal lanterns floated freely through the air, trailing drifting lines of pale gold. Streets radiated outward from a vast central courtyard, each one meticulously symmetrical, forming a pattern so harmonious it could have been carved from a star map.

Eidonrael.

Nilsa didn't know how she knew the name—but she did.
Deep in her bones.
Deep in her blood.

The air smelled of winter rain and heated metal, and something faintly floral she couldn't place. People bustled through the streets—figures in flowing tunics of shimmering fabric, clasped with star-shaped brooches. Some carried books. Some wore armor. Some walked with children whose eyes glowed faintly, like their pupils held starlight.

Everyone moved urgently.
Everyone looked upward.

Nilsa followed their gaze.

And her breath caught.

Above the city, suspended in the air like an artificial sun, hung a massive ring of silver light. Twelve points radiated outward like the spokes of a celestial wheel. The space where a thirteenth point should have been was fractured—broken—charred around the edges like a wound.

Lines of power streamed from each spoke into the city below, flowing like rivers of starlight into vast anchor-pillars of polished stone.

Nilsa felt awe and grief twist together in her chest.

It was beautiful.
It was broken.

Whispers filled the air.

"—the ring is unstable—"
"—they said it held for generations—"
"—the thirteenth point is collapsing—"
"—we must evacuate—"
"—where is the high regent—"
"—has anyone found the child—"

Nilsa stepped forward, heart racing. "I don't understand," she whispered.

Her voice didn't echo.
No one reacted.

They couldn't see her.

She was walking through memory, not time.

A sudden tremor shook the ground beneath her feet. The floating lanterns flickered wildly, then burst into sparks. Windows shattered. One of the crystalline bridges cracked.

The twelve-pointed ring above the city flickered—once, twice, and then with a violent shudder that sent a ripple of distortion down its length. A piece of it broke off—an entire spoke, a beam of pure silver—falling like a shard of a shattered star.

Screams erupted around her.

Nilsa flinched as the fragment plummeted toward the city—but instead of impacting the street, it dissolved into spiraling dust, absorbed by the air as if the world was trying to swallow its own dying magic.

Another tremor.
Another shudder.
Another piece fell.

Nilsa forced herself to move, pushing through the crowd even though she knew they couldn't feel her. Buildings blurred. Voices blurred. Everything blurred until she reached the wide central courtyard—a plaza paved with obsidian tiles that glowed faintly beneath her boots.

A massive structure stood at the courtyard's center.

A palace.
No—something older.
Something sacred.

Twelve tall arches encircled it, each engraved with runes representing a kingdom Nilsa had never seen on a map. She recognized none of the symbols.

Her breath hitched when she reached the thirteenth arch.

It was broken.

Half the stone lay in fragments on the ground.
The runes carved into it had been scorched away.
And above the ruined arch, filling the void where a symbol should be, hung a spiral of black smoke that writhed like a living thing.

Nilsa shivered violently.

A feeling—primal, instinctive—rose in her chest.

Get away.

But the vision pulled her forward.

Through the broken arch.
Into the sanctum beyond.

THE THRONE ROOM OF A DYING KINGDOM

The interior of the sanctum was enormous, shaped like a circular amphitheater with steps descending toward a central dais. Statues lined the walls—figures whose faces had been defaced or erased, some with their heads shattered entirely.

Blue fire burned in braziers around the room, casting ghostly illumination.

And at the very center, on a platform carved from obsidian and star-metal, sat a throne unlike any Nilsa had ever seen. It was tall, spined, impossibly intricate, as though forged from woven branches of night itself.

A man stood before it.

Or what remained of him.

His hair was silver, twisted back in braids that had come undone. His shoulders sagged beneath a mantle of dark, star-stitched fabric. His hands trembled as they rested on the pommel of a sword forged from pure radiant metal.

His eyes glowed faintly.

Nilsa didn't know how she recognized him.

She just did.

The last king of Eidonrael.

He lifted his head at a sound behind him.

Nilsa turned.

At the chamber entrance, a young woman ran through the archway, her arms clutched tightly around a small bundle. Her long dark hair streamed behind her, whipping like a shadow caught in wind. She stumbled to a stop before the king, gasping.

"She's coming," the woman cried. "We haven't much time."

"She shouldn't be here." The king's voice was frayed, yet steady. He sounded like every ounce of strength in him was borrowed from love alone. "Bring her to me."

The woman came forward.

Nilsa's heart hammered.

She wasn't holding a bundle.

She was holding a **child**.

A girl.
Toddler-aged.
Dark hair.

Soft cheeks.
Eyes—bright, silver-blue, glowing faintly even through tears.

The child stared at the king with innocent confusion, one small fist rubbing her eye.

Nilsa's throat tightened. "Is that—?"

It couldn't be. It couldn't.

The king pressed a trembling palm to the child's cheek. "It was not supposed to be her," he whispered. "The thirteenth light was never meant to fall to a daughter."

The woman gasped. "We must hide her before they breach the sanctum."

Nilsa shook her head slowly. "No... no, that child—she can't be—"

But the stone in her hands pulsed.

Hard.

The king pressed a kiss to the child's forehead. "She must be kept safe. Far from here. Far from this place." His eyes darkened. "Far from *him*."

"Him?" Nilsa whispered.

As if in answer—

A tremor tore through the chamber.
The braziers flickered.
The statues shook.
A sound—deep, resonant, like a roar made of pure magic—echoed through the sanctum.

The woman paled. "He's inside the citadel."

The king turned his gaze on her, urgent and raw. "Take the child. Go. Now."

The woman hesitated. "But—"

"NOW!"

She obeyed.

The child—tiny, luminous—cried out as she was carried away. Her hand stretched toward the king, fingers curled in silent plea. Nilsa felt something shatter inside her—a grief not her own, but so potent it stole her breath.

The woman vanished with the child through a hidden passage behind the throne.

The king turned toward the doors of the sanctum.

They burst inward before he took his second step.

THE ENEMY ENTERS

He walked in like a king returning to a throne that had always been his.

Tall.
Dark-clad.
Shoulders straight.
Hair black as obsidian, bound in a clasp shaped like a broken star.
His eyes—

Nilsa's heart stopped.

They glowed with pale silver light.

Just like hers.
Just like Erabor's had, in the shrine.

But colder.

Colder than winter.
Colder than death.

His shadow stretched long across the tiles—too long, too thin, too alive.

Nilsa had never felt fear like this.

It wasn't terror of the unknown.

It was terror of recognition.

She *knew* this man.

Not by memory—by blood.

Cold realization crawled up her spine, settling at the base of her skull like a hand of ice.

"No," she whispered. "No, he can't be—"

The king of Eidonrael raised his sword. "You should have died centuries ago."

The man in the doorway smiled.

And the chamber collapsed around them.

The chamber collapsed not with fire, nor with stone, but with **sound**—a sound so vast and violent it felt alive.

The air ripped open with a shuddering boom that slammed through the sanctum like a hurricane trapped in stone walls. Nilsa stumbled backward, hands flying to her ears though it did nothing to soften the roar. The walls shook as if the entire palace had been torn from its foundations; dust rained from the carved arches; braziers toppled and spilled blue flame across the floor.

Yet none of it touched the two figures standing at the center of the storm.

The last king of Eidonrael.

And the man with the broken-star clasp.

They stared at one another with the quiet intensity of enemies who had known each other too long—too deeply—to ever be anything else.

The air between them pulsed.

A web of cracks spread through the floor.

And then the dark-haired man stepped forward, each movement slow and deliberate, as though savoring the inevitability of what was coming.

"You should not be here," the king said again, voice hollow with grief.

"And yet," the stranger murmured, "here I am."

His voice carried no raised volume, no anger—only a terrible certainty. It echoed like a whisper in a vast cavern, soft but impossible to ignore.

Nilsa felt the hairs on her neck rise.

The stranger took another step.

Shadows pooled beneath his boots, spreading outward like ink spilled across stone. They crept toward the shattered thirteenth arch, toward the king's feet, toward the braziers whose flames sputtered in protest.

"You destroyed the thirteenth point," the king spat.

"I freed it," the stranger corrected.

The king's grip tightened on his sword. "You ended my people."

"No," the stranger murmured, eyes glowing brighter, "your people ended themselves when they clung to a destiny that was never theirs."

Another tremor shook the room. The statues along the walls split at their bases. The domed ceiling cracked. A thin beam of daylight speared through the fissure like a blade.

Nilsa could hardly breathe.

"How… how did this happen?" she whispered, but the memory swallowed her voice whole.

The king raised his sword.

The radiant metal flared with light—white, pure, blinding, burning. It cast the stranger's shadow into monstrous proportions across the wall behind him. The glow reflected in the king's eyes, illuminating a grief so raw she felt it in her own ribs.

"You will not have her," the king said.

The stranger tilted his head. "Her?"

Something cold crawled up Nilsa's spine.

The king raised the sword higher, voice cracking. "The child."

The stranger's lips twitched—not fully a smile, not fully a snarl. "You mean the last ember of a kingdom you failed to protect?"

A low sound—half grief, half fury—escaped the king.

The stranger continued, "She is the reason Eidonrael still breathes."

"She is the reason it must die," the king snapped.

The stranger stopped.

The temperature in the sanctum dropped instantly, frost crystallizing across the black tiles. The remaining braziers sputtered and dimmed until the entire room shone with only the twin lights of their eyes—silver against silver, starfire against starfire, but different in tone.

The king's was warm.
The stranger's was ice.

"You still do not understand," the stranger said quietly. "You never did."

Nilsa could not stop trembling. She didn't know which man terrified her more—the dying king whose heart broke before her eyes, or the stranger whose calmness burned colder than death.

"What do you want?" the king demanded.

The stranger took one final step, crossing into the center of the dais.

"Balance."

The word fell like a stone into the world's deepest well.

The king lunged.

He brought the star-forged blade down in a sweeping arc.

The stranger raised a hand.

And the sword—
solid, ancient, powerful—
shattered into a thousand shards that burst outward like exploding stars.

Nilsa screamed.

The force threw the king back. Shards embedded in the walls, in the statues, in the floor—glittering fragments of a weapon meant to defend the last hope of a dying kingdom. The air rippled from the blast. Blue flames extinguished. The ground cracked open beneath the king's boots.

He fell to one knee.

The stranger approached him with slow, measured steps, shadows swirling at his feet like living chains.

"You were never meant to hold the light of Eidonrael," he said. "That power was not yours. You stole it from those whose blood could bear it."

The king lifted his head with difficulty. "I protected her."

"No," the stranger said softly, almost tenderly. "You hid her. For a time."

Nilsa's lungs constricted painfully.

Her heart hammered.

Her stomach knotted.

She knew.
She knew who they meant.

The child carried out through the hidden passage.
The baby whose eyes glowed silver-blue.
The last ember of Eidonrael.

The child Nilsa had seen—

—had her eyes.

Her mouth.

Her hair.

Nilsa choked on a breath. "That was—"

Her voice drowned again in the memory.

The stranger stooped down before the king, shadows curling around him like a cloak.

"You cannot protect her," he said gently. "She is mine to claim."

The king spat blood. "She is no one's to claim."

"She is Eidonrael," the stranger whispered, as if tasting the word. "And Eidonrael belongs to me."

He lifted a hand.

Shadows surged.

And the king convulsed, body lifting from the ground as though pulled upward by invisible strings. His back arched, head thrown back, mouth open in a scream no sound could carry. His veins glowed through his skin—silver lines spreading from his heart outward, brightening, burning—

Nilsa clapped her hands over her mouth. Tears streamed down her cheeks. This was wrong. This was so wrong.

The king's chest ruptured in a burst of silver light.

Nilsa screamed with him—her knees buckling, the floor rushing up to meet her, the Memory Stone scorching her palms as it forced her to watch, to feel, to *know*.

But the vision didn't let her collapse.

It held her upright like a puppet on strings.

The stranger lowered the dead king's limp body back onto the cracked obsidian floor.

Then he turned his head—

and looked **directly at Nilsa**.

Not the people in the memory.

Not the king.

Her.

Nilsa's heartbeat stopped.

"You will not hide from me," he whispered.

Nilsa stumbled backward—actually stumbled, despite being inside a vision.

No.
No, this wasn't possible.
He couldn't see her.
He couldn't.

He smiled.

"Oh, but I can. You touch the stone. The stone touches me." His voice was velvet wrapped around a blade. "And through it, I taste you."

Nilsa's entire body went numb.

"Your fear," he murmured. "Your blood. Your light."

He stepped forward.

"And your shadow-guard."

Nilsa froze.

"No—" she whispered.

"Ah," he purred, "so you do not yet know what he is to you."

The chamber shattered.

Not slowly.
Not gradually.

In one violent, impossible instant—
the sanctum, the king, the stranger, the throne—
all exploded outward in a roar of starfire and shadow that tore the world apart.

Nilsa felt the Memory Stone rip free from her palms.

The world went white.

And she fell—

back into herself.

Nilsa hit the stone floor hard enough to knock the breath from her lungs, but the pain barely registered. Her entire world was pain—bright, sharp, blinding, a white-hot spike driving through the center of her skull.

Her fingers spasmed, scraping against the cold dais. Her heartbeat thundered in her ears, out of rhythm, staggering like a creature that had forgotten how to walk. The Memory Stone rolled away from her hands, clattering across the platform like a dropped ember.

Nilsa curled inward, choking on a sound that wasn't quite a sob and wasn't quite a scream.

Too much.
Too fast.
Too violent.

Her head felt as though the stranger's gaze still pressed against the inside of her skull. She couldn't breathe. She couldn't think. She couldn't—

"Princess!"

Hands caught her shoulders. The world spun. Light and shadow blurred. Her vision pulsed, washing in and out of focus like a lantern guttering in a storm.

"Nilsa—Nilsa, breathe!"

The voice—
familiar, desperate, warm—

Erabor.

Her eyes snapped open.

He wasn't fully awake.
No, not fully.

His body still trembled from the aftermath of the shrine. His shadow flickered weakly beneath him, stretched in patterns that didn't quite match his movements. His pupils were blown wide, unfocused, as though he was fighting through three layers of consciousness to reach her.

But he was there.

Alive.

Holding her.

She grabbed fistfuls of his tunic and dragged herself upright, burying her face against his chest as her lungs spasmed for air. His arms closed around her instinctively, fiercely, pulling her tight against him.

Her voice broke in a strangled whisper. "He saw me."

Erabor went still.

"Who?" he demanded, the single word low and dangerous.

Nilsa shook her head frantically. "I—I don't know his name. The stranger. The one in the vision. The one who—who killed the king."

Erabor tensed so sharply she felt every muscle in his body lock.

The Oracle was suddenly there beside them, kneeling gracefully, her veils whispering on the stone. "Pull back," she commanded Erabor. "You are not stable enough to anchor her. Your shadow is still fractured."

Erabor snarled—actual, feral defiance. "Try and move me."

Nilsa clung to him harder. She didn't want him to pull back. She needed him. Needed something warm, something real, something to hold onto before the memory dragged her screaming under again.

The Oracle hesitated.

Then she exhaled, short and tight. "Very well. But if your shadow flares—if it lashes at her—"

"It won't," Erabor growled.

Nilsa wasn't sure if he was right. His shadow trembled beneath him like a dying flame, flickering and stretching toward her in small, involuntary reaches. But it didn't touch her. It never crossed the boundary of his stance.

She gripped his tunic tighter.

Her voice barely scraped out. "He spoke to me."

Erabor stiffened. "The stranger in the vision?"

Nilsa nodded, shaking.

The Oracle inhaled sharply. "Impossible."

"No," Nilsa whispered, lifting her head to meet the Oracle's gaze. "He saw me. Through the Memory Stone. He looked right at me—and he said he could taste my fear."

Erabor's arms tightened around her too quickly to hide. His pulse hammered against her cheek. "Tell me what else he said."

Nilsa swallowed, fighting the nausea swirling up her throat. Images of the sanctum flashed behind her eyes—the glowing ring above the city, the child, the king's death, and finally the stranger's smile.

"He said I was the last ember of Eidonrael," she whispered. "And that Eidonrael belongs to him."

Erabor froze.

The Oracle did not.

Instead, her veils rippled in a sudden, sharp exhale, and she rose to her feet with a fluid motion that carried pure, unfiltered fear.

"Stand," she ordered. "Both of you."

Nilsa tried—but her legs buckled beneath her. Erabor caught her again, shifting his stance to support her weight despite his own trembling. His breath came shallow, but he planted himself beside her like a barricade.

The Oracle swept her arm toward the far wall.

The runes carved into the stone flared to life, spiraling outward, forming a constellation pattern identical to the floating sigil

Nilsa had seen in the shrine. The entire chamber brightened until shadows fled to the edges.

Nilsa shielded her eyes.

Erabor didn't.

He stared forward with a grim, dark recognition that chilled Nilsa's blood.

"What is that?" Nilsa whispered.

The Oracle didn't hesitate.

"The mark of the one who destroyed your kingdom."

The runes shifted, rearranging themselves until they formed the shape of a **broken star**, the edges jagged, the center burning with black light.

Nilsa's breath stuttered. "The clasp he wore—"

"Yes," the Oracle said.

Erabor hissed through his teeth. "He used that symbol before the Sundering. Before he betrayed—"

He cut himself off.

The Oracle turned so sharply her veils snapped. "You know his identity."

Erabor's jaw locked.

Nilsa grabbed his arm, pleading. "Tell us."

Erabor opened his mouth.

No sound came out.

Not because he refused—

—but because he **couldn't**.

His shadow seized sharply beneath him, rippling outward like a wounded creature trying to shield him from a threat.

Nilsa gasped. "Erabor—?"

The Oracle nodded slowly, a grim understanding dawning in her eyes. "He carries a binding oath. One woven into his very blood. He cannot answer directly."

Nilsa shot him a look of desperate confusion.

Erabor's expression twisted—not from pain this time, but from shame. He lowered his forehead to hers, voice trembling. "I can't say his name. I can't say what he is. The oath… it burns."

Nilsa cupped his cheek with shaking fingers.

"It's not your fault," she whispered.

His eyes closed, relief flooding his features at her words.

The Oracle lifted her staff.

"We do not need his name," she said. "We have something far more urgent."

Nilsa's voice cracked. "What?"

The Oracle stepped close—closer than before—her violet eyes glowing with a fear Nilsa had not seen in her until now.

"The Memory Stone is not prophetic. It is reflective. It shows only what was."

Nilsa swallowed.

"And?" she whispered.

"And yet the stranger saw you."

Nilsa's stomach dropped.

The Oracle's voice dropped to a trembling whisper. "Which means he is not trapped in memory. He is not bound to the past. He walks the living world."

Erabor's grip on Nilsa tightened.

Nilsa felt a wave of cold pass through her, sinking deep into her bones.

"And worse—" the Oracle continued.

Nilsa's throat closed.

The Oracle's next words were almost inaudible.

"He has found you."

Nilsa felt herself sway. Erabor caught her again, pulling her against him as her knees buckled. His hands shook, but his voice steadied with lethal resolve.

"Then we run."

The Oracle shook her head.

"You cannot run fast enough."

Nilsa's voice trembled. "Then what do we do?"

The Oracle looked at her with a solemnity so heavy it felt ancient.

"You do not hide. You do not beg. You do not bargain."

"What then?" Nilsa whispered.

The Oracle raised her staff.

"You prepare to fight the one who erased your kingdom."

A silence heavy as stone followed.

Then the Oracle turned to Erabor.

"And you," she said, "must begin to remember what you are."

Erabor's breath stopped.

Nilsa's heart did too.

The Oracle struck her staff against the stone floor.

The runes flared.

And the chapter ended with the echo reverberating through the chamber:

Remember.

CHAPTER TWENTY-SIX

What Moves in the Silver Pines

Nothing in Morrivan ever broke the silence of night.
Not wind.
Not animals.
Not even magic.

Night was the forest's sacred hour—its breath held in perfect stillness, its shadows soft and watchful, its silver needles whispering only when spoken to by moonlight.

Tonight, they whispered first.

Nilsa lay awake long after the Oracle had retreated to her meditation chamber. She sat beside Erabor's makeshift bed—her back against the cool stone wall, knees drawn to her chest, cloak pooled around her like a puddle of wine-dark fabric.

She had not left him since touching the Memory Stone.

She didn't think she could.

The air in the sanctuary felt heavy—not dangerous, not charged, but thick with exhaustion and aftershocks. It smelled faintly of moss and burning pine resin, with an undertone of cold stone that seeped into the bones.

Erabor breathed shallowly beneath the furs, the color returning slowly to his cheeks. His eyelashes trembled when he dreamed—little flickers of emotion passing across his closed lids.

Nilsa watched him quietly, her chest tight.

He had nearly died.

She had nearly died.

And the man who destroyed their kingdom—her kingdom—walked the world.

He saw her.

Her fingertips shook where they rested against her knee. She curled them into fists to hide the trembling. She didn't know what terrified her more: that she had seen him, or that he had seen back.

A soft sound broke the stillness.

A hum—distant, muffled, metal on stone.

It vibrated through her bones before her ears even registered it.

Nilsa stiffened.

At first, she thought it might be her memory of the shrine's pulse echoing in her skull again—but no. This sound was different, deeper, as if rising from the earth rather than descending from the air.

The runes etched along the wall to her left shivered—just once, a faint flicker of light traveling through them like a warning.

Nilsa rose slowly, hands braced on the floor to steady herself.

"Erabor…?"

Her voice was quiet, uncertain.

He didn't stir.

She moved closer, brushing a hand across his cheek.

"Erabor."

His breath hitched. His brow furrowed as if fighting to surface.

Nilsa looked toward the entrance to the sanctum. The tunnel was dark. Still. Silent.

Her heartbeat quickened.

Something was wrong.

The silence wasn't night-silence.
It was *pressure*.

A held breath.
A coiled spring.
A weight pressing against a door.

Nilsa backed away from Erabor, eyes on the tunnel, feeling every hair on her arms stand on end.

Another hum.

Louder.

Then—

CRACK.

A sharp sound echoed through the forest above—fast, violent, splitting the air like a tree trunk fracturing under lightning. The runes along the sanctum walls flared, each line of light brightening in a cascading wave.

Nilsa jolted violently.

Erabor's eyes snapped open.

He inhaled sharply, confusion flashing across his features, followed instantly by recognition.

Nilsa exhaled in relief. "Thank the stars—"

Erabor shot upright—not groggy, not weak, not tentative. Instinct. Pure animal instinct. He caught Nilsa's wrist in a tight grip, pulling her close before she could even finish her sentence.

"What happened?" he rasped.

Nilsa swallowed. "Something's wrong. The forest—"

Another crack.
Closer.
Louder.

Followed by a low, rolling groan that vibrated through the stone beneath them.

Erabor's grip tightened until his knuckles turned white. His eyes—still dark, still shaken—focused sharply, like a hunter scenting a threat.

"No," he whispered, voice rough. "No, he shouldn't be able to enter Morrivan. The wards—"

Nilsa's heart seized. "It's him?"

Erabor didn't answer.

He didn't need to.

The air in the sanctum turned cold enough that Nilsa's breath formed mist. Frost crawled across the stones from the entrance, delicate patterns forming in spirals before shattering under invisible pressure.

Somewhere deeper in the forest, a ward stone shattered.

The sound—
a haunting, bell-like ring—
vibrated deep into their ribs.

Erabor's eyes burned.

Nilsa's pulse spiked.

Before she could speak again, the Oracle swept into the chamber, veils trailing behind her like tattered banners caught in a storm. Her staff glowed violently at the tip, runes running down its length like molten lightning.

She did not look serene now.

She looked afraid.

"We must move," the Oracle said, voice sharp and strong despite the panic flickering at its edges. "Now."

Nilsa stood quickly. "What's happening?"

"The outer wards have been breached. Something has entered Morrivan's borders."

Erabor surged to his feet, nearly stumbling as his shadow flickered violently behind him. Nilsa caught his arm, steadying him by instinct.

"Something?" Erabor growled. "Say his name."

The Oracle snapped her head toward him. "I cannot. His name has not been spoken here for over three hundred years."

"He is here," Erabor said, breath ragged. "In the forest."

Nilsa felt her knees weaken.

The Oracle nodded grimly. "Yes. The hunter has arrived."

Nilsa's vision pulsed—no, her memory pulsed. The stranger's face. That smile. Those cold, silver eyes.

"He found me," she whispered.

"He followed the stone," the Oracle corrected. "He felt it awaken. He felt *you* awaken. Morrivan's magic slowed him, but it did not stop him."

A howl—low, distorted, inhuman—echoed through the trees above.

Nilsa flinched violently.

Erabor stepped in front of her without thinking, shield, barrier, instinct.

The Oracle raised her staff. "We leave. Immediately. The deeper sanctum wards cannot hold him."

Nilsa's voice trembled. "Where do we go?"

The Oracle pointed to the far side of the chamber.

The stone wall was dissolving.

Literally dissolving—grain by grain, rune by rune, as though the rock had turned to sand under some unseen command. Behind it, a narrow pathway formed—dark, spiraling upward through the earth like a secret artery of the forest.

"To the inner paths," the Oracle said. "They may buy us minutes."

Erabor snarled, "Minutes?"

"It is more than you have now."

Nilsa's voice cracked. "He's that close?"

As if in answer, the outer tunnel lights flickered—dimmed—then extinguished entirely, plunging the entrance into shadow.

Then—

A footstep.

Slow.
Deliberate.
Barely audible.

But the sound of it rattled through the stone like thunder.

Erabor and Nilsa both sucked in the same breath.

The Oracle spun, staff slicing the air in a wide, glowing arc. "Move!"

Nilsa grabbed Erabor's arm to help him.

He didn't let her.

Instead, he grabbed *her* hand—tight, steadying—and pulled her toward the dissolving passage.

Behind them, another ward stone shattered with a scream of magic ripped apart by force.

Nilsa wasn't sure if the sound came from the forest—

—or from the Oracle's own breaking heart.

The dissolving stone wall shivered one last time, then crumbled inward in a silent cascade of fine, glimmering dust. Cool air breathed out of the newly revealed passage—an old, stale breath, the scent of stone and ancient roots, water drips, and something faintly metallic that made Nilsa's tongue prickle.

The tunnel beyond sloped downward sharply, the walls narrowing into a twisting artery of polished rock shot through with glowing veins of silver-blue quartz. The patterns of the quartz were erratic—pulsing faintly like tiny, flickering lanterns embedded in the stone. Light wasn't steady here; it trembled as though frightened.

Nilsa didn't realize she was holding her breath until Erabor nudged her forward.

He still looked weakened from the shrine fight—his knees unsteady, his breathing uneven—but he stayed ahead of her, one hand braced against the tunnel wall when needed, the other gripping her wrist as if he feared she might vanish if he let go.

Behind them, the Oracle swept inside last, veils fluttering in the unnatural wind that chased them. Her staff glowed violently, the runes spiraling along its length like frantic, terrified creatures trying to escape.

"Move quickly," she said. "Do not let the light falter."

"Why?" Nilsa breathed, voice barely carrying.

"Because what follows us thrives in dark places."

Erabor swore under his breath and quickened his steps, shadows beneath him writhing in agitated bursts.

The tunnel constricted just enough that Nilsa's shoulders brushed the rock. That metallic scent thickened—sharp, iron-laced, as if the air itself remembered blood spilled in this space long before any of them were born.

Footsteps echoed behind them.

Not from the Oracle.

Not from any warden.

From **above**.

A heavy footstep.
Then another.
Slow.

Rhythmic.
Measured.

Nilsa flinched with each one.

Erabor's grip tightened to the point of pain. He pulled her close, nearly shielding her with his body as they pressed deeper into the twisting corridor.

"The hunter is in Morrivan," Nilsa whispered, as if saying it too loudly would summon him faster.

"He is everywhere in Morrivan now," the Oracle said. "The forest bends around him. The wards cannot read him. The light cannot track him. He has walked these paths before."

Nilsa shivered violently. "When?"

"When he buried Eidonrael's heart beneath our roots."

The blood drained from Nilsa's face.

Ahead, the quartz veins flickered wildly—brightening, dimming, brightening again in erratic pulses. The light faltered for a full second.

Erabor stopped so suddenly Nilsa nearly collided with him.

"NO," he snapped, voice sharp with fear far too raw to be hidden.

But the quartz light returned, weakly, trembling against the stone.

Erabor exhaled through his teeth and forced himself to move again.

Nilsa reached up and touched his shoulder, voice shaking. "You don't have to keep me behind you. You're still—"

He cut her off without turning. "I'm fine."

"You're barely standing."

"Then you walking behind me would make us both easy prey."

"But—"

He spun toward her—eyes dark, fierce, terrified.

"I will not lose you," he said, the words cracking on the edges like they had been pried out of him forcibly.

Nilsa forgot how to breathe.

The Oracle stepped between them before she could respond. "Do not stop. The paths twist at irregular intervals. If you pause too long, they may shift."

Nilsa blinked. "Shift?"

"Yes," the Oracle said, sweeping her staff along the wall. "These tunnels were shaped by the forest centuries ago. They realign when threatened."

"And they think we're the threat?" Nilsa asked.

"No. They think **he** is."

A distant roar—not loud, but deep, resonant, vibrating down the stone like thunder muffled by miles—rattled the tunnel. Dust drifted from the ceiling in slow, trembling spirals.

Nilsa jerked forward, her heart pounding.

"What was that?"

"The outer wards have fallen," the Oracle said.

Erabor swore again, harsher this time.

Nilsa stumbled ahead, running her hands along the walls for balance as the corridor began to tilt beneath her feet. The stone rippled under her palms—just slightly, like the pulse of a giant creature lying dormant beneath the earth.

"How long," she whispered, "before he reaches the inner sanctum?"

The Oracle did not answer.

Which was an answer in itself.

They rounded a bend so sharp Nilsa scraped her shoulder on the stone. The walls narrowed again, pressing them into a single-file path. Erabor stayed ahead, leaning heavily on the wall when his legs trembled, but never faltering enough to slow.

Nilsa pressed her palm against his back lightly. "You're shaking."

"So are you."

"That's not an answer."

"Neither was your question."

Nilsa scowled—and then flinched as the light ahead flickered again.

Flicker.
Flicker.
Dark.

The tunnel plunged into absolute blackness.

Nilsa gasped. "Erabor—!"

His hand shot behind him immediately, locking around her wrist in a bruising grip.

"Here," he said, voice low and taut. "I'm here."

The Oracle slammed her staff onto the rock floor.

A burst of silver fire rippled outward—brief, weak, flickering—but enough to illuminate a few feet ahead.

Enough to reveal movement.

Nilsa's blood froze.

Shadows crawled along the walls—thin, elongated, reaching shapes that moved without bodies.

They slithered.

They stretched.

They pooled.

Not ordinary shadows.

Searching shadows.

"He's already in the tunnels," Erabor breathed, voice shaking with fury and terror.

"No," the Oracle said sharply. "Not fully. These are fragments—pieces of him. Probes. He is looking for you."

Nilsa's breath hitched.

"For me," she whispered, horrified.

"Yes," the Oracle said. "He can feel your bloodline. He can taste your fear through the stone."

Nilsa staggered.

Erabor turned, cupping her face with both hands despite his weakened state. "Look at me. Look at me, Nilsa—not the shadows."

She did.

His eyes—dark, human—not glowing, not monstrous—steadied her.

His thumbs brushed her cheeks. "Do you trust me?"

"Yes," she breathed without hesitation.

"Then breathe with me."

The shadows thickened behind them.

Closer.
Closer.

Nilsa matched his breathing, forcing her lungs to obey even as fear clawed at her chest.

In—
Out—
In—
Out—

The shadows stilled.

But only for a heartbeat.

Then they surged forward.

The Oracle thrust her staff downward, and a shockwave of brilliant silver light exploded through the tunnel, incinerating the first tendrils of darkness that reached for Nilsa.

"RUN!" the Oracle screamed.

Erabor didn't wait.

He grabbed Nilsa's wrist and pulled—hard—dragging her down the twisting path, his shadow flaring dangerously behind him, trying to protect her, trying to stay solid despite the threat tearing at him from every direction.

Nilsa stumbled, caught herself, and ran.

The tunnel tilted downward sharply, stone slick beneath their boots, forcing them into a semi-controlled slide. Quartz veins flickered wildly around them, lighting their path in broken, frantic flashes.

Behind them, something entered the tunnel fully.

Not a fragment.

Not a shadow.

Something massive.

The stone groaned.
The walls shuddered.
The air *curved* around the presence.

Nilsa couldn't help herself—
she looked back.

For one fraction of a heartbeat, she saw:

A silhouette.
Tall.
Straight-backed.
Moving with impossible calm.

Eyes like cold silver fire.

Her blood went cold.

"Erabor," she whispered, voice cracking. "He's here."

Erabor didn't look back.

He just ran faster—not away, but toward something deeper, older, hidden beneath Morrivan.

The Oracle's voice echoed from behind them—shouting, chanting, commanding the tunnel to seal, the stone to close, the roots to rise.

But the hunter kept coming.

Slow.
Patient.
Impossibly sure.

As though he had already won.

The tunnel funneled downward in a spiraling rush, stone walls slick beneath their palms as Nilsa and Erabor half-ran, half-slid through the tightening passage. The quartz fractures lighting the tunnel pulsed harder now—like a heartbeat straining under pain.

Boom.
Boom.
Boom.

And behind every pulse, the echo of *footsteps* followed them.

Slow.
Measured.
Deliberate.

A hunter never needed to run.

Nilsa stumbled as the tunnel floor shifted under her boots, rippling like a creature turning in restless sleep. Erabor caught her with one hand, fingers slipping against her wrist from the sweat and dust and fear that coated their skin. He hauled her upright and kept moving, leaning heavily against the wall when his knees buckled.

He was shaking again.

Not from exhaustion—
this was something deeper.

A tremor running along his bones.

His shadow cracked behind him, fizzing with sparks of black-blue light that flickered erratically. Each time the hunter's footsteps echoed again, Erabor's shadow spasmed in response, as if dragged on an invisible leash.

Nilsa grabbed his forearm, voice trembling, "Erabor—your shadow—"

"I know," he rasped. "Just move."

She didn't let go.

Not even when the tunnel jolted beneath them, sending loose quartz fragments skittering across the floor like shrapnel. She steadied him and together they forced their way down the narrowing corridor.

Behind them, the Oracle chanted under her breath, her staff raised high as she raced after them. The tip of it burned like a white-hot star, illuminating her veiled face in rapid, stuttering flashes. Her voice shook—not with fear, but with effort—as she forced the tunnel's ancient wards to respond.

"Close!" she commanded, slamming her staff onto the stone.

The walls behind her convulsed—
shivered—
and began to seal like a gash pulling shut.

But the sealing wasn't quick enough.

A ripple of shadow slipped through the narrowing gap—thin as smoke, sharp as claws. It scraped along the stone with a sound that made Nilsa's teeth ache.

The Oracle grimaced and thrust more power into the collapsing passage.

The gap slammed shut with a deafening crack.

But the sealed wall vibrated—
once—
twice—
three times—

As if something pressed its palm on the other side and simply waited for the right moment to tear through.

Nilsa's skin crawled.

"Don't stop!" the Oracle shouted.

They didn't.

The tunnel widened abruptly into a small cavern—a sphere of stone supported by thick, twisting root pillars carved smooth by centuries of forest magic. Blue phosphorescent moss glowed along the ceiling in shimmering patches, casting wavering light across the chamber.

In the center stood a door.

Or rather, a gate.

Tall.

Circular.

Made purely of living root and silver-veined stone.

The air around it shimmered faintly, humming with ancient wards.

Erabor nearly collapsed when he saw it. He braced himself against one of the root-pillars, panting, sweat sliding down his neck.

Nilsa rushed to him. "Are you alright?"

"No," he said honestly, resting his forehead against the cool bark. "But I will be."

His hand shook when he reached for hers. She didn't comment. She just slipped her fingers into his, squeezing tightly until his breathing steadied.

The Oracle walked past them, staring at the sealed gate with a cold, assessing gaze.

"This is the Last Gate of Morrivan," she said. "If anything crosses this threshold, the forest itself will die."

Nilsa's heart dropped.

Erabor's eyes darkened.

A deep thud echoed down the tunnel behind them—slow, heavy, resonating through the stone like a heartbeat that didn't belong to anything living.

Thud.

Nilsa flinched.

Thud.

The Oracle spun toward the tunnel. "No…"

Thud.

Erabor staggered upright.

The Oracle lifted her staff.

And then—
as if gently placing a hand on a table—
something pressed against the sealed wall and **pushed**.

The stone bulged inward.

Cracked.

Hairline fractures spiderwebbed across the surface in branching veins of darkness.

Nilsa felt her lungs seize.

The Oracle took a step forward. "You cannot break that ward."

A voice answered.

Velvety.
Calm.
So close it felt whispered directly against Nilsa's ear.

"Cannot?"

The cracks deepened.

"Or will not try?"

Nilsa screamed before she knew she was doing it.

The Oracle snapped her staff downward. Wards flared across the entire cavern—lines of brilliant silver fire tracing along the ceiling, walls, and root-pillars. The very air trembled under the force.

But the cracks in the sealed wall only spread faster.

The wall wasn't resisting.

It was *failing*.

"He's too strong," Nilsa gasped. "Oracle—what do we do?"

The Oracle tilted her head slightly, listening to something Nilsa couldn't hear, as if calculating how long the ward would hold—and deciding that it wasn't enough.

Then she turned to Erabor.

"Shadow-bound one," she said softly.

Erabor's entire body flinched.

Nilsa's breath caught.

The Oracle met his eyes. "It is time."

"No," he snapped instantly. "I'm not ready—I can't—"

"There is no choice," the Oracle said. "He is tearing through a ward carved by the first Morrivan priesthood. You must remember what you are."

Erabor backed up, shaking his head fiercely. "No. No, if I fall into it now—if I slip in front of her—"

"You won't hurt me," Nilsa whispered.

His breath hitched—sharp, pained. "You don't know that."

Nilsa grabbed his face between her palms, pulling him down to her level. "Then I trust you for both of us."

Erabor froze.

His shadow reeled behind him—twisting, convulsing, as though unsure whether to collapse or ignite.

Nilsa held his face, trembling.

"Erabor," she whispered. "Come back to yourself."

He pressed his forehead to hers.

And breathed once.
Twice.
A third time.

The shaking eased.

But only a little.

The sealed wall cracked down the center with a deafening roar—

CRAAACK—BOOM.

Dust shot into the cavern. The roots trembled. The moss dimmed. The gate behind them flickered, its wards weakening under the surge.

Nilsa's scream caught in her throat.

The Oracle raised her staff with both hands, runes blazing so bright they left afterimages streaking across the air.

"Stand back!"

She drove the staff into the ground.

A dome of silver light erupted outward, encasing them in a shimmering barrier.

The wall exploded inward.

Shards of ancient stone flew across the chamber like thrown daggers. Several struck the Oracle's barrier and vaporized, scattering into glittering dust. Nilsa shielded her face as the wind slammed into them—cold, sharp, carrying the scent of pine, blood, and something like winter without sunlight.

Then—
the dust settled.

The barrier flickered.

And through the settling haze…

He stepped inside.

The hunter.

Tall.
Straight-backed.
Calm.

Wearing a cloak of midnight and silver-threaded shadow.

His hair was dark as storm clouds.
His eyes glowed like two shards of cold starfire.

He looked at the Oracle first.

Then Nilsa.

And then—
slowly—
his gaze drifted to Erabor.

Erabor's entire body locked as though hit by a physical blow.

Nilsa grabbed his hand.

The hunter stopped walking.

And spoke with awful, terrifying calm.

"Found you."

Nilsa's heart plummeted.

Erabor's breath shattered in his chest.

The hunter's smile sharpened.

"You ran," he murmured. "You hid. And yet—here you are."

He took another step forward.

The Oracle slammed her staff down again.

"You tread on holy ground," she warned.

The hunter didn't even look at her.

"It is unwise," the Oracle continued, "to challenge Morrivan."

The hunter lifted his gaze to her, almost pitying.

"Morrivan is dying," he said softly. "Just as Eidonrael did."

Nilsa's knees nearly buckled.

Erabor moved in front of her.

The hunter's eyes narrowed.

"You defy me again, shadow-born."

Erabor bared his teeth, silent.

The hunter tilted his head as if studying a puzzle that should not exist. "You should have died centuries ago."

Erabor didn't move.

The hunter's smile widened.

"Very well," he murmured.

"If I cannot claim your corpse, I will claim—"

His gaze slid to Nilsa.

"—your heir."

Nilsa's world spun.

Erabor lunged forward with a snarl so raw it ripped through the chamber like tearing fabric. His shadow erupted behind him—massive, winged, jagged—before collapsing under its own weight.

The Oracle screamed, "NOT HERE—NOT NOW—"

The hunter raised a hand.

And the cavern shook.

The cavern lurched so violently Nilsa thought the entire forest had been ripped from its roots and hurled sideways. The stone groaned, pillars buckled, quartz veins burst in a shower of cold blue sparks. She slammed against Erabor as the ground split beneath their feet, a jagged fissure tearing through the center of the chamber.

The hunter's raised hand pulsed with cold light.

He was not even trying.

Not yet.

"Stay behind me," Erabor breathed, though his voice trembled and his knees shook and his shadow writhed behind him like a creature trying desperately to remember how to exist.

Nilsa's fingers clung to him; she didn't know when she'd grabbed him, only that she could not let go.

The Oracle stepped forward, the runes on her staff blazing as she slammed the bottom of it into the cracking floor. The blow rang like a bell struck underwater—deep, soft, resonant—and for a moment the cavern steadied.

A protective dome flared around them again, the silver barrier trembling with strain but holding.

The hunter tilted his head, as if impressed.

"A shrine-born Oracle stands with a dying kingdom's last ember." His eyes gleamed with dark amusement. "How poetic. How futile."

The Oracle didn't respond. Her jaw clenched beneath her veils, shoulders trembling from the force she was channeling. Sweat slid down her temples as she kept her arms raised, staff pointed at the intruder like a spear of starfire.

Nilsa swallowed the rising panic, forcing her voice steady. "What do you want from me?"

The hunter smiled—slow, terrible, inevitable.

"Everything."

Nilsa stepped back; Erabor stepped forward; the hunter's smile sharpened.

"You are the last piece," he murmured. "The final spark. The bloodline that slipped through my grasp." His gaze softened, almost gentle. "I have waited… far too long."

Erabor growled—a sound Nilsa had never heard from him before, animal-deep, instinct-sharp. His shadow flinched behind him, wings twitching in half-formed spasms as if something ancient struggled to break free.

The hunter's gaze shifted.

"Ah," he breathed. "There you are."

Fear stabbed through Nilsa like ice.

He wasn't talking to her.

He was talking to Erabor's shadow.

"You hid him well, child of Morrivan," the hunter said to the Oracle. "But not well enough."

The Oracle's knuckles whitened around her staff. Her voice shook but did not break. "You cannot take him. Not again."

"Take him?" the hunter echoed with a soft laugh. "My dear Oracle… he was never yours."

He stepped forward.

The dome shuddered violently, cracks spiderwebbing across its surface.

Erabor flinched, stumbling. His breath came in ragged gasps as if the pressure alone was crushing him. Nilsa grabbed his sleeve, voice breaking.

"Erabor—look at me—look at me—"

He did.

His eyes—dark, human, terrified—locked onto hers.

Her heart clenched.

He was fighting something she could not see.

Something massive.
Something old.
Something inside him.

The hunter's voice curled through the cavern like smoke.

"Submit, shadow-born. Your oath is mine."

Erabor's face twisted in agony. His hands clawed at the air, at his chest, at his own shadow as it writhed beneath him, stretching out like hands grasping blindly.

"No," he gasped. "No—no—don't—"

His knees buckled.

Nilsa caught him before he hit the ground, pulling his weight into her arms though he was heavier than she expected. His forehead pressed against her collarbone, sweat dampening her cloak. His breathing was ragged, too fast, too shallow.

"Stay with me," she whispered, her voice cracking. "Erabor—stay with me."

He trembled violently.

Nilsa cupped the back of his neck, grounding him.

The hunter's expression softened—not with compassion, but with a chilling kind of satisfaction.

"You feel it, don't you?" he murmured. "The truth whispering through your bones. Calling. Claiming. You are mine."

Something inside Erabor snapped.

Not physically—
but Nilsa felt it.

Like a thread pulled taut
and breaking
inside his soul.

His shadow convulsed, shooting outward in jagged, uncontrolled bursts. It slammed against the barrier, against the root pillars, against the hunter's approaching figure in raw, desperate defiance.

The hunter didn't even flinch.

The Oracle did.

"Oh stars," she whispered. "He is awakening too soon."

Erabor screamed.

Not loud.
Not long.
But Nilsa felt the agony of it down to her bones.

His shadow split in two.
Then three.
Then a frenzied tangle of broken wings and clawed silhouettes that flickered around him like shards of night fighting to become whole.

Nilsa held him harder.

He clutched her cloak, knuckles white, voice cracking through clenched teeth. "Don't let go—don't—Nilsa—I can't—"

"I'm here," she breathed, pulling him close, anchoring him with every ounce of strength she had.

The hunter's eyes softened in cold triumph.

"Yes," he murmured. "Hold him still."

"NO!" Nilsa screamed, throwing herself between them, instinct taking over faster than fear.

The hunter's smile vanished.

And for the first time—
he looked surprised.

The Oracle seized that moment.

She thrust her staff forward.

The runes blazed with blinding light—

—and the cavern EXPLODED with a shockwave of raw, ancient magic.

Nilsa was thrown backward. She hit the ground hard, Erabor pulled with her as he clung to her cloak. Stones rained from the ceiling. The root-pillars groaned and cracked. Mossfire flickered violently.

The hunter stumbled.

Only slightly.

But enough.

"Run!" the Oracle roared, her voice echoing like thunder through the cavern. "Go, children of Eidonrael and shadow! GO!"

She slammed her staff into the ground again.

The floor split open.

A narrow passage—dark and buried deep beneath the roots—ripped itself from the stone.

Nilsa stared in horror. "Oracle—what about you?"

The Oracle turned toward the hunter, raising her staff, her veils fluttering as the wind of her power whipped around her.

"I will hold him," she said. "For as long as I can."

Erabor shook violently in Nilsa's grasp. "No—we can't leave you—"

"You must," the Oracle said.

The hunter straightened, brushing dust from his cloak with calm irritation.

"You cannot stop me," he said.

"No," the Oracle whispered. "But I can delay you."

She raised her staff.

And the entire cavern ignited.

Roots erupted from the floor, twisting upward in massive spirals, forming barricades and walls and tangles of living wood that wrapped around the hunter like a cage.

He snapped one root with a flick of his fingers.

But more rose.

And more.

And more.

The Oracle stood like a pillar of light in the midst of chaos.

Nilsa grabbed Erabor and pulled him toward the newly opened passage. "Come on—we have to go!"

Erabor stumbled, eyes unfocused, shadow trembling.

But he followed her.

Because she was the only thing he could still see clearly.

They reached the mouth of the tunnel.

Nilsa hesitated—looking back.

The Oracle met her gaze once.

And in that single moment, Nilsa understood:

The Oracle knew she would die.

And she was choosing to.

"For Eidonrael," the Oracle whispered.

"For the child."

Before Nilsa could speak—
before she could protest—
before she could even scream—

Erabor grabbed her hand and pulled.
Hard.

The tunnel walls slammed shut behind them.

Cutting off the Oracle.
Cutting off the hunter.
Cutting off the light.

They plunged into darkness.

Nilsa clutched Erabor's hand, her voice trembling in the suffocating silence.

"Erabor… where does this tunnel go?"

His breath shuddered against her ear.

"To the one place," he whispered, "the hunter never wanted us to reach."

CHAPTER TWENTY-SEVEN

Beneath the Roots

The tunnel swallowed them in a darkness so complete it felt living—thick, velvet-coated, swallowing the last echoes of their breath and the final scream of stone as Morrivan sealed them inside. Nilsa's fingers clutched Erabor's hand like a lifeline, her heart racing a brutal rhythm against her ribs. She could no longer feel the forest above, no longer sense the Oracle's blinding magic or the crushing presence of the hunter. Here, beneath layers of ancient earth and root, the world grew still again.

Too still.

Erabor stumbled beside her, shoulders shaking with the aftermath of what he'd been forced to hold back. His breath came in rough, erratic bursts, each one edged with pain. She could feel the tremors traveling through his arm, feel how close he still was to losing himself—to slipping back into that crackling, dangerous space his shadow had exploded from.

Nilsa slowed them both, pressing her free hand against the wall until her palm slid over a surface smoother than stone. It felt almost like flesh—warm, pulsing faintly with a heartbeat that wasn't her own. She swallowed hard and forced her voice steady.

"Erabor… we have to stop. Just for a moment."

He shook his head immediately, breath shuddering. "No. We keep moving. He'll find us if we stop."

Nilsa drew closer, her shoulder brushing his arm. "You can barely stand."

He exhaled—sharp, frustrated. "I'm fine."

"You're lying."

He swayed on his feet.

Nilsa caught his other arm before he could fall, bracing him with her body. His head dropped forward against her shoulder, breath hot against her collarbone, fingers tightening around her wrist as though holding onto her kept him from slipping into something else entirely.

The air trembled faintly.

Not with danger.
With exhaustion.

Erabor's voice cracked against her ear. "If I lose control in here… Nilsa, there's nowhere for it to go. No air. No space. No wards. I don't know what I'll—"

"You won't hurt me," she whispered fiercely.

His breath stuttered. "You don't know that."

"I do."

Silence followed—heavy, dense, thrumming with something that felt too important to name. His forehead pressed against her shoulder again, and this time he didn't pull away.

Nilsa pulled him closer, steadying his hips with her thigh so he wouldn't collapse fully. His entire body shook—not cold, not fear, but something deeper. Something he'd been holding back since the shrine. Something tearing at him from inside.

She ran a hand down his spine, feeling the way each muscle fought to remain human.

Outside the walls of the tunnel, far above them, the world roared faintly—distant thunder, distant battle, distant death. Here, beneath the roots, the air was thick as honey, warm and damp, smelling of earth and sap, as though they had stepped inside the ribcage of a sleeping giant.

"Erabor," she said softly. "We need to find somewhere safe."

He lifted his head—slowly, reluctantly. His face looked carved from moonlight and pain, sweat tracing lines down dust-scattered skin. His pupils were still too wide, the whites of his eyes tinged with the faintest grey-blue sheen she didn't understand.

But gods, he looked human.
He looked breakable.
And yet he clung to her like she was the only thing tethering him to the world.

Nilsa squeezed his hand. "This tunnel must lead somewhere. The Oracle wouldn't have opened it if it dead-ended."

Erabor swallowed, throat tight. "It leads to the root chamber…"

"The what?"

He pushed off the wall, barely standing, and nodded deeper into the tunnel. "The oldest heart of Morrivan. A sanctuary for the dying. A tomb for the sacred. A refuge for the hunted—when the forest still had teeth to defend itself."

"And now?"

"It's quiet," he whispered. "Has been for centuries."

That frightened her more than anything.

Still, Nilsa slid under his arm, letting him lean on her fully now. She took his weight, bracing her feet against the uneven stone. He didn't apologize. And she didn't need him to.

They continued forward.

The darkness began to glow—softly at first, thin threads of silver-blue light weaving along the walls like veins awakening. The deeper they walked, the stronger the glow became, illuminating swirling patterns carved into the living roots that supported the tunnel. Nilsa brushed her fingertips along one of them and felt warmth pulse beneath the bark.

Like a heartbeat.

Erabor exhaled roughly. "We're close."

"How can you tell?"

He didn't answer immediately. His fingers tightened around hers. His voice, when it came, was low, strained.

"Because it feels like a memory."

Nilsa didn't ask.

She didn't push.

He was already unraveling in her arms.

The tunnel widened abruptly, the air growing warmer, heavier, scented with floral sweetness and something like old magic clinging to the very dust. A faint luminescent glow seeped from the circular entrance ahead.

Nilsa's pulse quickened.

"That's it?" she whispered.

"Yes," Erabor breathed. "The Rootheart."

Nilsa rounded the final curve—

—then stopped breathing.

The chamber opened before them like the inside of a world-forgotten cathedral—vast, soaring, hollowed out by time and magic rather than mortal hands. Nilsa froze on the threshold, breath catching in her throat as the Rootheart revealed itself in layers of glow and shadow.

The ceiling stretched high above, vanishing into darkness that shimmered like deep water. Thick roots—massive as tree trunks—wove down from that darkness and spiraled into the chamber floor, crossing and tangling and interlocking in patterns older than any kingdom. They formed archways and pillars, bridges and hollows, a lattice of living architecture that pulsed with a faint, silvery luminescence.

And in the very center—

A pool.

Circular.
Still.
Glass-clear.

Its surface reflected the glow of the roots above, turning the entire chamber into a mirrored cradle of silver-blue light. The air felt thick, humid, heavy with the scent of sap and mineral-rich water—clean, sweet, ancient.

Nilsa stepped forward involuntarily.

She felt Erabor's weight lean on her harder.

His breath hitched—harsh, strangled, barely controlled. His fingers spasmed around hers, then slid from her grip entirely as his knees buckled.

"Erabor!" Nilsa caught him under the arms, but his body folded like something had simply shut off inside him. She lowered him to the root-woven floor, cradling his shoulders, heart pounding so hard she thought it might burst from her ribs.

His skin was clammy.
His breathing ragged.
His eyes squeezed shut, jaw clenched against pain.

Nilsa brushed damp strands of hair back from his forehead. "Talk to me. Erabor—look at me."

His eyes opened a fraction.

The pupils were blown wide, swallowing almost all color.

He didn't look at her.

He looked through her.

"Erabor…"

She pressed her palm to his cheek—it burned cold. A cold that wasn't natural. A cold that felt familiar now.

The same cold that spilled through the shrine.
The same cold that snapped through the cavern when the hunter breached the ward.
The same cold that lived in the stranger's gaze.

Erabor's body trembled violently, muscles locking then releasing, then locking again as if fighting invisible chains.

Nilsa leaned closer, voice shaking. "You're safe now. The hunter isn't here. He can't reach you in this place."

Erabor exhaled through his teeth, breath gusting hot against her throat. "He's… not the danger."

"What?"

His fingers twitched around her sleeve, gripping tight. "I am."

Nilsa's heart twisted. She took his face in both hands. "No. I will not accept that."

"You don't—" His voice cracked, breath shuddering. "You don't understand. The oath… the binding… when he calls—when he pulls—it tries to tear me apart."

"But you resisted him."

"Barely," he rasped. "Barely, Nilsa."

Nilsa felt her throat tighten. His fear wasn't for himself. It was for her.

She slid closer, threading her legs beneath his shoulders so she could prop him upright. Her cloak pooled around them like spilled wine-red silk. She pressed her forehead to his, grounding him with warmth, with touch, with the steadiness he had used to ground her so many times before.

"Then let me help you," she whispered.

Erabor's breath caught. "You already are."

He shook again—harder this time. His shadow flickered along the roots beneath them, stretching and shrinking erratically like a creature trying to decide whether to breathe or break. Nilsa grabbed his wrist and held tight.

"Erabor," she breathed. "Listen to me."

His eyes opened fully now—dark, wild, rimmed with a faint silver glow that made her stomach drop and her heart lurch all at once.

She cupped his face, thumbs stroking the sharp angles of his cheekbones. "You are not his. Do you hear me? You are not his."

His breath hit the back of her throat as he whispered, nearly breaking, "I don't know what I am anymore."

Nilsa drew his forehead against her shoulder, cradling him like she would a child fighting nightmares they couldn't wake from. She slid her arms around him, pulling him into her lap, guiding his head against her chest where he could hear her heartbeat.

Her heart was steady.
Strong.
Human.

And she knew instinctively he needed that sound.

"You're Erabor," she said softly but with fierce certainty. "That's who you are. And I am not letting you fall apart in my arms. Not now. Not ever."

He shuddered again, breath cracking in his throat like he was swallowing a sob he didn't want her to hear.

She heard it anyway.

Nilsa pressed her lips to the crown of his head—a light, instinctive touch. His hands curled into the fabric of her tunic, clinging to her like an anchor in a storm.

Minutes—or hours, she didn't know—passed with him trembling quietly against her. The Rootheart glowed around them in gentle waves, as if the chamber itself recognized the brokenness in him and shifted to cradle them both.

Eventually, his breathing slowed.

The violent shaking eased.

His weight softened against her.

He wasn't fine. Not even close.

But the tearing inside him had stopped.

Nilsa kept her arms tight around him, brushing her fingers through his hair, feeling him finally—finally—fall into an exhausted, fragile sleep.

For the first time since the cavern, his shadow lay still.

Nilsa exhaled shakily, forehead resting against his temple. "You're safe," she whispered again. "I swear it."

Whether to him or to herself, she wasn't sure.

But the Rootheart listened.

And something ancient stirred beneath the pool.

Nilsa did not know how long she held him—only that time in the Rootheart flowed differently, thick as honey, slow as tree sap. The air hummed with an almost tender vibration, as though the chamber recognized the wounded things cradled within its ribs. Erabor slept with his head resting in the hollow of her shoulder, breath brushing lightly against her collarbone, his hands curled instinctively around the fabric of her cloak.

He looked younger like this.
Not in years—
in vulnerability.

A boy abandoned.
A soldier broken.
A creature trying desperately to be human.

Nilsa's fingers brushed a damp lock of hair from his forehead, her chest tight with something that frightened her more than the hunter's pursuit had.

Care.
Deep, aching care.

Her gaze drifted to the pool at the center of the Rootheart.

The surface reflected the room perfectly—roots, glowing veins, silver-blue light—but nothing moved in the water. Not ripples. Not shadows. Not even dust motes drifting across the air.

It looked like a mirror made of liquid moonlight.

And something pulled at her—
a gentle tug
just behind her ribs.

Nilsa looked down at Erabor, then gently lowered him onto her cloak, making a soft pillow with the folded fabric beneath his head. His breath hitched in protest for an instant—his fingers catching her wrist as if afraid she would disappear—but she whispered softly, stroking his hair.

"I'm not going far. I promise."

His hand loosened.

Nilsa rose carefully, knees stiff from holding him so long. Her boots made no sound on the root-woven ground. The air felt warmer near the pool, like stepping close to a fire on a winter night.

The light brightened as she approached—
soft, welcoming, ancient.

Nilsa knelt at the water's edge.

Her reflection looked back at her—
pale, shaken, dust-smeared, circlet askew—
but behind her reflection, something else shimmered.

She leaned closer.

The pool brightened.
Then darkened.
Then brightened again.
As though it were breathing.

"Hello?" she whispered before she could stop herself.

The pool responded.

The water did not break.
It did not ripple.
It simply *shifted,* as though her reflection had been brushed aside by an unseen hand.

Nilsa gasped.

The surface now showed a throne room she had never seen—
white marble pillars,
tall windows draped in silver veils,
a throne carved of pale stone shaped like blooming crystal.

Her breath stalled.

A woman sat on that throne.

Not the Oracle.
Not her mother.
Not anyone she recognized.

Tall.
Regal.
With hair the color of spun moonlight, falling in long sheets down her back. Her skin glowed faintly, her gown woven of pure luminescence. A circlet of twelve points rested on her brow—twelve, not eleven.

Nilsa's heart fluttered.

The queen in the vision lifted her face.

Her eyes glowed a brilliant silver-blue.

Nilsa's breath tore free.

Those eyes—
that glow—
that exact shade—

Nilsa had seen them once before.
On the child carried from Eidonrael's burning sanctuary.

Her reflection shimmered in the pool's surface, overlapping the queen's face for a brief instant.

Nilsa jerked back.

"No," she whispered. "No, it can't—"

She reached toward the pool again—

but a hand closed around her wrist.

Softly.
Gently.
Trembling.

Nilsa gasped and turned.

Erabor had pushed himself upright, though his arms shook with the effort. His hair fell wild across his forehead, shadows clinging to his shoulders like something reluctant to let go.

His eyes—dark, tired, burning faintly—fixed on her with a strange, conflicted intensity.

"Do not touch the pool," he rasped.

Nilsa swallowed, pulse racing. "Why? What is it?"

He shook his head, jaw tightening. "It shows truths. But not all truths are meant to be touched. Some… bind."

Bind.

Nilsa's stomach twisted. "But it showed me—"

"It showed you what you were ready to see," he interrupted softly. "Nothing more."

Nilsa stared at him, breath shaking. "Erabor… that woman. That throne. Was that—"

He closed his eyes, pain flickering across his face. "I can't say."

"Because of the oath."

He nodded.

Nilsa knelt beside him again, brushing her thumb over the back of his hand. "But you know."

Erabor swallowed hard, voice low. "I know enough to fear what comes next."

Nilsa's throat constricted. "Is the woman in the pool related to me?"

He inhaled sharply—
too sharply—
shoulders tensing as though struck by invisible force.

His shadow jerked behind him, stretching suddenly, almost violently, its edges sparking with black-blue light.

Nilsa reached for him again—but stopped as the shadow arched behind him like a half-formed wing.

Her breath left her in a rush.

"Erabor…"

He gritted his teeth, jaw clenched, hands digging into the roots beneath him as he fought to keep control. Sweat slid down his temples, breath ragged, body shaking with effort so intense it looked painful.

Nilsa cupped his face, forcing him to look at her. "Focus on me. Don't fight it alone."

His eyes snapped to hers—wild, dark, pleading.

"I won't lose control," he ground out, voice strained. "Not here. Not in front of you."

"You're not losing control," she whispered. "You're holding on."

He stared at her.

Long.
Silent.
As if memorizing her face.

The shadow behind him slowly folded inward.

Collapsed.

Stilled.

Erabor dropped his forehead into her shoulder again, breath shaking with relief.

Nilsa stroked the back of his neck gently, grounding him as the Rootheart thrummed softly around them.

After a moment, she whispered, "The pool showed me Eidonrael's queen, didn't it? The last true queen. Before the Sundering."

Erabor didn't look up.

But the way his breath hitched told her everything she needed to know.

Nilsa exhaled slowly, heart racing.

The pool had shown her a queen with her eyes.

Her blood.

Her light.

Her legacy.

Nilsa pressed a trembling hand to the pool's mirrored surface—

—but the moment her fingers came close, the water flashed white.

She jerked back as a whisper—thin as breath, ancient as stone—rose from the depths.

"Child of the thirteenth star…"

Nilsa froze.

Erabor's head snapped up.

The water pulsed.

"…find what was broken."

Nilsa's skin prickled.

"…restore what was lost."

Then the pool went dark.

Completely.

As though nothing had ever spoken.

Nilsa shook, staring at the blank surface. "What… what am I supposed to do?"

Erabor reached out with trembling fingers
and laced them tightly through hers.

"You," he whispered, voice low with fear and awe,
"are meant to change everything."

For a long moment after the pool's final words sank into the humming quiet, Nilsa and Erabor simply sat together on the woven roots, holding onto one another as though the world outside no longer existed. Nilsa's heartbeat slowly steadied, her breath falling in time with Erabor's as the magic-heavy air wrapped around them like a living cocoon.

But the peace didn't last.

A tremor ran through the Rootheart—subtle at first, no more than a soft vibration beneath their palms. Nilsa lifted her head and looked around the chamber, brow furrowing. The glowing veins along the arching roots dimmed, flickered, then steadied—brighter than before, and pulsing in a rapid rhythm that reminded her of fear.

Erabor stiffened in her arms.

His fingers dug involuntarily into her waist, not enough to hurt, but enough to say he'd felt the shift long before she had.

"Erabor?" she whispered.

His eyes darkened, pupils dilating until only the faintest ring of color remained. "He's searching."

Nilsa's breath hitched. "Here?"

"No." He swallowed tightly. "Not yet. But he's closer. Close enough that the forest's pulse has changed."

Nilsa glanced at the pool—the way the once mirror-like surface now churned faintly, threads of silver curling like smoke beneath the water. The chamber seemed to draw inward on itself, the air thickening with urgency, with a kind of old, cracking grief.

"The Rootheart is afraid," she breathed.

Erabor exhaled shakily. "Yes."

Another tremor pulsed through the roots, this one stronger, rattling loose dust from high above. The pool brightened—then darkened almost to black. Nilsa felt the hair on her arms lift, a primal, instinctive reaction to something older than fear.

Erabor pushed himself upright, though his legs trembled under him, and his shadow jerked sharply across the floor. Nilsa moved with him, steadier this time, her hand gripping his shoulder in instinctive support.

"Don't stand yet," she murmured. "You're not fully—"

"We can't stay here," he said, voice hoarse but resolute. "The Rootheart hid us long enough to catch our breath. But it wasn't meant for... this." His gaze flicked upward, toward the unseen depths of Morrivan. "He's breaking through the sanctum."

Nilsa's heart twisted painfully. "The Oracle..."

Erabor flinched at her voice, a flash of grief crossing his features. "She knew the cost when she stayed behind."

Nilsa bowed her head, absorbing that truth. The silence that followed hurt worse than the fear. She squeezed her eyes shut against the tight sting of loss—not just for the Oracle, but for the forest itself. Morrivan had protected countless refugees, outcasts, hunted souls for generations. To think of it falling—of its wards being shredded like thin parchment—felt like losing another kingdom all over again.

The roots pulsed again—rapid, urgent.

This time the tremor traveled up Nilsa's spine like a whispered warning.

Choose.
Move.
Now.

Erabor gripped her hand, tighter this time, his palm warm and calloused and shaking with the effort to remain grounded. "Nilsa... the pool didn't speak idly. If it showed you Eidonrael's last queen... if it called you the child of the thirteenth star..."

Nilsa felt her pulse thud. "Then it wants me to find something."

"Yes," he said softly. "Something lost. Something broken. Something hidden in the bones of the world."

"And you can't tell me what it is."

He breathed out hard. "No. The oath holds. But I can guide you toward it. I can protect you while you seek it." His gaze softened with something almost unbearably vulnerable. "If you'll let me."

Nilsa reached up and brushed her thumb along his jawline, wiping away a streak of dust. "Then we do this together."

He closed his eyes—and the tension in his shoulders eased, just barely.

Another tremor rippled through the chamber—strong enough to send ripples across the pool's surface. The glowing roots dimmed, then surged brighter, then dimmed again in a frantic rhythm that felt like the beating of a heart pushed too far.

Erabor's shadow convulsed. His breath hitched sharply. He gripped Nilsa's hand harder.

"He's breaching the second wardline," he said quietly. "The one that guards Morrivan's inner sanctum."

Nilsa felt panic claw up her throat. "Then we need to move. Now."

Erabor nodded, though his legs trembled with the effort to remain upright. "There's an exit through the far side of the Rootheart. A tunnel that leads out of Morrivan's oldest boundary."

"Will it be safe?"

"No," he said honestly. "But it will be away from him."

Nilsa swallowed hard. "Lead the way."

He turned—slowly, painfully—but stopped as the pool brightened a final time. The water shimmered, then cleared, revealing not a vision but something small at the bottom:

A medallion.

Round.
Silver.
Inscribed with the twelve-pointed star.

Only this star had **thirteen** faint lines in its shape—the thirteenth carved so lightly it was almost invisible.

Nilsa knelt, breath trembling. "What is that?"

Erabor didn't speak.
He couldn't.

His oath sealed his throat.

But his eyes—dark, wide, shaken—fixed on the medallion with naked reverence.

Nilsa reached into the pool.
The water parted around her hand like silk.
Her fingers closed around the medallion's cool surface.

When she lifted it free, the pool went dark again.

Deadly silent.

Nilsa stared at the medallion in her palm—its weight startling for its size, as though she held more than metal… as though she held memory. Legacy. Truth.

"It was meant for you," Erabor said softly.

Her heart pounded. "Why?"

But he didn't answer.

He couldn't.

And the Rootheart gave a final, violent tremor—roots shuddering, moss lights dimming to near-black.

Erabor seized her hand. "We have to go NOW."

Nilsa nodded, fastening the medallion around her neck with trembling fingers.

Together, they rushed across the chamber toward the far archway—roots shifting under their feet, guiding them, urging them forward.

At the threshold Nilsa dared one final look back.

The pool was still.
Dark.
Silent.

The last sanctuary of Morrivan… dimming like a dying ember.

Nilsa swallowed hard and whispered, "Thank you."

Then she turned and followed Erabor into the narrow, living tunnel—
the exit sealing behind them
with the sound of a heartbeat breaking.

CHAPTER TWENTY-EIGHT

The Path That Bleeds Light

The tunnel beyond the Rootheart narrowed almost immediately into a winding passage of stone and root that felt less like a corridor and more like the inside of something ancient crawling through the earth. Every surface pulsed faintly with life, small veins of soft blue luminescence threading through the walls like glowing strands of hair. Nilsa kept one hand against the wall to steady herself—its warmth was unsettling, but it grounded her through the trembling in her legs and the echo of the Rootheart's voice lingering in her bones.

Erabor moved ahead of her, though "moved" was generous. His steps were uneven, the tremor still present in his limbs, his shadow stuttering beneath him like a fragile flame fighting wind. But he refused to lean on her again—some mix of pride, instinct, and fear she didn't yet understand.

Nilsa watched him closely, heart tight. Every few steps he'd press his palm to the wall, steadying himself against the living roots, breath thin and shallow. She wanted to help. She wanted to wrap her arm around his waist and let him lean as heavily as he needed. But she knew he was fighting the remnants of the oath pulling at him, fighting the hunter's shadow still gnawing at the edges of his mind.

And fighting the truth that the Rootheart had almost pulled out of him.

So she kept close behind him, her hand hovering just inches from his back, ready to catch him if he stumbled again.

The tunnel bent sharply to the left, then rose in a steep incline. The air grew colder, thinner, smelling faintly of rain-soaked bark and distant lightning. Nilsa's breath fogged slightly when she exhaled. The walls here were darker, the glowing veins thinner and less frequent. Shadows thickened in the corners—quiet, watching, patient.

"Where does this lead?" Nilsa asked softly.

Erabor didn't turn, but his voice—when he finally replied—was low and strained.

"Out of Morrivan's heartland. Into the wild border where the forest still remembers how to fight." He paused, steadying himself against an outcropping of smooth stone. "It's not safe. But it's the only path that leads away from him long enough to breathe."

Nilsa swallowed hard. "How long until he finds the entrance?"

"He already knows the direction," Erabor murmured. "But these tunnels coil like living things. They close behind us. They shift when hunted. He'll have to tear his way through the Rootheart itself, and that will slow him…"

He hesitated.

Nilsa stepped closer. "But not stop him."

Erabor's silence confirmed it.

The tunnel walls suddenly widened into a rough cavern—low-ceilinged, glittering with mineral clusters that caught the faint blue light and fractured it into thousands of tiny, shimmering reflections. Nilsa slowed, breath catching at the way the cavern glittered around them—like being inside a sky full of frozen stars.

Erabor did not slow.

His shadow flickered uneasily across the star-like reflections.

Nilsa followed him out the far side of the cavern, where the tunnel steepened once more. The incline grew sharper with each step until they nearly climbed. The air grew colder still. The light dimmed until Nilsa had to touch the wall with each step to avoid slipping.

Her foot hit open air.

Nilsa gasped and jerked back.

Erabor caught her wrist instantly, pulling her toward him. "Careful."

Nilsa looked down. The tunnel ended abruptly, opening into a jagged crevasse that dropped into pitch-black nothingness. Cold wind surged up from the depths, carrying the scent of old rain, crushed stone, and something sharp and metallic.

"What is this?" Nilsa whispered.

Erabor exhaled shakily. "The Boundary Split."

Nilsa's pulse quickened. "The what?"

"The break between Morrivan and the uncharted forest. A wound carved centuries ago when the forest tore itself apart to escape the hunter." His grip tightened on her wrist. "It never healed."

Nilsa swallowed hard. "How do we cross it?"

Erabor looked across the chasm.

Nilsa followed his gaze—

—and her stomach dropped.

A bridge.
If it could be called that.

Two impossibly thin roots stretched across the gulf, twisting around each other like braids of dark wood. They swayed faintly in the cold wind, fragile as threads, connecting the tunnel they stood in to another across the abyss.

Nilsa's hand flew to her mouth. "That can't hold us."

"It will," Erabor said. But his voice held no confidence—only necessity.

Nilsa shook her head. "That's not a bridge. That's a wish."

Erabor stepped toward it anyway.

Nilsa grabbed his wrist. "Erabor, you can barely stand."

He looked at her then—finally really looked—and she saw the truth he'd been hiding behind determination and fear.

He didn't expect to make it across.

He expected to fall.
Or worse.

"Nilsa," he said softly, "we don't have another choice."

The wind howled up from the crevasse, colder now, sharper, as if sensing the coming decision. The roots groaned faintly beneath their weightless sway.

Nilsa stepped toward him, placing her hand firmly against his heart—feeling its frantic, uneven rhythm beneath her palm.

"We don't separate," she said. "Not across this. Not ever. We go together."

His eyebrow lifted slightly. "Together?"

She nodded once. Firm. Unshaken. "I'm not letting go."

His throat worked. "Nilsa…"

"No," she whispered, her voice trembling but resolute. "You saved me in the cavern. You held us both together in the tunnel. Let me hold you now."

He stared at her—long enough for her heart to pound painfully, long enough for the wind to cut cold between them, long enough for the roots to sway like warning fingers.

Then he reached up and covered her hand with his.

"Together," he agreed.

Nilsa exhaled shakily. "Then we need a plan."

Erabor turned to the bridge again. "One at a time won't work. The roots respond to balance. To paired steps. They were built for two."

Nilsa blinked. "How do you know that?"

He tensed. "I've crossed one before."

"When?" Nilsa asked softly.

He didn't answer.

Oath-bound.

Again.

Nilsa slid her arm around his waist, fitting herself against his side, steady and warm. "Then show me how."

He swallowed hard. "Hold on to me."

"I am."

"Hold tighter."

Nilsa did—and felt his breath stutter at the closeness.

The chasm breathed cold air up at them.
The roots swayed.
The darkness below deepened like an open mouth.

Nilsa pressed her forehead briefly to Erabor's arm. "If we fall…"

"We won't," he said. "Because you're holding on."

She nodded.

They stepped together onto the living bridge.

The moment Nilsa and Erabor stepped onto the living roots, the bridge reacted.
Not gently.
Not like a trail welcoming travelers.

It **writhed** beneath their feet—shifting, twisting, tightening its braided strands as if tasting their weight, deciding whether to hold them… or reject them.

Nilsa's stomach lurched as the roots dipped three inches with their combined step. Erabor braced her instantly, his arm tightening around her waist, his other hand gripping one of the twisted branches for balance.

"Don't look down," he murmured.

Nilsa looked down.

The crevasse stretched beneath them like a wound carved into the world—too deep to see the bottom, too dark to reflect even the faint silver glow bleeding from the roots that framed the chasm walls.

Wind surged upward, cold enough to sting her eyes. The darkness below… breathed. Slowly. Deeply. Something down there exhaled like a sleeping beast uncurling in its lair.

Nilsa shivered and pressed herself closer to Erabor, clasping his tunic in one fist.

"I told you not to look," he said, voice uneven—not irritated, not mocking—just strained.

"I didn't mean to," she whispered. "The dark pulls at me."

Erabor's gaze flicked downward involuntarily, then he snapped his eyes forward again. "Don't let it. That's how this place works. The chasm wants you to look. Wants you to imagine what's beneath. Want is its first weapon."

Nilsa swallowed. "And its second?"

"Falling."

A nerve in Nilsa's cheek twitched. "Wonderful."

The wind howled again—louder now. The roots swayed beneath them, the movement more pronounced than before. Nilsa's foot slipped and she gasped, nails scraping the rough bark as she tried to steady herself.

Erabor immediately adjusted his stance, shifting his weight to counterbalance hers. He pulled her flush against his side, one arm anchoring her, the other clutching a root strand so tight his knuckles whitened.

"I have you," he murmured. "Breathe. Match me."

Nilsa did—
in,
out,

in,
out—

His chest rose and fell beside her, warm and steady even as the roots shivered beneath them.

Together they took another step.

The bridge lurched violently.

Nilsa yelped as her boots skidded. Erabor grabbed her thigh to steady her, his grip firm, urgent, unhesitating. The contact sent her pulse racing, but the terror overwhelmed any awareness of closeness.

"Slow," he whispered. "Don't fight the sway. Move with it."

Nilsa nodded, heart pounding hard enough to vibrate through her bones.

They stepped again.

And again.

Four feet across.
Six.
Ten.

The bridge tightened with every inch, the roots shifting from pliant to rigid, as if responding to their determination. The light of the tunnel behind them dimmed, swallowed by distance. Ahead, only the faint outline of another cave mouth broke the shadowed cliff face.

"We're halfway," Nilsa breathed.

"Don't say that," Erabor muttered. "Never say that."

She might have laughed if her voice weren't locked in her throat.

The wind hit them again—this time, hard enough to nearly knock them sideways. Nilsa's boot slipped off the root entirely and she screamed as her foot dangled over open void.

Erabor reacted faster than thought.

He seized her waist in both hands and yanked her tight against him, pulling her back onto the roots. His body pressed fully against hers, bracing them both as the bridge bucked beneath the force of the gust.

"Nilsa!" His voice cracked with pure terror.

"I'm okay," she gasped. "I'm okay—Erabor, it's alright—"

"Don't say that either," he said. His voice shook.

Nilsa clung to him, breathing hard, her face pressed against his chest. His heart hammered in uneven, powerful beats beneath her cheek. He numbly stroked the back of her head once—instinctive comfort—before pulling his hand away as if afraid of what it meant.

She pulled back just enough to look at him, brushing a strand of hair from his eyes. "We're getting across. Together. I told you."

His jaw flexed. "You shouldn't have followed me onto this bridge."

"I'm not letting you walk it alone."

He flinched—even now, even amidst danger—as though those words hit him where he was softest.

Before either could say more, the roots groaned beneath them.

A deep, shuddering sound.

Like a belly rumbling.

Erabor went still.

Nilsa held her breath.

Another groan followed—lower, heavier—rising from deep, deep beneath the chasm.

A cold realization slid down Nilsa's spine.

"Something's down there," she whispered.

Erabor's voice barely carried. "Something old."

The dark moved.

Not fast.
Not suddenly.

A slow unfurling.
A ripple.
A shift in the endless black, as if a faint light glimmered far below—then vanished.

Nilsa's throat closed. "Erabor, what is that?"

"I don't know," he said. "And I don't want to."

The roots lurched again—upward this time, as if pulled from below by a sudden tug.

Nilsa screamed.

Erabor gripped her tighter and snarled, "Move! NOW!"

They hurried forward, steps frantic and unsteady as the bridge writhed beneath them. The roots jerked violently—once, twice—like something was thrashing below, disturbing the ancient architecture that kept the chasm bridged.

Nilsa stumbled forward, forcing herself not to look at the shifting dark below, forcing her gaze to lock onto the opposite cave mouth.

Almost there.
Almost—

Erabor suddenly staggered, knees buckling. His shadow spasmed behind him in a violent arc, slamming into the roots with a crack of energy.

"Erabor!" Nilsa grabbed him, her arm around his waist, dragging him upright. "Stay with me—stay—"

His head dropped, breath ragged. "The oath—he's calling—"

Nilsa's pulse spiked. "Ignore it. Focus on me."

"I'm trying."

The bridge twisted.

Nilsa gasped as both of them lost footing. Erabor lunged, grabbing a rising root strand with both hands, muscles straining with the effort. He swung them sideways, pressing Nilsa between his body and the living wood as the bridge dipped dangerously.

Nilsa clutched his tunic with trembling fingers. "We have to jump. We're close enough. The cave lip is right there—"

He looked—saw the distance—then nodded. "On my count."

Nilsa nodded back. "Three?"

"No. One."

She blinked. "Erabor—"

"One!"

He pushed off the root.

They leapt.

Nilsa felt air tear past her ears, the wind a cold scream against her skin. For a heartbeat they hung over the void—weightless, suspended, everything silent except her pounding heart—

Then Erabor shoved her upward, throwing her toward the ledge.

Nilsa caught the stone lip—barely—fingers scraping raw as she clung, kicking desperately.

"Erabor!" she cried.

He hit the stone beside her—but his grip slipped immediately. His fingers clawed at the ledge, his boots skidding on the wet stone, his shadow flaring in chaotic panic as he dangled above the abyss.

Nilsa screamed. "I've got you!"

She grabbed his wrist with both hands.

He jerked violently downward—too heavy, too strong, his weight nearly tearing her from the rock.

"No—no—Nilsa, let go—"

"I am not letting you fall!"

His eyes—dark, ghosted with silver—locked onto hers in horror.

"You'll be pulled with me—"

"Then we fall together!"

A tremor of raw emotion broke across his face.

He didn't deserve her faith.
He'd never had it before.
And he didn't know how to hold it.

But Nilsa did not let go.

He roared in pain—or fear—or both—and kicked hard against the stone. Nilsa hauled upward with everything she had, her arms screaming, her fingers slipping, her back arching with the effort.

Her shoulder nearly popped—

Then he surged up.

She dragged him over the ledge.

They collapsed together on the stone floor just inside the narrow passage, Nilsa sprawled half across his chest, Erabor gripping her waist with shaking hands as though making sure they were both actually, truly alive.

The roots behind them snapped
and fell
into the chasm.

Nilsa pressed her forehead to Erabor's chest, breath coming in gasps.

"We made it," she whispered.

He exhaled, trembling beneath her.

"No," he said hoarsely. "You made it. You pulled us both across."

She lifted her face, brushing her fingers along his jaw. "Together, remember?"

He swallowed hard, eyes dark and unbearably soft. "I won't forget."

Below them, something moved in the darkness—slow, massive, patient.

Waiting.

Erabor pulled Nilsa fully against him, shielding her from the cold wind.

"We need to keep moving," he murmured. "Before whatever that is decides to climb."

Nilsa nodded against him.

But she didn't move yet.

For one moment more, she let herself feel the way his arms wrapped around her—tight, protective, grounding.

A moment stolen from fear.

A moment that shouldn't exist.

A moment she needed.

Then she whispered, "Where now?"

Erabor exhaled slowly, eyes fixed on the narrow, twisting passage ahead—no safer than what they'd just faced, but away from the chasm.

"Now," he said, "we choose the path that should never be walked."

For a while, neither of them moved.

The stone beneath them was cold, slick with moisture, and the ceiling of the narrow passage soared upward into jagged curves like the ribs of some ancient beast. The wind from the chasm behind them continued to breathe its slow, icy rhythm—exhale, inhale, exhale—carrying the scent of something old and hungry from below. Nilsa listened to Erabor's uneven breaths beneath her cheek, her fingers still tangled in his tunic, the memory of nearly losing him replaying again and again in her mind.

His heartbeat hadn't slowed.
Her own hadn't either.

But slowly—very slowly—they pulled themselves upright.

Nilsa settled onto her knees, pushing her hair from her face, her fingers trembling from the strain of hauling him to safety. She looked at Erabor, expecting the usual quiet composure, the contained strength—but what she saw instead was exhaustion carved deep into his features.

He was pale.
Too pale.

The shadows under his eyes were darker. His hands, braced against the stone, still shook faintly. For a brief moment his shadow flickered behind him—out of rhythm with his body—like it was breathing separately from him.

Nilsa reached out and touched his shoulder. "You're not well."

He flinched at the honesty of it but didn't pull away. "I'm... recovering."

"You almost fell into a bottomless chasm."

"You pulled me out."

"I shouldn't have had to."

Erabor looked at her then—really looked—and the rawness in his eyes stilled her heart. "Nilsa… if you hadn't been there, I would have jumped alone. I would have tried to force you back. You shouldn't—"

"Don't finish that sentence," she said sharply. "We're doing this together. I'm not losing you in these tunnels."

A muscle in his jaw tightened. He opened his mouth, closed it again, then exhaled slowly. "Then we need to keep moving."

Nilsa nodded reluctantly. "Which way?"

He looked ahead.

The passage narrowed and stretched into darkness—an unsettling silence hanging heavy in the air. No wind. No drip of water. No glow of moss. Just a straight, suffocating tunnel swallowed by shadow.

"The safe path is to turn back into Morrivan's northern ridge," Erabor murmured. "We could try to reenter the forest's upper level. The wards would still be damaged, but there are pockets of refuge. Old hollows. Survivor dens."

Nilsa frowned. "But that keeps us too close to him."

"Yes."

"Then we need the other path."

Erabor's breath misted in the cold air. His eyes flickered with conflict. "The forbidden road."

Nilsa's pulse quickened. "What is it?"

He didn't answer immediately. He stood, steadier now but still tense with the lingering aftershock of the oath pulling on him.

Nilsa rose with him, brushing the dust and bark from her clothes.

Erabor stepped forward until he stood at the mouth of the narrowing passage. His silhouette was slim, tall, framed by the faint glow from the bridge behind them. He lifted his hand and let it hover an inch from the entrance.

The air beyond shimmered slightly.
Barely visible unless Nilsa squinted.
Like a thin veil of mist clinging to the stone.

Nilsa stepped closer. "What is that?"

"A wardline," he said quietly. "Old. Damaged. But still… aware."

"Will it stop us?"

"No."
A soft hesitation.
"Yes. But not physically."

Nilsa's brow furrowed. "Erabor, you're not making sense."

He drew a slow breath. "This passage is one of Morrivan's forbidden routes. A severed corridor that once led to the old Shadowgate—the place where Morrivan touched another kingdom before the Sundering."

Her heart squeezed. "Which kingdom?"

He hesitated again.

Nilsa's breath caught. "Erabor. Which one?"

He closed his eyes.
She saw agony tighten his features.
Then he whispered, "Eidonrael."

Nilsa froze.

The air seemed to still.
The cold deepened.
Her heartbeat thudded once—twice—slow and thunderous in her ears.

"Eidonrael," she repeated. "The thirteenth kingdom."

He nodded once.

Nilsa stepped back a single pace, her fingers trembling. "And you didn't tell me—"

"I couldn't," he said, voice raw. "The oath—"

"I know," she cut in. She reached up and touched the medallion that now hung around her neck—the silver piece with the thirteenth carving faint etched into its surface. It felt heavier suddenly, as if hearing the name of its origin.

Nilsa swallowed hard. "Is this path dangerous?"

"Yes," he breathed. "More than the chasm. More than the hunter. This road was abandoned for a reason. Morrivan severed it so nothing from the Shadowgate could ever reach the heartwood again."

"What kind of things?"

Erabor looked at her with an expression she'd never seen on him before.

Pure fear.

"Things that remember Eidonrael," he whispered. "Things that kept its secrets. Things that survived its fall."

A shiver crawled down Nilsa's spine. "And we're going to walk toward them."

Erabor exhaled slowly. "It is the only path he will not follow."

Nilsa blinked. "The hunter won't go there?"

"No." His voice hardened. "He fears it."

"Why?"

He shook his head. "I can't say. But I know this—if he fears what lies ahead more than losing us, that means it's the only place we might gain time. Answers. A chance."

Nilsa looked at the narrow passage, at the faint shimmer of the wardline.
Her heart pounded.
Her fingertips tingled.
Something deep in her bones stirred—something old, something waiting.

A whisper brushed the back of her mind.
Not a word.
A pull.

"Erabor," she said softly, "I think that passage wants me."

His breath hitched.

Nilsa pressed her hand to her chest. "I feel it. Like… like something calling. Faint but steady."

He stepped toward her, lifting a trembling hand to brush a stray curl from her cheek. His touch was gentle—careful—like he feared breaking her. "It's not calling you to safety. It's calling you to truth. That is always more dangerous."

Nilsa lifted her chin. "Then we walk it."

Erabor's throat worked. "Nilsa…"

"You said we need answers," she said. "The Rootheart told me the past isn't gentle. If this path leads closer to Eidonrael, then it leads closer to answers."

He exhaled shakily. "I should argue. I should stop you."

"Can you?"

His silence said everything.

Nilsa stepped forward and held out her hand. "Walk with me."

His fingers closed around hers—slow, reluctant, reverent. Like he knew this was a crossroads he could never undo.

The wardline ahead shimmered brighter, reacting to their nearness.

Nilsa took a breath and whispered, "On three?"

Erabor shook his head, voice low and tense. "No. On one."

Despite everything—fear, exhaustion, the chasm they had almost fallen into—she smiled faintly. "Just like the jump."

He managed a small, pained smile back. "Yes. Exactly like the jump."

She tightened her grip.

"Then let's jump again," she said.

And before she could lose her courage, before he could lose his resolve—

She stepped with him through the wardline.

The world changed.

Instantly.

Violently.

Completely.

The moment Nilsa and Erabor crossed the wardline, the ground lurched beneath their feet as if the earth had inhaled sharply. The air thickened, congealing around them like cold sap, pulling at their skin and clothes with a slow, sticky drag. Nilsa felt her heartbeat stutter as an invisible pressure pressed against her chest—heavy, insistent, ancient.

She gasped for breath.

Erabor's grip on her hand tightened instantly, anchoring her against the sudden shift. He pulled her closer, body angled to shield her from a threat they could not yet see. His voice reached her through the distortion, roughened with both strain and instinctive protectiveness.

"Stay with me. Don't let go."

He didn't need to say it twice. Nilsa clung to him, fingers gripping his tunic, the medallion at her throat burning faintly against her skin.

The corridor around them warped.

The stone walls, moments ago narrow and cold, began to stretch upward—lengthening, thinning—twisting into spirals of pale stone threaded with veins of silvery-black mineral. The passage widened, then constricted suddenly, then widened again in rhythmic pulses, as if breathing.

Nilsa swallowed hard, dizzy as her perception shifted with every movement of the walls. "This… this feels alive."

"It is," Erabor murmured. "These corridors were carved with magic older than Morrivan. They don't react to footsteps. They react to lineage."

Nilsa's pulse fluttered. "Mine?"

His jaw tightened. "Yes."

The corridor twisted again—this time not upward, but inward, like two spiraling pathways suddenly converging. Light bled from cracks in the ceiling—thin, ghostly beams that flickered like candleflames in a storm. The illumination was weak, but it painted the space in hues of silver and smoke, giving everything a dreamlike unreality.

Or a nightmare's clarity.

Nilsa kept her eyes forward, refusing to let the shifting walls disorient her. "This is Eidonrael's old passage, isn't it?"

Erabor nodded once, jaw clenched. "One of them."

"And we're inside it."

"Yes."

Nilsa tried to steady her breath, but the air fought her—thick and heavy, flavored with something metallic and cold. It tasted like storm-soaked iron and the echo of lightning. A scent that didn't belong in Morrivan.

"Why does it feel like this?" she whispered.

"Because Eidonrael never died cleanly," Erabor said. "The kingdom's fall wasn't a collapse—it was a tearing. A ripping from the world. Its magic didn't fade. It bled."

A chill crawled down Nilsa's spine. "And we're walking through the place where it bled out."

"Yes."

The corridor shuddered beneath their feet.

This time the tremor wasn't the faint pulse of living roots—it was a deep, thrumming vibration that rolled through the stone like a heartbeat. Nilsa staggered, nearly falling, but Erabor pulled her close again, his arm tight around her waist.

His whisper brushed her ear. "Don't react to the sound. Don't mirror the rhythm."

Nilsa blinked. "Why not?"

"The corridor listens. If you match its pulse… it might think you're answering."

Nilsa swallowed hard. "And that would be bad?"

He exhaled. "Very."

They continued forward, Nilsa now hyper-aware of every sound, every breath, every echo of her heartbeat. She forced her lungs to move on her own rhythm—steady, quiet, calm—not the throbbing pulse thrumming beneath the floor.

But then the corridor narrowed again.

Not just visually.

It **pressed** inward.

The walls leaned toward them, shadows deepening, the silver veins in the stone glowing faintly like blood pulsing beneath skin. Nilsa felt pressure at her temples—subtle at first, then tightening, then compressing into a painful band across her skull.

She winced. "Erabor…"

He didn't answer.

She snapped her head toward him—and fear struck through her.

His eyes had gone fully black.

Not with shadow magic.

Not with feral instinct.

Not with danger.

But with **recognition**.

"Erabor?" she whispered.

No response.

Not even a blink.

His body went rigid beside her, breath freezing in his chest. His shadow stretched behind him, not violently—slowly, like ink spreading across parchment.

Nilsa's heart pounded. "Erabor, look at me."

Nothing.

His head tilted slightly—as if listening to something she couldn't hear.

His lips parted.

A whisper crawled out—barely audible. "It knows."

Nilsa's stomach lurched. "What knows?"

He didn't answer.

Instead, his gaze—those empty, fathomless, black eyes—drifted past her, following something moving in the shadows of the corridor ahead.

Nilsa turned slowly.

A long, thin crack appeared in the far wall—splitting downward from ceiling to floor with a soft, crystalline **chime**.

Something inside the crack glowed.

Not brightly.
Not warmly.
A faint, cold shimmer—like moonlight reflecting off a blade.

Nilsa's breath hitched. "What is that?"

Erabor exhaled a single, trembling word.
A word that made the medallion at her throat burn hot against her skin.

"A memory."

The crack widened.

The silver light spilled across the corridor floor—not in beams or patterns, but in delicate, drifting particles, like dust caught in a sunbeam. They floated outward, settling on the stone like frost.

Nilsa stared in awe. "It's beautiful."

Erabor's hand tightened painfully around hers. "Don't trust the beauty."

"It's… a vision, isn't it?"

"Not a vision." His voice trembled. "A remnant."

The floating particles thickened—shimmering like silver ash—swirling together until they formed the faint outline of a doorway.

Not a real one.
Not yet.
But almost.

Nilsa's pulse slowed.

Her breath steadied.

A whisper brushed her mind—so faint she thought she imagined it.

Nilsa.

She blinked sharply. "Did you hear that?"

Erabor's voice rasped. "Don't answer it."

The whisper came again.

Nilsa.

Closer.

More urgent.

More familiar.

She stepped back. "Erabor… that voice… I've heard it before."

"Nilsa, look at me," he said, gripping her shoulders. "Don't listen. That voice isn't real. It isn't someone you know. It's the corridor. It's the bleed. It's Eidonrael's death echoing."

Nilsa's throat tightened. "But it sounded like—"

"All echoes sound like someone," Erabor said. "It's how the corridor pulls you deeper."

She stared at him, pulse racing. "Why didn't Morrivan destroy this place entirely? Why leave any of it standing?"

He swallowed hard. "Because some memories cannot be destroyed. They only hide."

The silver particles thickened further, swirling into a shape—a silhouette.

Tall.
Slender.
Cloaked.

Nilsa froze.

"Who is that?" she whispered.

Erabor didn't answer.

His breath hitched.

His shadow recoiled behind him.

Nilsa stared at the shimmering figure as its outline sharpened—and a strange pull tightened in her chest, the same sensation she'd felt when she first held the medallion.

The silhouette lifted its head.

Nilsa felt her pulse stop.

A third whisper—gentle, broken, breathless—slid across her mind.

Come home.

Nilsa staggered backward into Erabor, her breath crushed from her lungs.

"Erabor… Erabor, it called me—"

His arms wrapped around her immediately—one around her waist, the other gripping the back of her neck as though physically shielding her from the unseen pull.

"I know," he whispered against her hair. "I know. That's why we have to move. Now."

"But—"

"No." His voice shook with something deeper than fear. "Nilsa, that is not someone calling you home. That is the echo of a kingdom that died screaming. And if you answer it—if you even *listen* too long—it will take you where you can't return."

Nilsa swallowed hard, feeling his heartbeat thundering against her back.

"But it knows my name."

"I know." He wrapped her tighter. "And that's the most dangerous part."

The silhouette shifted again—lifting a hand toward them.

Silver particles drifted off its form like pieces of moonlight burning away.

The corridor vibrated.

The walls pulsed.

The medallion at Nilsa's throat turned ice-cold.

Erabor didn't hesitate.

He grabbed her hand, pulled her forward, and whispered with a voice strained by both fear and a loyalty so fierce it hurt:

"Run. Don't look back."

They ran.

Together.

Into the corridor that led deeper still—
toward the truth Morrivan died to hide.

CHAPTER TWENTY-NINE

The Kingdom That Calls Through Ruin

Nilsa wasn't sure how long they ran.

The corridor twisted into strange, spiraling shapes that made every step disorienting, as though the floor were tilting beneath them and the walls were shifting around their bodies. The silver silhouette's whisper had faded behind them, but the echo of it still clung to Nilsa's spine like the last cold breath of a dying realm.

Her lungs burned. Her hair clung to her cheeks in damp strands. The medallion at her throat throbbed in sharp pulses that didn't match her heartbeat.

Erabor pulled her through another sharp bend in the corridor. The air changed—growing colder, thinner, tasting faintly of night and pine resin. Nilsa stumbled once, nearly falling, but Erabor's grip tightened around her hand, steadying her instantly.

"How much farther?" she whispered between breaths.

"Not far," he said, though his voice was strained. "The corridor bends toward the northern rim. Morrivan ends soon."

"Ends?" Nilsa sucked in a breath. "What do you mean ends?"

"You'll see."

He didn't elaborate, and she didn't push him. His shadow was flickering again—panting in sharp stutters beneath him like an exhausted creature fighting a leash. Whatever the Eidonrael echo did to him… it hadn't fully released him.

Nilsa moved closer, pressing her shoulder to his. "Are you… alright?"

He didn't answer at first. His breath shook. Then—

"No."

Nilsa's heart tightened. "Erabor—"

"I can hear him," he whispered. "The hunter. Closer than before."

Her stomach dropped. "Here? In this corridor?"

"No." His voice sharpened with fear. "He's above. Breaking through the northern canopy. Morrivan's wards are nearly gone."

Nilsa swallowed a rising wave of panic. "Then we need to reach the exit before he does."

"We will." Erabor squeezed her hand. "We have to."

They ran again.

The corridor widened, then narrowed, then split into two twisting forks wreathed in shimmering dust. Erabor yanked Nilsa left without hesitation, trusting something she couldn't see—instinct, knowledge, or memory.

The air grew warmer.

Lighter.

More real.

Nilsa's pulse brightened with hope. "We're close?"

"Yes."

A faint glow appeared ahead—cool and white, spilling down from a jagged opening in the ceiling. The corridor near it trembled as if tugged by wind. Nilsa felt the promise of open air sweep toward them.

But she also felt something else.

A new rhythm.

A pulse.

A low, heavy thud that vibrated the walls.

"Erabor…" Nilsa slowed. "What is that sound?"

He didn't slow.

"That," he said darkly, "is the forest screaming."

The sound deepened—like a tree trunk cracking under enormous weight.

Then a second crack.
Then a roar—raw, ancient, not belonging to anything human.

Erabor grabbed Nilsa's waist and shoved her forward. "Go. Don't stop."

Nilsa stumbled up a slope of broken stone and twisted vines, her hand grazing the cool mineral surface as she climbed toward the faint white glow of daylight. The earth trembled beneath her palms.

"Erabor—what's happening?"

"The hunter is ripping the boundary open."

Nilsa's breath caught. "I thought he wouldn't follow us onto this path."

"He won't." Erabor jumped the last few feet, landing beside her with unsettling grace. "But he can break Morrivan to find where it ends."

"And we're heading straight for that break?"

He nodded once. "Yes."

Nilsa swallowed against the rising panic. "And we have no other way out."

"No."

He offered his hand.

Nilsa slid hers into it, fingers locking tightly with his, grounding both of them.

The corridor's ceiling opened overhead, jagged like a wound, revealing fractured beams of cold daylight. The wind rushed through the gap, carrying the scent of pine, frost, and smoke—smoke from ancient trees burning under magical strain.

Nilsa climbed through, helped by Erabor's steady pull, until she reached the surface.

The moment her boots touched open earth, she straightened and froze.

They stood at the northern edge of Morrivan—
or what remained of it.

The forest beyond the chasm was no longer lush green or shimmering silver. Entire portions of the upper canopy had collapsed. Enormous trees lay broken, their trunks split open like ruptured ribs. Moss that once glowed was now darkened to ash-gray. Thick smoke drifted from cracks in the forest floor as if the earth itself were exhaling its dying breath.

Above them, the sky churned with swirling black clouds—the same unnatural storms Nilsa had seen over Drakhalen and Bryndara in old travel tomes. Magic storms. An omen of a curse fully awakened.

Nilsa's throat tightened. "Morrivan…"

Erabor stepped beside her, his voice quiet and hollow. "This is what it looks like when a kingdom's wards fail."

Nilsa hugged her arms around herself. "We did this."

"No." He shook his head sharply. "He did this. And you warned them in time. The Oracle died for that warning to spread."

Nilsa's chest ached. "And will the kingdom survive? Can anything be saved?"

Erabor didn't answer.

Nilsa turned to him sharply. "Erabor?"

His silence said everything.

The kingdom of shadows and truth—Morrivan, the sanctuary for the hunted—would not rise from this breaking.

Not the way it once was.

Nilsa stared out across the wounded landscape, swallowing the sting of grief. The trees were still trembling, some bending sharply before righting themselves. Others groaned under pressure from invisible forces.

"How do we get out?" she asked softly.

Erabor lifted his hand and pointed toward a slanted ridge rising at the forest's far end—steep, treacherous, still intact.

"That path," he said. "It leads to the ridgeline between Morrivan and Havrelin."

"Havrelin..." Nilsa whispered.

The kingdom where horses sicken before journeys.
The kingdom closest to Ashova.
The kingdom that would test them in new ways.

She nodded once, jaw tightening. "We go to Havrelin."

But Erabor didn't nod.

His eyes were fixed on the sky—warily, urgently—tracking something Nilsa couldn't yet see.

"Erabor?" she whispered.

He took a slow step toward her, body tensing. "Nilsa… don't move."

The wind shifted.
The tree line shuddered.
Something massive landed in the distance with a force that rattled the ground beneath their feet.

Nilsa's breath seized.

Erabor stepped in front of her, his body a wall of heat and strength and trembling fury. "He found us."

"No," Nilsa whispered. "No, not now—"

Erabor grabbed her hand. "Run."

Nilsa looked up—

And saw a shadow crest the burning tree line.

Tall.
Humanoid.
Wrong.

A figure of roiling darkness, taller than any man, draped in smoky tendrils that writhed like living serpents.

The hunter.

Not fully formed—
but formed enough.

He lifted his head, and the air in Nilsa's lungs froze solid.

Erabor snapped, "RUN!"

Nilsa didn't question him this time.

She ran, her heart slamming against her ribs, Erabor's hand locked around hers as the final chapter of Morrivan collapsed behind them—

and the hunter stepped into the dying forest.

Nilsa had never run like this.

Not even during the ambush in the whispering glade.
Not across the writhing bridge.
Not through the collapsing Rootheart.

This was different—this was pure, primal survival, driven by the knowledge that the thing behind them was not chasing them out of hunger, or instinct, or vengeance…

…but purpose.

The forest floor shook beneath her boots as she sprinted alongside Erabor, branches snapping like bones, fallen leaves exploding upward in icy gusts. Smoke wafted through the air in thin spirals, carrying the scent of burning moss and splintered bark. Wind keened between the skeletal trunks as if the forest were screaming a warning too late.

Erabor's grip on her hand was iron, his other arm angled protectively across her back as though shielding her from arrows that hadn't yet been fired.

"Don't trip," he murmured harshly.
He wasn't warning—he was pleading.

Nilsa forced her legs to move faster, though each step felt heavier, as if the earth were dragging at her ankles. "I'm not—"

A tremor split the ground behind them before she could finish.

Nilsa stumbled and looked back—

—and her blood went cold.

The hunter stepped into full view.

He was taller than any living man by two heads at least—broad-shouldered, lank-limbed, his form wrapped in roiling, oily shadow. His "cloak" writhed as though filled with snakes. His face—if it could be called that—was a mask of deep, malformed darkness, without features except for two narrow slits of pale, unnatural light.

Eyes, Nilsa realized with a shudder.
Eyes that held no soul.
Only hunger.

A hunger that wasn't for flesh.
A hunger for **lineage**.

The hunter's head tilted, listening to the heartbeat of the air.

Then he moved.

Not with a run.
Not with a walk.

He simply—
shifted.

One moment he stood fifty yards back.
The next he flickered forward, suddenly twenty yards away.

Nilsa's breath hitched. "Erabor—he's—"

"I know," he snapped. "Don't look at him. Look at the ground. Don't fall."

Nilsa tore her gaze away just as a black tendril shot toward them, slicing through a tree trunk like butter. The tree toppled, crashing to the earth behind them. Bark and splinters rained down.

Erabor yanked her aside just before another tendril struck the ground where she'd been standing.

"Keep moving!" he growled.

They wove between trees—dead ones, dying ones, ones shuddering as if pulled by invisible strings. The sky above lashed with lightning, illuminating the hunter's silhouette in flashes that made him appear to flicker in and out of existence.

Nilsa gasped for breath. "Where are we going—?"

"The ridge!" Erabor yelled. "If we reach the ridge, he can't—"

A crack like snapping bone boomed across the forest.

Erabor swore under his breath. "He's cutting us off."

Nilsa looked up.

One of the massive ancient trees—the thousand-year guardians of Morrivan—began to fall. Slowly at first, then faster, crashing down across their path with a horrifying groan. Roots ripped from the soil, soil exploded upward in a shower, and the trunk thundered toward them like a collapsing tower.

Erabor grabbed Nilsa around the waist and **threw** them both sideways, rolling beneath the falling trunk a split second before it smashed into the ground with earth-shaking force.

Nilsa's ears rang. Dust choked the air. Something sharp grazed her cheek.

Erabor was half on top of her, shielding her with his body, breath ragged.
"Are you hurt?"

"No," she whispered, dizzy. "Are you?"

"No."

She didn't believe him—but there was no time to argue.

The hunter appeared on the other side of the fallen tree, turning its faceless gaze down at the trunk as if considering whether to climb or simply pass through it.

Then it slid forward again, gliding around the obstacle like smoke.

Nilsa's heart lurched. "He's faster."

"Yes."

"And closer."

"Yes."

"Erabor—"

"I know!"

He pulled her to her feet and scrambled up the bark of the fallen tree, dragging her with him. They ran across its length, leaping down the other side. Nilsa's boots skidded on broken wood but Erabor steadied her again, refusing to let her fall.

The forest ahead began to thin.
The trees grew farther apart.
The ground tilted upward.

"The ridge!" Nilsa gasped.

"Yes!"

They pushed harder.

The hunter followed.

The shadows around him lengthened unnaturally, reaching across roots and stones like searching fingers. Each time they grazed bark, that bark blackened. Each time they brushed the forest floor, moss withered in a spreading circle.

He wasn't simply chasing them.
He was **unmaking** Morrivan.

Nilsa choked on rising terror. "Why does he want me?"

Erabor gritted his teeth. "Because of what you are."

Her heart stuttered. "And what am I?"

He didn't answer.

Not because he refused.
Because he *couldn't*.

Nilsa's lungs burned. Her legs ached. Her shoulders screamed from the strain of being pulled through every twist of the broken forest.

But she kept running.

Because in the distance, where the tree line broke, a faint glow of daylight spilled across a steep slope. Beyond that—barely visible—rose the first ridgeline stones. The border between kingdoms.

Freedom.

Safety.

Answers.

All of it within reach—

The ground suddenly bucked.

A crater exploded open behind them, showering them with dirt as the hunter slammed a tendril into the earth, pulling himself forward with horrific ease.

He was **ten paces away**.

Too close.

Nilsa cried out, stumbling. "Erabor—"

"I know!" His arm locked around her waist again. "Almost—don't stop—don't look—"

"Erabor!" she screamed as the hunter lashed a tendril straight toward her spine.

Erabor spun without thinking, shoving her forward and twisting his body to meet the attack.

The tendril struck his back—

—then vanished.

Nilsa gasped and froze. "What—?"

Erabor's back heaved—shoulders trembling violently—as if something had been deflected.

Or stopped.

Or absorbed.

Slowly, he turned his head toward her, breath shaking, eyes bright with something raw and terrified and ancient.

Nilsa whispered, "How did you—"

He cut her off with a single word.

"Run."

Nilsa obeyed.

They tore up the slope, boots slipping on loose stone, lungs burning. The ridge rose before them like a jagged crown of weathered rock. Beyond it, the horizon stretched into unknown lands—a thin strip of pale gold sky cutting through the ruins of Morrivan.

Nilsa reached the first ridge stone.

Erabor reached her side.

They tumbled over the crest together—

Just as the hunter slammed into the ridge behind them with enough force to split the earth.

Nilsa twisted around.

And saw it.

The hunter could not cross the ridge.

He clawed at the stone, shadows contorting, tendrils flailing in jagged pulses. His faceless head turned toward Nilsa with burning, hungry focus.

He couldn't enter.

But he wasn't leaving.

Nilsa stood trembling at the ridge's edge as the ground beneath the hunter cracked, shadows spilling from the wounds like black flame.

He raised an arm.

A tendril burst across the air—
but stopped just short of the ridge stone.

As if frozen mid-strike.

Nilsa's breath caught.

The hunter tilted his head.

Slowly.

Horribly slowly.

Then he whispered—not into the air, but directly into Nilsa's mind.

Thirteenth star…

Nilsa's blood turned to ice.

I see you.

Her knees buckled.

Erabor caught her instantly, pulling her back from the ridge, shielding her with his body.

The hunter lowered his head, shadows writhing around him like a rising storm.

You cannot run forever.

A crack split the ridge stone beneath his hand.

He smiled.

Nilsa knew it was a smile.

Then—

He vanished.

Not in smoke.

Not in wind.

He simply ceased to be.

Nilsa collapsed against Erabor's chest, shaking violently.

He held her tightly, whispering,

"It's alright. He can't cross. He can't follow us here."

But Nilsa trembled, eyes fixed on the stone the hunter cracked with a single touch.

"Erabor," she whispered, "if he breaks the ridge…"

Erabor swallowed hard.

His silence was answer enough.

For several long moments after the hunter vanished, the world fell strangely silent.

Not safe.
Not calm.
Just silent.

The kind of silence that follows a scream.

Nilsa remained pressed against Erabor's chest, her fingers curled instinctively into the fabric of his tunic as if anchoring herself was the only way to keep from shaking apart. His breath rumbled unevenly beneath her cheek—too fast, too sharp—his muscles still taut with the strain of protecting her.

Wind swept over the ridge, lifting loose strands of Nilsa's hair and carrying the scent of burnt forest behind them and open world ahead.

Only when her lungs finally remembered how to work did she whisper, "He knew my name."

Erabor's hand tightened gently against her back. Not possessive. Not fearful of her running.
Reassuring.
Human.

"He shouldn't have," he said softly.

Nilsa lifted her head to look at him—really look. His face was pale, a sheen of sweat along his brow, and his eyes held a brightness that wasn't all shadow, wasn't all magic. Fear lived there. Not for himself.

For her.

"What does that mean?" she asked. "Why can he speak to me? Why does he want me?"

His throat worked. "Nilsa…"

"I know you can't tell me everything," she said, her voice steadier than she felt. "But you can tell me this: does he want to kill me?"

"No," Erabor said immediately.

Nilsa's breath hitched. "Then what does he want?"

Erabor looked away—toward the ruined forest they'd fled, toward the crack in the ridge stone, toward the path the hunter could not cross but had nearly broken.

"Not death," he whispered. "He wants to bring you back."

"Back where?"

Erabor flinched as if burned by the question.

Nilsa's heart hammered against her ribs. "To Eidonrael."

He closed his eyes.

"Erabor," she breathed.

"I can't," he choked. "The oath—"

"I know," she said, pressing her forehead to his. "I know."

They stood like that for a moment—foreheads touching, breaths mingling, bodies trembling with the echo of the chase and the weight of the unspoken truth between them.

Then Nilsa pulled back slowly, her fingers brushing down the line of his jaw. "He said I cannot run forever."

Erabor opened his eyes, and for the first time she saw the exhaustion he'd been hiding.
Not the physical exhaustion.
The cost.

"You can," he said. "You will. For as long as it takes to find the answers. And I will keep you ahead of him."

Nilsa swallowed. "Even if it kills you?"

"Yes."

The answer came too fast.
Too raw.

Nilsa's breath caught. "Don't say that."

"It's true."

"You're not allowed to die for me."

"I already decided I would."

She stared at him, stunned by the quiet ferocity in his voice—by the way he said it not like a vow made in crisis, but a truth that had lived in him long before today.

"Erabor…" she whispered.

He looked away first.

They walked farther down the ridge, leaving the cracked stone behind and climbing toward the crest where the view widened. As they ascended, the world shifted. The air grew cooler, more open. The smell of burning forest faded into a distant ghost, replaced by the crisp scent of untouched soil and wind-swept grass.

When they reached the highest point, Nilsa drew in a sharp breath.

The world stretched before them.

Rolling foothills.
A patchwork of meadows and outcroppings.
Lonely roads snaking between sparse clusters of trees.
A misty horizon painted in soft shades of amber and pale blue.

And far, far off—glinting faintly in the distance like a silver thread woven between hills—lay the borders of **Havrelin**.

Nilsa stood in awe, heart battered from fear but softening at the beauty. "It's... peaceful."

"It won't be," Erabor said quietly. "Havrelin has its own curse. One that doesn't hide in shadows. It shows its teeth early."

Nilsa turned to him. "Will it attack us?"

"The curse affects movement. Travel. Horses. Journeys planned or taken. It tries to stop those who cross its borders with purpose."

Nilsa nodded. "Then we'll do what we've done since Orlanthia."

"What's that?"

She reached for his hand again. "We will not stop moving."

His fingers laced with hers unconsciously.

And for a few breaths, they simply stood together on the ridge with the wind curling around them—two battered souls pushed onward by broken kingdoms and ancient hunger.

But as they descended the ridge toward the border path, Nilsa noticed something unsettling.

Erabor was limping.

And not his normal exhaustion limp.

This one was wrong—tight, controlled, as though he were hiding it from her. She slowed her pace until she was beside him, brushing her shoulder against his gently.

"You're injured."

"No."

"You are."

He didn't respond.

Nilsa stopped moving entirely.

"Erabor."

He froze too—shoulders tense, hands curled slightly, jaw clenched.

She stepped in front of him, lifting her hand to his chest again. "What did the hunter do to you?"

Erabor closed his eyes.

"Nothing."

"Erabor—"

"Nothing I can't endure."

"Then why didn't the tendril hit you?"

He opened his eyes.

And she saw it.

The truth.

The fear.

The secret.

"Because," he whispered, "he cannot harm me."

Nilsa's breath caught. "What?"

He looked past her, gaze hollowed by centuries of unspoken truth.

"He cannot harm me," Erabor repeated quietly. "But he can hurt you through me."

Nilsa felt the earth shift beneath her.

"Why can't he hurt you?" she asked.

Erabor swallowed.

His voice broke.

"Because he made me."

Nilsa's heart stopped.

"Erabor…"

He shook his head. "Don't ask me more. Not yet. The oath—"

Nilsa reached for him, cupping his face between her hands. "Erabor, look at me."

He did.

And in his dark eyes, she saw it—

not evil,
not corruption,
not the hunter's shadow—

but agony.

Agony of someone who had lived in chains too long.

Agony of someone terrified to lose the one person he wasn't supposed to care for.

Nilsa whispered, "You are not him."

His breath shuddered. "I know."

"You are not his."

He closed his eyes. "I try not to be."

"You are not defined by him."

He flinched. "But he defined what I am."

Nilsa's voice softened, trembling. "Then let me redefine it."

His eyes opened—slowly, painfully, as though he'd never thought he deserved such a thing.

Nilsa brushed her thumb over his cheek. "Come with me into Havrelin. Whatever truth waits for us—you won't face it alone."

His answer was a broken exhale.

They stood there for a heartbeat.
Then another.
Then another.

Until the wind shifted.

Carrying a new scent.

Not Morrivan's dying moss.
Not smoke.
Not shadow.

But something sharp, bitter, metallic.

The scent of a curse awakening.

Erabor tensed. "Havrelin knows we're approaching."

Nilsa exhaled. "Then we keep walking."

Erabor nodded once, stepping beside her as they descended the last stretch of ridge.

But just before they crossed the threshold into the next land, Nilsa glanced over her shoulder.

The ridge stone cracked by the hunter emitted a thin, spidering fissure of shadow—
barely visible,
but spreading.

Nilsa whispered, "He's breaking through."

Erabor's breath shook. "Not yet. But soon."

And together—
holding each other up,
broken but unbowed—
they stepped into **Havrelin**.

They crossed the ridge into Havrelin as the wind shifted—changing direction so abruptly it felt as if the kingdom itself inhaled them.

The air here was different.
Thinner.
Sharper.
Carrying the faint smell of iron and wilted grass.

Nilsa's boots hit Havrelin's soil with a soft crunch. The ground felt almost hollow beneath her feet—like something important had been dug up long ago and never filled in properly. A faint tension coiled in the air around them, a tight, buzzing stillness that made the tiny hairs on her arms rise.

The ridge behind them groaned.
A low, ominous sound.
Not breaking yet.
But cracking just a little deeper.

Nilsa shivered.

Erabor placed a steadying hand on her back, guiding her forward. "Don't look behind," he murmured. "Not now."

Nilsa nodded, tearing her gaze away from Morrivan's broken edge and focusing on the new landscape before her.

Havrelin stretched out in rolling, wind-carved hills—some bare, some covered in harsh, low brush, others in wild, struggling grasses that bent under a restless breeze. Weathered stone spires rose from the earth like the bones of ancient titans, jutting crookedly toward the sky. In the valley below, a lonely road wound like a pale scar through empty, undulating land.

No birds.
No distant voices.
No rustle of forest creatures.

Just wind.
And earth.
And the quiet, suffocating sense that something here was wrong.

Nilsa swallowed hard. "It feels… empty."

Erabor shook his head. "Not empty. Waiting."

Nilsa's pulse quickened. "For what?"

He didn't answer. He stepped in front of her instead, scanning the horizon with narrowed eyes, posture tense, shadow low against the ground. The effort of holding himself together after the hunter encounter showed in every movement—every careful breath, every tightening of his jaw.

Nilsa reached for his hand without thinking.
He took it instantly without hesitation.

For a heartbeat they simply stood, joined by hands, facing Havrelin together.

"Which way?" Nilsa asked softly.

Erabor pointed toward the distant valley. "We follow that road until we reach the first stone arch. Havrelin's heartland lies beyond it."

Nilsa nodded and began walking—but the moment her boot pressed deeper into Havrelin's soil, something shifted in the air.

A heavy, sudden weight settled over her shoulders.

She staggered.

"N—"
She couldn't finish the word.

Her legs buckled.
Her breath stuttered.
Her vision blurred around the edges.

Erabor caught her before she hit the ground. "Nilsa!"

She clung to him, her fingers curling desperately into his sleeve as the world warped around her. The sky dimmed, the wind thickened, and the air grew dense—pressing against her lungs like invisible hands.

"Erabor—" she choked, "I can't—"

"Havrelin's curse," he said sharply. "It senses your intention. It's trying to stop you."

Nilsa gasped. "My… what?"

"Your purpose," Erabor whispered. "The curse weakens those who enter with the intention to change their fate, to challenge destiny, to unravel truths."

Nilsa tried to breathe, but the curse pressed harder, crushing her chest, bending her knees.

"I can't—"

Her voice broke on a tremor of pain.

"Erabor—I can't breathe—"

He wrapped his arms fully around her, lifting her half off the ground in a protective embrace. "Listen to me. Stay with me. Fight it. This is just the threshold. It cannot break you."

Nilsa pressed her forehead to his shoulder, her breath coming in thin, ragged gasps. "How... do I fight something I can't see?"

Erabor lowered his lips to her ear, voice trembling, desperate. "Look at me."

She forced her eyes open—and met his.

Dark.
Burning.
Terrified.

And fiercely loyal.

"Breathe with me," he whispered, chest rising against hers. "Match me. Let me anchor you."

She did.

Slowly.

Painfully.

Once.
Twice.
Again.

The pressure eased just enough that she could gasp for air. Erabor kept her pressed against him, one hand gripping the back of her neck, the other firm around her waist.

He didn't hide his shaking.
He didn't hide his fear.
He didn't hide anything.

"Good," he whispered. "Nilsa… good…"

Her fingers curled into his tunic, knuckles white. "Does Havrelin always do this?"

"Only to those who are destined to change something," he murmured. "Its curse feels purpose like a threat."

Nilsa swallowed. "And we are… threats?"

He brushed his cheek against her hair—an unconscious gesture, full of instinct and longing. "You are."

She shuddered, gripping him tighter.

But the curse wasn't done.

A sudden chill rippled across her spine—sharp as a blade.

The air behind them warped.

Nilsa gasped and twisted her head back—

—and saw a thin crack of shadow spreading at the top of the ridge stone.

Not wide.
Not deep.
But spreading.

Slow.
Patient.
Inevitable.

Nilsa's mouth went dry. "Erabor…"

He followed her gaze—and his breath stuttered.

The ridge stone cracked again—
a faint, hairline fracture tracing a jagged path downward.

"He's breaking through," Nilsa whispered.

"Not yet," Erabor said—too fast.

Nilsa turned her face toward him. "Erabor, I saw it. He's breaking the boundary. He'll follow us."

"Not now," Erabor insisted, but his voice trembled. "He needs more time. Hours, at least—maybe longer—"

Nilsa stared at him, pulse hammering. "You don't believe that."

The fear in his eyes confirmed it.

Nilsa trembled in his arms. "Then we have to run."

"Yes," Erabor whispered. "But not blindly. Havrelin's curse won't let you sprint across its land without breaking you." He cupped her face gently, reverently, forcing her to meet his gaze. "We move slowly. Carefully. Together."

Nilsa nodded through shaking breath. "Okay."

He lowered his forehead to hers, grounding them both. "I won't lose you. I swear it."

The vow pressed warm against her skin—even though his voice trembled.

For a moment, Nilsa felt anchored in him.
Steady.
Held.
Protected.

Then the wind shifted again—this time blowing from Morrivan—and with it came a whisper.

Not a voice.
A vibration.
A low, thrumming warning.

Nilsa stiffened. "Erabor…"

He felt it too. His grip tightened. "I know."

Nilsa turned her eyes toward the horizon of Havrelin—and gasped.

There—distant but visible—a faint shape moved across the wind-carved hills.

Not human.
Not animal.
Not shadow.

A figure—hooded, golden-lit, wandering slowly as if searching for something.

Nilsa's breath hitched. "What is that?"

Erabor's voice cracked.
"That… is trouble."

Nilsa stared harder.

The figure stopped.

Lifted its head.

Looked directly at her.

Nilsa staggered. "He sees us."

"No." Erabor pulled her back, panic flaring in his eyes. "Not *him*. Something else. Something worse."

Nilsa clutched his arm. "Erabor—who is that?"

He shook his head. "I don't know. But I know what kingdom that's from."

"Which?"

He exhaled.

Hollow.

Terrified.

"Ashova."

Nilsa felt her blood freeze.

"Ashova," she whispered. "The kingdom where the animals go mad under moonlight."

Erabor nodded once.

"And we just crossed into Havrelin."

Nilsa swallowed hard. "Why would someone from Ashova be waiting for us?"

Erabor's answer was a whisper that wasn't a whisper—
a warning,
a promise,
a prophecy unraveling.

"Because, Nilsa," he said, "your fate is not tied to Morrivan or Havrelin alone. The kingdoms are aligning. The curses are waking. And the moment you stepped across the ridge—every kingdom that can feel you… now does."

Nilsa's heart dropped.

The figure lifted a hand—
beckoning.

Erabor pulled her behind him, shielding her again.

"No," he whispered fiercely. "No, no, no—Nilsa, we have to go. NOW."

"Where?" she gasped.

"Anywhere but toward him."

Nilsa looked at the distant figure one last time—

and saw the faint glow around its head split into two sharp points
like twisted horns
glimmering under the afternoon light.

She choked on air. "Erabor—what is he?"

His voice broke.

"Someone who shouldn't exist."

The wind roared.

The ridge stone cracked behind them.

Made in the USA
Coppell, TX
20 January 2026